unnerving

twelve stories for a monthly dose of shivers

BLUE FORGE PRESS
Port Orchard, Washington

Unnerving Wicked
Twelve Stories for a Monthly Dose of Shivers
Copyright 2022
by Blue Forge Press

Cover art by Brianne DiMarco

First Print Edition, August 2022
Second Print Edition, February 2023

ISBN 978-1-59092-912-4

For information about film, reprint or other subsidiary rights, contact blueforgegroup@gmail.com

Blue Forge Press is the print division of the volunteer-run, federal 501(c)3 nonprofit company, Blue Legacy, founded in 1989 and dedicated to bringing light to the shadows and voice to the silence. We strive to empower storytellers across all walks of life with our four divisions: Blue Forge Press, Blue Forge Films, Blue Forge Gaming, and Blue Forge Records. Find out more at www.MyBlueLegacy.org

Blue Forge Press
7419 Ebbert Drive Southeast
Port Orchard, Washington 98367
blueforgepress@gmail.com
360-550-2071 ph.txt

*To all those who navigate
the deep, dark abyss
and live to tell the tale*

CONTENT WARNING

This book is intended for mature audiences as these stories are purposefully meant to unsettle the reader. If one month's story is too intense, skip that month. While the editor and Blue Forge Press have selected and edited each of these stories, ultimately you are responsible for curating what you read.

For a full list of triggers by story, please write to:
blueforgepress@gmail.com

table of contents

unnerving

twelve stories for a monthly dose of shivers

January

Butterfly Effect
Bree Indigo

Violet

I am pulled from a dream
with a jolt—electricity
          like that summer
          under the pale buttermilk sun
but the chill across my skin
reminds me that it's January
          not July
though the low, crackling hum
                    does remind me of the electric horse fence
          that was supposed to be off

I try to sit up
or scramble away
but I am leaden, limbs
heavy and immovable

the static rises behind me
reverberating down my vertebrae

a sharp cacophony of white noise
                    creeping closer, growing louder
            and with a shudder like a dry-heave
                            I feel it pass over my shoulder

my screams build
            thick with panic
                    and stuck in my throat
my ears burn
            stomach knotted in anticipation
                    skin pricked with cold and fear
my heart pounds
            a rhythm vibrating beneath my breast
                    a deep pulse of life
                    threatened by this primordial darkness

this can't be real
I think
but it feels
            so
            very
            real

only a breath away from me
her piercing gaze
pale blue, cold and empty
            like staring into the sapphire depths
                    of a glacial abyss

her hair is a dark halo
    unburdened by gravity
her body suspended
    just inches above me
she doesn't touch me
    and yet, still
        I can't move

Lilith
my breath is your breath
waxing and waning
our tides controlled
by moonshadow

be as water—
    cry, release, flow
be as air—
    breath and listen
be as earth—
    ground, give, heal
be as fire—
    burn and ignite

you will be brought low
your voice shall come
from the ground
and from the dust
your speech shall
w h i s p e r

Violet

my heart threatens
        to break my sternum
                a wild thing trying to escape
                        its bony cage

I keep thinking I'm awake
        finally awake
and then it happens
        again
                and again
                        and again

and then—
        s
                i
                        l
                                e
                                        n
                                                c
                                                        e

my pulse is a butterfly
        trapped in my carotid

                                but the static
                                        is finally
                                                gone

I cautiously start to move
push myself into a sitting position
and force myself to take
        deep

        slow

        breaths

an antique mirror is hung
        on the wall across from me
a familiar darkness blooms
          along the edge of the glass
            stained with truths
              deceptions
                and memories

I shiver, run my hands
          down my arms where
        something else blooms
            under my skin
purple ringed with chartreuse
          like a tattoo
        in soft focus

the bathroom door slammed open
and I jumped
        almost dropping the towel
        I was wrapping around myself
skin still warm and damp
        wet tendrils of hair
        dripping down my bare shoulders

I'm getting really fucking tired
of being the breadwinner in this house
  I stared at Taylor for a moment
  taken off-guard by her sudden words
    and she took a step forward
    the space in our small bathroom
    starting to shrink
Cat got your tongue? *she asked*
  and my mind started spinning
  trying to pick the right response
    a maze of answers
      and only one of them
        would lead to the exit

I kept my voice level
neutral and casual
and reminded her
  Uber pays on Thursday
Taylor scoffed but I continued
  And Dad's housekeeper
  canceled this morning—
    their kid woke up with a fever

she rolled her chestnut eyes
  Lazy bitch *she spat out callously*

I swallowed hard, continuing
  So I'm going to head out
  to Olalla tonight; it'll be a couple hundred
    since it was a holiday booking
    and they stayed more than a week

Taylor sucked her teeth
and finally asked
          How long
          will you be gone?
her tone hadn't changed but
something shifted in her eyes
and she looked younger for a moment
like the child she used to be
back when we shared
          stickers and secrets
          instead of a bed

I'll be home tomorrow night
after Dad stops by with the check
          I let out a breath
          relaxed my shoulders
          and smiled, asking
                    Come with me?

she smiled sweetly
          and closed the distance between us
                    her fingertips trailing along
                              the rivulets of water
                                        that fell down my arm
                              I shivered as she pulled close
                    tightening her grip
          she leaned in to whisper
                    Then who would go to work
                              and pay the fucking rent?

I wipe away the memories
spilling down my cheeks
and my reflection stares back at me
        but offers no solutions
        only a sigh of resignation
                as she stands and walks away

Lilith

mother, maiden, crone
triple goddess tesseract
an eternal lotus
in endless cycles
blooming, dying
a celtic knot
forever repeating
an everlasting circle
tied together
foretold by fate
and bound by blood
she and you and
we are one

Violet

I am halfway through dusting
the pictures along the mantel
        small metal frames proudly
        displaying our lineage
when I feel another jolt
        but I'm not asleep
                and it isn't a dream
                this time

my arm spasms
knocking a bronze frame
     to the floor
         with a loud, sharp clatter
and I spin, expecting
     to fend off
         a ghost or a taser
   but I am still
     just
      a l o n e

three deep breaths
and I'm already trying
to convince myself
it hadn't just happened
     maybe I fell asleep I think
but I don't really believe me
     maybe I need to sleep
sounds more like the truth
whatever rest I found
last night was lost
     to endless rounds
        of sleep paralysis

I turn and reach down
     picking up the frame
thankful the glass is
     still whole

I joke *Nice try, Grandma*
     but my voice is thin
        and cracks

my grandmother Rose
stands arm-in-arm with her sister Lily
		wide smiles under wide-brimmed hats
		shading finger-waved curls
				that framed their nearly
				identical faces

Did you know? I wonder and
			I think of her at my age
			walking down Fourth Avenue
					under the glittering lights
					of the Admiral Theatre

what if instead of
			meeting the young sailor
					she married three months later
			Rose had stayed home
					or missed the bus
					or simply not hit it off
							with the man
							I would call Grandpa

one small decision
			and suddenly my mother
					my siblings
					and I
							are just g o n e
			having never
					existed
						in the first place

what decisions would she make
                if she knew the pain
        she could avoid?

her husband's early departure
        which left her without him
                for more years than they shared
        like so many of the widows
of nuclear plant workers
        whose death certificates
                read *natural causes*

or her daughter's battle
        with AIDS
                contracted because
                        my mother's boyfriend
                may have loved her
        to the moon and back
but not enough
        to get tested

I set the frame
        down gently
                back on the mantel
        and cross my arms
suddenly chilled

Cassia...

I hear my grandmother
        calling my mother's name
    but this haunting
       is more memory
          than spectre
   and not as corporeal
     as the flowers
        on their graves

twin bouquets
of pale pink roses
golden cassia blossoms
and a single violet
bound together
with red raffia ribbon
already decaying
in their plain brown
butcher paper wrap

exhaustion pulls me
    back to the present
and I sink into the couch
    willfully escaping reality
      and the clarity
      of consciousness

my eyelids close
    as I succumb
      to sleep
        once more

Lilith

drowning in the murky depths
      of your own undoing
tossed by waves
      frigid and paralyzing
         you live at the
         mercy of the storm

nurture the shadows
        let them pour into your
     cracked and broken places
         but don't
       sanction the consumption
          of your light

Violet

her cobalt gaze
bores into me
and every nerve is
     screaming, teeming
       with apprehension

she slowly floats
down from the ceiling
closing in on my
      powerless
        c a t a t o n i c
           f o r m

my throat fills
        with silenced screams
once again
I try to move
        but I am frozen
forced to witness
her slow descent
        creeping
                ever
                    closer

her mouth opens
        with a low, guttural moan
and I watch as
a fine crimson mist
escapes her parted lips
        reaching toward me
                unfurling smoky tendrils
threatening to invade
my mouth and nose

something pushes
up from my core
and I hear the static
        beginning quietly
rising from my sacrum
        and up though my throat
the static grows louder
until it breaks
        the dam of my silence

my lips parting
      to scream
            No!
my voice is a roar
that wakes me
skin slick with sweat
as I scream
      over and over
      and over
         No no no
         noooo!
my breath is loud
coming in haggard
      gasps of air
my face wet with
      tears and relief
my throat raw
and I keep
      screaming
      until I am
         e m p t y

my phone chimes
and I eye it warily
from my crumpled position
but I reach for it
      with a sigh
      I can feel
      deep in my breast

Taylor's text
only says
> *Call me*

and before I can
second guess myself
I write back
a single word:
> No

Funny she responds
quickly adding
> *Seriously, call me*

my hands are shaking
but I quickly type
> *I can't do this anymore*

and her reply is instant
> *Violet, call me NOW*

> No

> *I'll do anything*
> *Just tell me what to do*

> No

> *I know I got mad*
> *the other day*
> *but it won't*
> *happen again*

> No

> *I need you*

> No

> *Violet!!*
> *Just fucking call me!!*

I type *No* once more
     but delete it
     replacing the words
     with what should have
     started the conversation
I'm moving out
I'll be gone
before you're home tonight

Lilith

I opened my eyes and let out a breath I hadn't realized I was holding. My reflection fogged for a moment but the glass cleared quickly, revealing my own familiar cornflower eyes and my sister's jade gaze, illuminated only by the light of the tall pillar candles circling us. I turned to her and her face was uncertain.

"What is it?" I asked, my brows creasing.

She frowned, looking away for a moment. "I just don't know if I believe it." She finally turned to look back at me. "I'm not some Dumb Dora, you know," she added contritely and I laughed gently.

"Rose!" I scolded. "Of course you're not. And you're the only one I trust with... *this*," I finished lamely.

Hearing the sound of the front door closing, I let out a small startled gasp. "They're back," I announced in a hushed whisper and we both moved to quickly blow out the candles before our parents called up to us.

Rose and I each took hold of either side of the heavy oval mirror and carefully lifted to place it back on the large iron nails protruding from the wall beside the door.

"Lily! Rose!" Our names echoed up the narrow wooden stairs that led to the second floor and Rose turned to call back,

"Yes, Mother, we'll be right there!"

At the doorway, Rose turned to me once more. "I just don't understand who it was supposed to be," she shared in a soft voice.

I shook my head, wishing I understood more. "I kept seeing my symbol for grandmother, but..."

"But our grandmothers were named Frances and Lillian," Rose finished and I smiled at the mention of my namesake. Rose was less amused. "That just doesn't make any sense at all, Lilith."

My eyes grew wide and I shushed her. "Don't let them hear–" Rose interrupted me, sticking out her tongue childishly and I couldn't help but laugh as I tried again. "Don't let them hear you call me that... Rowena," I added quietly.

Rose smiled at her secret name before heading out the bedroom door, leaving me alone with my reflection. My voice was soft as I asked, "Who were you, Violet?" before I walked away, closing the door behind me.

february

The February that was Not

Gregor Fjellrev

It has returned from the void, once again to make known its presence. It churns forth again as mercilessly as time itself; that ensures its cyclical nature. It is prepared to sunder minds and reduce genius to madness alike, and—whether by way of its insipid soldiers spitting its drivel or by sundering the sole survivalists who find themselves in the crossfire—blithering madness awaits for all in the end the same.

A cycle of doom, and not even the good kind, is rained upon one's enemies. A cycle of death, and not even the good kind that is rained upon one's foes. A cycle of madness, madness indeed, threatens countless with prospects of the unfathomable abyss. Abyss, abyss, abyss...

Prepare yourself, warrior. Prepare yourself as you always have. The stalwart steel and indomitable doom has weathered this storm. Year after year it has dared attempt to tear your will to shreds, with its shearing winds as though it carried a current of glass to cut your mind to ribbons.

But it has yet to win, this beast that comes each year. It has yet to claim your life, as it has yet to claim mine. We are all that stands against it, in battle and in solitude, and when it comes to pass, we shall raise our glasses to those who were felled, those whose minds were not as prepared, as staunch as ours.

I know, warrior. I know this beast of dire legend grows cleverer every year of its passing. I know that it gets stronger, its strikes more precise, toned and trained, tailored to crumbling the fortress walls that protect us from its wrath. I know that its hide becomes stronger every year, callused by the slings and arrows we rain upon it in our defense. But so do we.

Our defense has become more trained, our accuracy higher, and our weapons sharper. But then again, just as we train ourselves for this inevitable storm that is brought forth by what this time stands for, so too does it. It grows in its cleverness just as we do. It grows in determination just as our spite and defiance does the same. And I know, warrior, I know that dread because I feel it too: That one day, it shall outpace and overcome us, and then our names will be added to the ever-growing list of those it has claimed in its horror and the delirium it brings. That our names shall be among those in the unfathomable abyss. The only hope we have, warrior, is that we may die of any other death before then.

We have fought this fight as we have been trained, and we have been trained well by our own methods. We taught ourselves to defeat this beast, we taught ourselves how to defeat it each year that it comes for us, it comes for our sanity, it comes for our very souls...

But we will not falter. We have yet to, and thus we shall not this time. Each year this oncoming doom has dared hunt us, we have beaten it back for another year, so what's one more year that we must? That question we ask ourselves every year, and though I know it infuriates that it must always be asked and never permanently answered, our answer can be 'yes' yet again, because it has always been so far, and thus those are our tools to ensure it always will be.

Training... tools... oaths we swear and vow and reaffirm, all means to the end. I know, warrior, that you are as weary as I, if not more so. This abomination grows in fervor each cycle, each damnable and merciless cycle, as does grow its determination and zeal to tear us asunder. There are only so many ways I can say that we shall defeat it again and always. There are only so many words I can say that mean the same thing: We shall prevail. I hope. I know I will, at the very least.

It is the most infuriating kind of cycle, I know. The cycle whose permanence of answer can only be brought about by failure. A cycle to prevent madness that is itself madness, I know, warrior. My only hope is that by my words and my address of your title, that it steels your will enough to survive along with me. Survive in the name of those who have not. Survive out of spite, the most powerful force of motivation in all of creation. I know this, because it is my own tool, one I gladly lend you if it means that you fight back and win once more.

What wouldn't I give, warrior, to train you myself, or at least grant you the chance to train and fight alongside me? Indeed. I write these words as the arrival of the beast looms, the eve of the great battle for the both of us. For all of us, invisible kinsmen in combat, brothers and sisters alike in battle. And not even the kind with the decency to be a battle of swords and spears, of fists and feet. That would be too easy, wouldn't it? But I digress.

The beast comes, warrior. It comes for you as it comes for me. But know this, if nothing else; that we fight this battle simultaneously if not together and back-to-back, that we fight this battle and win as we always have, that if nothing else in all of creation, though you fight this battle alone, you are not its sole fighter. Know that I will survive, and that I challenge you to do the same. I do not do so under the pretense of us meeting one day, shaking hands, exchanging bows and raising glasses. That would be patronizing and we both know it. I do not do so under the even more egregious and unfathomably insulting pretense of similarly insipid spittle to the drones of the privileged, that say the battle might one day end. That would be even more insulting than if I were to relieve myself on the graves of every fallen warrior like us, who gave out under the sheer crushing blows and swipes of the beast we both fight.

I do not even ask or beg of you to survive as I will. I only tell you that I will survive, and I challenge you to do the same. Wield spite as your weapon. You might even outlast me.

Our mercy is the same as the creature's, which is why we shall prevail. This is why the cycle of this eternal battle will not falter this time. That level of pity for our foes we share is none at all.

Count the seconds. If nothing else in all of creation, count the seconds. The window of this doom's time is finite, and the number of seconds that must be counted can only go down as they are counted up. The horror that awaits us cannot remain in this realm forever. And when that time is over, we have bought ourselves until the next year to train harder, further, stronger, until it falls itself, if it can. Even if it can't... We're still one step ahead after all this time. We still outmatch the enemy. All we have to do is simply not fall behind. All we have to do is not fail.

The bell has struck midnight....

The fourteenth has begun.

MARCH

The Bowerbird

James Lowell Snyder

It was a windy day in March, but it's always windy in Southern Arizona in March. This one was the kind of day kids over in Tucson would be flying kites. Deputy Sheriff Roberto J. Arvizu sort of wished he was flying a kite right now. His eyes followed the sweep of the San Pedro River Valley up to the beautiful Galiuro Mountains in the east. Bob loved this view of his home. He could spend hours just looking at it.

Bob had a degree in psychology from the University of Arizona. Some people had been surprised when he took a deputy's job with the County Sheriff's Office, but his close friends knew it was the perfect place for him. Bob was a genuinely nice guy who loved this place and the people with whom he shared it.

Bob snapped out of his reverie and started the engine of his old Ford patrol car. His break was over, it was time to continue his patrol.

William Conner was working on the Conner ranch with a calf which got into some cactus. Will was patiently removing the teddy-bear cholla segments from around the calf's mouth with pliers when a stranger approached him. The stranger was a wanderer, a young man. He had the sad look of someone who had witnessed tragedy. It was the look often seen in soldiers. The Korean War had ended not long ago and soldiers were back home and looking for new places where they could just forget the war and get on with living.

March is a cusp in the Sonoran Desert, a time when winter is winding down and the wind heralds the coming of spring. There was much work to be done on the ranch before the heat of summer arrived. If this stranger was looking for work, though, he would be disappointed. The Conners were young and not yet to the point with their ranch where they could afford hired help.

Will assumed the man approaching him was looking for work, so he wasn't surprised the stranger's first words were, "Sir, do you own this land?"

"Yes, I'm William Conner. My wife, Jenny, and I own this ranch."

The stranger pulled out a tattered map, gestured to the east toward the Galiuro Mountains, and asked, "Is any of the land over there available?"

Will studied the man and his map, then said, "Yes, some of it is government land which is still available for homesteading." Will continued, "It's marginal desert land. Good only for grazing and not great even for that. At the higher elevations things shift from desert to forest. The First People called those beautiful cool high places Sky Islands, but you don't hear that term much anymore. Now the high land up there is controlled by the Forest Service, and it can't be homesteaded."

The man wondered aloud, "Are there any folks living there about on that lower land?"

"No, nobody lives out there. An occasional hiker wanders through once in a while. No one else."

The stranger said, "Thank you, Sir." Then turned east and started off toward the Galiuros.

Will stopped the man and cautioned him, "It's hard land out there, be careful. Come on back here if you have any trouble. By the way, what's your name?"

"Oh, I'm sorry I didn't say. I'm Jacob Clevenger, Mr. Conner."

Half an hour after Jacob Clevenger departed, Deputy Sheriff Arvizu pulled off the road when he saw Will Conner working with the calf. Bob turned off his old Ford patrol car's engine, got out and put on his Stetson, then walked toward Will. "Hey, Will," he said. "Problem with the calf?"

"Nope, nothing serious, just a mouth full of cactus," said the rancher as he let the calf go. "You need anything, Bob?"

"No. I'm just patrolling the south road," the deputy replied. "Anything new here?"

"Matter of fact there is, Bob. I just spoke to a young man passing through. He looked like a soldier just out of service. Said he was looking for land to homestead. He headed off toward the Galiuros."

"The Galiuros, huh. It's hard out there," murmured Bob.

"I warned him," said Will. "Told him to come back here if he had any trouble.

Three months or so later, Jacob walked up to the Connor's corral and asked Will if he could fill his canteen with water. "Sure," said Will. "Let's go in the kitchen."

"Oh, I can't come in your house. I'm all dirty," said the man, clutching his dusty hat in his hand.

Will responded, "Come up on the porch out of the sun. I'll

call my wife. She'd like to meet you. We don't get many visitors out here."

Will walked to the porch, stepped up and strode across to the ranch house door, opened it and called, "Jenny, we have company and he needs his canteen filled."

Jenny appeared a moment later, she had the look of a woman far stronger than this desert where she lived.

"Who do we have here?" Jenny said in a surprisingly powerful contralto voice.

Visibly stunned by Jenny's voice and demeanor, the stranger stammered, "I... I'm Jacob Clevenger."

"Well, I'm Jenny Conner. Come on in and rest a bit," she offered.

"Oh, I don't need to come in. I just need some water," said Jacob.

"Come on, Jacob. Get yourself in here and take a load off. Rest a bit while I fill your canteen for you. You sure you don't want something to eat? Coffee, maybe?"

"Oh, yeah, I ran out of coffee a month ago. A cup would be real good," Jacob responded as he followed Jenny into the house.

Jenny placed three steaming cups of coffee on the table and the three of them sat down.

"Did you find what you were searching for, Jacob?" asked Will.

"Yes, sir, I think I did. I'm heading over to the Federal Land Office in Tucson to see if I can file for homestead on it," was Jacob's answer.

Three weeks passed and Will saw Jacob leading two heavily laden mules toward the Galiuro Mountains, so he rode over to talk to him.

"Hey, Jacob," Will shouted as he approached. "Did you get your land?"

"Yes, Sir, Mr. Conner, I surely did. I have acres and acres of cactus, mesquite, and golden grass, all mine," Jacob said with a big smile.

"Congratulations, Jacob. Welcome home," said Will. Then he added, "Jacob, like I said before, this is hard land. If you ever need help, just give us a holler."

"Thank you, sir. I'll remember," Jacob replied as he led his mules off toward the Galiuros.

Will thought of Jacob from time to time and wondered if he was still out there in his acres of cactus, mesquite, and golden grass. Nearly three years passed before Jacob appeared again.

Surprisingly, on a pleasant March morning, there was Jacob coming across the range on one of his mules. He was burnt so deep from the sun Will hardly recognized him. Jacob's first words were, "Good day, Mr. Conner. Do you know if there's a doctor, or a hospital anywhere around here?"

"The closest doctor is in San Manuel, but is there any way I may be able to help? What's the problem?" said Will.

Jacob didn't answer. He just sat there on the mule with a strange, puzzled look on his face.

"Jacob, are you okay?" Will inquired.

Jacob stammered, then he almost began to cry and finally said, "I don't know, sir. She just ain't right!"

"Who's not right?" Will asked, suddenly alarmed. "Are you talking about a woman or an animal?"

"She just came one night," Jacob started. "She needed help, but I couldn't understand what she was trying to tell me.

After a bit she just went to sleep. She slept for a couple of days. Then she sort of woke up, but not completely. She's kind of confused-like, but I still can't figure out what all's wrong with her."

Will moved closer to Jacob and got his attention and asked, "Jacob, where is this woman? Is she at your place?"

"I don't think she's a regular woman, Mr. William," Jacob mumbled.

"Do you mean she's a girl?" Will inquired.

"No, well, I don't know. She's not like us," was Jacob's reply.

"Could she be from Mexico? Maybe she speaks Spanish. Jacob, do you understand any Spanish?" Will asked.

"No! No, it ain't like that," Jacob mumbled, now almost sobbing. Then Jacob shouted, "She ain't regular people!"

Will was stumped. What in the world was Jacob talking about?

"What do you mean 'she ain't regular people?'" Will queried. "How did you meet her?" he continued.

Jacob, still confused, stammered then said, "She came in a boat thing one night. It was all lit up with lights—flashing lights. Then it smashed into the hill." Jacob's voice trailed off.

Will asked, "Was it an airplane?" Getting no answer, Will said, "What happened? What did you do?"

"I went outside to see what all the lights and commotion was about. There wasn't any fire, just some of the lights still working. Willow was just lying there on the ground."

"Willow?" asked Will.

"I call her 'Willow' because she is so thin and graceful like a willow tree. I don't know her real name. There were three others, but they all were dead. Willow was the only one who moved. I took her to my cabin and tried to talk with her, but she passed out." Jacob paused a long time, then he continued, "I tried talking to her, but she just didn't understand me. Later, I decided to come to your place for help."

Will wondered if Jacob was drunk, or hallucinating, or was something else happening out there in the Galiuros? As Will helped Jacob into his home he called to Jenny. "Honey, Jacob is here and he's in some serious distress."

Jenny dropped what she was doing and raced to the kitchen where Will had taken Jacob. "What's going on?" she asked as she helped Will get Jacob seated at the kitchen table.

"I really don't know what's wrong with him," Will answered as he pulled Jenny aside. "He keeps talking about 'her' but he's not clear about who 'she' is. He started by asking me if there is a doctor or a hospital nearby. Then he told me how bad off 'she' was, but I couldn't get him to say who she is, except he calls her 'Willow' because he thinks she's thin and graceful like a willow tree. He finally said she's not 'regular people'... but I don't know what he meant by it."

"How'd she get up there?" Jenny asked.

"I don't know, he's really confused by whatever happened up there in the hills. I think maybe we should call the sheriff," concluded Will.

"That's exactly what I was thinking," said Jenny as she walked in the office and picked up their phone.

A few minutes later Jenny returned to the kitchen and said, "They're going to send Bob Arvizu out. He's the best in this kind of a situation."

Deputy Sheriff Arvizu pulled up in front of the Conner ranch house in his new Dodge Coronet patrol car, shut off the engine, stepped out, put on his Stetson, and paused a moment to appreciate the vastness and beauty of the Galiuro panorama spread out before him. Smiling, Bob remembered his job, then turned and started toward the porch which spanned the entire north side of the Conner home. Will was waiting for Bob as he strode up the steps.

"Hi, Will. What's the problem?" he said.

"Bob, I don't even know where to start," replied Will. "You remember me telling you about the loner who moved in up near the Galiuros a few years ago? His name is Jacob Clevenger."

"Yeah, you said he looked like a lonesome soldier," Bob replied.

"Well, he's in our living room and he's really upset about someone, or something, he found up there by his place. He's incoherent. Jenny and I can't make sense of what he tells us. He keeps talking about someone he calls 'Willow' but we can't figure out exactly what he means."

"Let me take a look at him, Will," Bob replied.

The deputy removed his hat and hung it on the hat rack near the door as the two men stepped into the Conner living room. Jenny stood up and said, "Hi, Bob, we're so glad you're here."

Jenny gestured toward the deputy and said, "Jacob, this is Deputy Sheriff Bob Arvizu. Bob's here to help us with Willow." Jenny had dropped her voice into a soft, slow cadence which seemed to soothe Jacob.

Jacob sat slouched on the sofa, his head tilted downward with his chin nearly on his chest. He looked as if he had been crying.

Bob pulled the ottoman in front of Jacob and sat on it, an easy smile spreading across Bob's face as he said, "It's nice to meet you, Jacob. Let's talk about Willow. How did you meet her?"

"They crashed into a hill near my place a few nights ago. There was a lot of dust, and noise, and smoke and lights flashing. I went out to see what was going on."

"Okay, Jacob. Were they in an airplane?" said Bob.

"No, it didn't look like any airplane I ever saw. It looked more like a boat with flashing lights."

"Jacob, could it have been a helicopter?" Bob inquired.

"I guess, maybe, but it didn't look like the ones I saw in Korea."

"Maybe it was a newer model than those in Korea. It's been a few years since you were in Korea, hasn't it?"

"Yeah, I guess so," was Jacob's response.

Bob asked, "Was anybody with Willow in the machine?"

"Yes, there were three others, but they never moved," Jacob said firmly. "They were dead. I'm sure."

"What did you do with those three?"

"I didn't do anything with them. They're still in the–uh, the, uh, helicopter thing."

"But you took Willow into your cabin. Am I correct?"

"Yes, you're right. I took her into my cabin. Those other ones never moved. I checked them again before I came down here to Mr. William and his wife's ranch."

Bob made notes of everything Jacob said. Next, he asked, "What did you do with Willow?"

"I put her in my bed. I propped her up so she'd be comfortable as I could make her."

Bob's next question was, "What else did you do for her?"

"Oh, I wrapped her left leg and left arm up, so they were comfortable. They looked broken. Then I gave her water and some food. She drank the water, but she didn't eat any food. I tried to talk to her, but I don't think she knew what I was saying.

She made sounds but I still couldn't understand her. Finally, she just passed out. I covered her with a blanket and then I went to sleep in my chair. When I woke up in the morning, she was watching me."

Then Bob asked gently, "Jacob, tell me what Willow looked like. Take your time and just describe her in your own words."

"Oh, she was beautiful. She was real tall and thin. Her skin was different, soft and smooth, but it had little lines all over."

"I don't understand. Do you mean lines like a net on her?" Bob asked.

"Oh, no, kind of like the lines of a jigsaw puzzle after it's put together. I couldn't see much of her skin, just her face and hands. Her hands weren't like ours. She just had four fingers on her hands, and they were separated two by two. It looked odd the way her fingers twisted when she took the cup to drink water." Jacob moved his fingers awkwardly trying to imitate the way Willow had moved her hand to grasp the cup.

"What sort of clothing was she wearing?" the Sheriff asked.

"She was wearing gold coveralls. Her hair was cut short and it was white and real soft like cotton, and her eyes…" Jacob stopped and was staring off as if visualizing.

"Jacob, go on and tell us about Willow's eyes," the deputy encouraged.

"Yeah, they were lavender color. My momma had a dress that color. Momma always said her lavender dress was her favorite and she only wore it on special occasions," whispered Jacob.

"Lavender eyes," repeated Bob. "Unusual. Sounds beautiful."

"Oh, yeah," said Jacob. "Those eyes sure were pretty. They were so clear. It was almost like I could see inside her."

"Jacob," said Bob. "Tell me about the other three people. How were they different from Willow?"

"First off," Jacob began. "Two were bigger and the other one was smaller, more like Willow. They all wore uniforms."

"What color were the uniforms? Were their eyes, hair, and skin like Willow's?" asked the deputy.

"The uniforms were light blue," said Jacob. "Their eyes were all closed, and I couldn't see them, but everything else was the same as Willow, same white hair and little lines all over their skin, except they all wore brown boots. Willow didn't have boots. Her coveralls had feet coverings, like little kids' sleeper suits and she had little purple slippers over those."

"Okay, Jacob, when you fell asleep how long did you sleep?" Bob asked.

"I guess it was the next morning. The sun was up and there I was in my chair next to the bed near Willow," Jacob replied as his voice trailed off.

"What did you do after you woke up?" Bob asked.

"I went and got some fresh water for Willow. She drank some of it, then she passed out again. Then I decided to go check on the other people."

Bob asked, "Was there any change in them?"

"No, Sir," said Jacob. "They were exactly like they were the night before. It didn't look like they had moved at all."

"What did you do the rest of the day?" asked the deputy.

"I checked my livestock, fed and watered them. Made sure everything around the cabin was okay. I checked Willow every once in a while, to make sure she was all right," Jacob said.

"Did you leave the cabin area any time that day, Jacob?"

asked Bob.

"No, Sir, I did not," was Jacob's response.

"Jacob, when did you decide to come to the Conner ranch for help?" asked the Sheriff.

"The next day, I decided to come down here and ask Mr. William and his wife for help. Willow wasn't getting any better and I figured they would know what to do."

Once again, Bob spoke very gently and said, "Coming here was the best thing you could have done, Jacob." He looked over his notes for a few moments, then he added, "I think it would be best if we all went to Jacob's place together to see how Willow is getting along. Jenny and Will, can you come with us? I may need your help." The deputy was frowning and it was quite clear he was very concerned about Jacob's situation and whatever had transpired at Jacob's cabin.

"I'll have to make some arrangements for the kids. They're in school, but it shouldn't be a problem," said Jenny. "I'll call the school and the neighbors to have the kids dropped off there."

Will said, "We'll need horses. I'll go saddle them." Will turned to Bob and asked, "How many do you think we'll need?"

Bob replied, "Three should do. Jacob has a mount, doesn't he?"

Will nodded.

"If Willow needs to come out, I'll call for Air Evac," said Bob, thinking of the new air rescue service the county had acquired.

In twenty minutes the four of them were prepared for riding and on their way, with Jacob in the lead on his mule.

Bob called to Jacob, "How long does it usually take you to make this trip?"

"Around an hour and a half on the mule," was his reply.

As the group moved eastward across the Conner Ranch the vegetation changed. First, the grass thinned some and mesquite and creosote bushes became more noticeable. Further on more cactus showed up. In the higher land to the east the giant saguaros became prominent.

True to his word, in just an hour and a half Jacob pulled up on the mule's reins and pointed to his cabin on the other side of a beautiful little stream.

"There's my place," he said, but he hesitated to continue.

"Is something wrong, Jacob?" said the deputy sensing Jacob's hesitancy.

"Yes, sir, everything's wrong. Their stuff is all gone and there was a big hole there in the side of the hill where the wreckage was." Jacob was quickly becoming agitated. He jumped off the mule and ran across the stream and into the cabin.

In a few seconds Jacob was back outside. He was crying and he said, "They came and took her away. They took my Willow!"

Jacob was sobbing now. Jenny went to him and hugged him. She rocked him from side to side trying to comfort him. Suddenly, Jacob's legs buckled and he slipped out of Jenny's arms and fell to the ground. He was sobbing inconsolably. Jenny knelt beside him and rubbed his shoulders to comfort him.

Will raised his eyebrows and looked over at Bob questioningly.

Bob shrugged and said, "I don't know. Your guess is as good as mine as to what really happened here. Did someone come back to get her and take time to clean up evidence of their visit, or did Jacob dream the whole thing? I just don't know, Will." Almost to himself he murmured, "Who would do something like this and where did they come from?"

"What do we do now?" said Will, obviously at a complete loss.

"Legally, I'm supposed to report this," said Bob with a bit of sadness in his voice. "If I do, the sheriff will have to elevate it up to state, and probably even up to the Feds."

The two men stood looking at each other and Will said, "Something weird is going on here, Bob."

"Yeah," Bob replied, then he added, "Something like visitors from far, far away. We've never had anything like this here, but when the story got out about that guy who saw 'flying saucers' up near Mount Rainier in 1947 everybody went crazy. Suddenly, there were reports of sightings all over the world."

"I'm afraid if this story gets out, the government, the press, and a swarm of loonies will show up out here and trample everything. Unless we suppress it, they'll strip this beautiful place for souvenirs. They'll ruin Jacob's home." Bob sighed. "Sometimes I hate this job and this is one of those times."

Jenny walked up, having overheard what Bob said. "Can't you just say it was a false alarm? Tell your boss Jacob had a bad dream?" she asked. "Will and I won't say otherwise."

"That's tempting," said the deputy. "But... no, let's take a closer look around. Let's start with the cabin."

The exterior walls of Jacob's cabin were made of stone. The cabin was crowned with a very serviceable hand-crafted shake roof. The window shutters and doors were finely built of native woods. They found the interior was divided into four rooms: The main room, a bedroom, a kitchen, and a storage room. The bedroom and storeroom had doors which matched the entry door in the main room. The kitchen had a small door in the back which led outside to the rear of the structure.

Bob and Will wondered how Jacob had built all this himself. The little building was sturdy, efficient, and beautiful in a rustic way. Where had Jacob learned how to do all this? Where did he get the tools to do it? Will's father was a carpenter and Will recognized how much time and craftmanship this work would require.

Both men were amazed by the bed in the bedroom. It was a work of art with intricately carved vines and flowers, although the straw mat and Army surplus sleeping bag on it were a bit incongruous. Also, there was a small home-made table and a comfortable-looking home-made chair, both with carvings to match the bed. A shelf mounted on the wall which held two Army surplus blankets and clothing, all neatly folded, was intricately carved, as well.

Jenny walked into the bedroom while Bob and Will were examining it. She stopped short stunned by the beauty of the decor and exclaimed, "This place is luscious. Jacob's a bowerbird!"

Bob exclaimed, "Oh, yeah! You're right. I never thought of a bowerbird."

Will's response was lower key. "What? What kind of bird?"

Bob jumped in with the answer, "It's a tropical bird. The males build lavish nests to attract females. It's exactly what Jacob has done. I don't know if he's aware of it or not, but he has built this cabin for a woman. This place is a love nest. The poor guy must be lonely being out here all by himself."

The three of them stood there looking at each other for a few moments, until Will said, "Let's go look at the kitchen."

The kitchen contained a wood burning stove, a box of firewood, and a wooden workbench attached to one wall. Shelves lined another wall, which served as Jacob's pantry and *batterie de cuisine*. In the center of the room was a modest dining table with benches on either side.

Jenny commented, "Jacob's kitchen is better equipped than mine. Where'd he get all this stuff and how'd he get it up here?"

The trio moved on to the little storeroom, which contained a variety of woodworking tools: There were hammers, hatchets, saws, several wooden mallets, a drill brace with a canvas roll of drill bits, a rack of chisels, a froe, three woodworkers' bearded axes, three draw knives all neatly hung on the walls. On shelves were boxes and boxes of nails, screws, and other hardware. Will, Jenny, and Deputy Bob realized how Jacob had built the cabin and its contents, but had he hauled all this up to the cabin on his mules? Also, where had he acquired all the skills to use these tools?

Everything in the entire cabin was neat and orderly. There was no sign of any other inhabitants. Will and Bob decided to go outside.

"I can't believe this. It's amazing," said Bob. "Will, did you know he had all those tools and was a skilled carpenter?"

"No. I just assumed he was a poor veteran living up here in a shack or a cave. Jenny and I just thought he was a vet with some mental distress and nobody important in his life. He always seemed kind of unaware of what was going on most of the time. You know, kind of out of touch. Let's find Jacob," said Will.

The horses and Jacob's mules were in the corral and they found Jacob tending to a flock of chickens in a pen nearby. Jacob had about a dozen hens and one nasty rooster which constantly ordered the humans to vacate his domain.

Bob said, "Let's go back in front of the cabin and find

Jenny. We need to talk."

They found Jenny in the front room and the four of them gathered outside in front of the cabin and Deputy Arvizu spoke, "Jacob, do you always keep your home this neat."

"Yes, sir. My momma and daddy liked things this way. I learned the Army liked things this way, too. They always said how important it was to keep your stuff neat and clean and orderly."

"Well, you certainly do a good job of it," said Bob. "Where did you learn how to work with wood and use tools so well?"

"My daddy is real good with tools. He used to let me help him," said Jacob. "I helped him a lot and learned a lot growing up."

His curiosity assuaged, Bob changed the subject. "Jacob, was everything here exactly the way it was when you left to get help for Willow?"

"Yes, sir," Jacob replied. "Except the wrecked helicopter thing was on the hillside."

"But you're sure everything in the house was just like this?" the deputy queried.

"Well, except Willow was in the bed and one of the blankets from the shelf was spread over her," Jacob answered.

"Okay," said the deputy. "Let's look at the hillside."

As the four of them walked up the hillside Jacob said, "They sure smoothed it out nice. It's a lot smoother than it was before."

Jacob pointed to a large boulder at the bottom of the hill, "That rock down there used to be right here on the edge of this smooth place."

Bob looked at the rock and estimated it had rolled sixty feet from where Jacob said it had been. He walked down to the rock and examined it closely. He saw nothing unusual, so he trudged back up to his companions. Bob said to the group, "I've seen nothing to convince me something happened here, but I am surprised everything is so neat and clean. It looks like it's been scrubbed by a special crew, which is the most suspicious part. This just looks too good. Jacob, except for Willow being gone and the blanket you said covered her now being folded up on the shelf, and everything being so neat and clean, is there anything else you can think of to prove Willow was here?"

"No, sir, I can't think of anything... Oh, wait, there was a cup!"

"What cup?" the others questioned almost in unison.

"There was a cup I found in the helicopter thing when I checked the other people. I used it to get water for Willow. It might be by the spring," Jacob said.

"What spring?" asked Jenny.

"There's a spring up the hill a bit. I get drinking water up there when the stream isn't clean," was Jacob's reply.

"Show us," said the deputy.

Jacob led them up the hill to a spot where a small trickle of water bubbled out of a rock face and flowed about twenty feet down to join the creek.

There on the ground beside the trickle of water was a little cup. "There it is," said Jacob. "It's what I used to get clean water for Willow while she was here."

"You got this cup from the machine they arrived in? Am I right?" Bob asked Jacob.

Jacob nodded.

Bob carefully picked up the little cup and they all marveled at it. None of them had ever seen anything quite so delicate, so translucent, so oddly colored. Something about the little cup made it seem exotic and precious. Bob rotated the cup in his hand

and then flicked it with his finger. It rang like a bell.

"This didn't come from anywhere around here," murmured Bob.

Bob stared at the remarkable little container for a long time, then he nodded his head, turned, and handed the cup to Jacob and said, "Jacob, you should keep this to remember Willow."

Deputy Sheriff Arvizu had made a decision. He was, above all, a man of honor. He thought to himself, *Jacob is a simple man who has a special home and a beautiful, if lonely, life here in the foothills of the Galiuros. Jacob should be allowed to keep what he has built. There is no good reason to destroy it by telling the world about it. The Conners have a lovely ranch, a ranch which could be spectacular if it is allowed to grow and prosper for a few years.*

Bob knew what would happen if he reported a flying saucer here in the Galiuros. The memory of the hysteria which came with the Mount Rainier sightings in 1947, and sightings near Washington, DC in 1952, gave Bob chills. Bob knew Jacob's home, the Connors' ranch, the whole area of the beautiful San Pedro Valley and Galiuro Mountains would be overrun with crazies if he went back to San Manuel and reported a flying saucer.

Bob led the way back to Jacob's cabin where the horses were waiting. While Will and Jenny checked the horses, Bob said goodbye to Jacob. "This is a lovely little home you have, Jacob, you take care of this place and yourself. Jacob, did you learn to keep a secret in the Army?"

"Yes, sir, I did. Why?" he replied.

"Good. It would be a good idea to keep Willow's visit a secret. She should be your private secret. It's important. Will you do this, Jacob?"

"Yes, sir. I will, Sheriff," Jacob said quietly.

"Good man," said Bob as he reached out to shake Jacob's hand.

The deputy turned and walked to where Will Conner held the horses. Jenny was already mounted. Bob took the reins Will offered and the two men mounted their horses. The three riders pulled their hats down tight, waved to Jacob, then urged the horses to move, and they crossed the little creek and headed west.

Their journey back to the Conner Ranch was quiet. The trio remained silent; nobody said a word. Bob spent the hour and a half ride pondering everything he had heard and witnessed. Deputy Sheriff Roberto J. Arvizu, man of honor, decided to re-write and falsify his report. He could not bring himself to tell the truth of what had happened to Jacob Clevenger, nor could he repeat what Jacob said he had seen. Aliens with lavender eyes, cotton hair and reticulated skin patterns traveling in a flying saucer was just too much. If he filed such a report the consequences would be disastrous. Bob refused to become the instrument to destroy the land he and his friends loved so much.

When Arvizu closed the door of his Dodge Coronet he paused, rolled down the window, turned to the Conners and said, "A couple of times a week we should check on Jacob. I'll be back day after tomorrow to see how he's doing. I'll take care of all the paperwork on all of this. It was great to see both of you, and I can never thank the two of you enough for your help today."

As the deputy drove away Jenny said to her husband, "I'm sure glad Bob got the call today. Will you go with Bob when he comes to check on Jacob?"

Will said, "Sure, I'll go. I wouldn't miss it."

Two days later Bob showed up at the Conner ranch. Jenny took him a cup of hot coffee as Will went to saddle two horses. After Bob finished his coffee the two men set off for Jacob's cabin, wondering in what condition they would find the poor man. They were soon more confused and distressed than ever. The livestock had disappeared. They could not find Jacob, nor could they find his cabin or any trace of him. They were certain they were in the right place, the creek was there and the big rock was at the bottom of the hill, but all was as if Jacob had never been there.

The two men dismounted and walked around the place. Had those who had taken Willow taken the Bowerbird as well? If so, they had also erased all evidence of Jacob's having been there. Everything connected with him was gone. It appeared as if all the labor Jacob had invested in his home had never happened. Had the man and his lovely bower ever existed? Why had it all been taken away, and to where could it have been taken, and how?

Then Will saw the little cup on the ground where the cabin had been. Had it been overlooked, or had someone left it deliberately? As Will picked up the cup and handed it to the deputy he asked, "What do we do now?"

"I don't know, Will," Bob replied. "Let's go home." He handed the cup back to Will.

The two men mounted their horses and rode slowly back toward the Conner ranch. Neither man spoke for the entire trip back. As they rode up to the Conner home Jenny came out. When she saw the faces of the two men she knew something was wrong. "What happened?" Jenny asked with a note of alarm in her voice.

"Everything is gone," said Will.

"What do you mean? How could it be gone?"

she demanded.

"We don't know what happened. Everything that was there is not there now," said Bob.

Jenny looked back and forth at the two men unable to believe what they were saying.

"We don't have an answer. It looks like no one ever lived there," Will said, his voice shaky.

The two men just looked at Jenny, then Will handed her the little cup.

"Is this something we should be afraid of?" Jenny asked nervously.

APRIL

April Showers May Bring Monsters
Lauren Patzer

The dappled sunlight on the road shifted and twisted as the wind lightly blew through the trees. Ed kept his eyes on the road but shook his head every once in a while to shake off the mesmerizing effect of the light show in front of him. He pressed a finger on the cell phone mounted on the dash.

Still have signal, he thought. *Probably should call her.*

His finger hovered over the phone icon for a few moments but then he lowered it and grasped the wheel tightly.

"She'll understand," he murmured through gritted teeth. "She always *understands.*"

He pressed his foot on the accelerator and his speed jumped up well over the speed limit for the winding country road. He went through several winding turns before he felt himself lose control a little and the tires squealed. He relaxed his foot on the accelerator and reduced his speed below the limit. There were no other cars on the road, so even his slight drifting into the oncoming lane had been unsafe but not particularly dangerous. He expected there to be more traffic especially on such a nice day.

The cell phone rang and he looked at it—incoming call from Tina. He sighed and pressed the phone to answer the call.

"Hey," he said putting on a cheery bravado.

"Baby, I didn't know you had left," Tina replied, her baby doll voice setting his nerves on edge.

Ed had seen the pictures the private investigator had delivered. She was *in flagrante* with his cousin Darren at the bastard's apartment. Smart move to not have their flings at the house he shared with her.

"I had to go. There's a check-in time at the B and B, so I had to leave. Sorry I couldn't see you before you got back from—" *Fucking his brains out.* "—shopping," he finished and forced a grin on his face, hoping it came through in his voice.

"I understand," she replied. "I just, I needed to tell you I was going to go to Vegas for a few days with the girls. I'm leaving Achtung with your parents."

Their shared Rottweiler, Achtung, was a big sweetheart. Just for a moment, he imagined the dog getting violent and tearing her throat out, blood spraying everywhere in unreasonable amounts, coating everything in the living room and pooling on the ground until it poured into the kitchen.

"Well, they love Achtung. I'm sure he'll be fine. Who you going with?"

"Oh, it's just some girls from the sorority, you haven't met them. We're just going to have a little party to celebrate our college days, you know."

Didn't know Darren went to your sorority!

"Sounds great," Ed replied. "I'll be gone for two weeks, so I certainly won't miss you being at home."

"Okay, just wanted to let you know."

"Look, the cell service up here is likely to be spotty, so I'll call you when I get service. Okay?"

"Sure thing, baby," Tina chuckled. "I may be on the casino

floor when you call, so no guarantees I will answer immediately."

Or up in a hotel room getting reamed by Darren.

"Fair enough," he said and felt his smile become a grimace. "I'll leave a voicemail. Have fun."

"Don't I always?" she asked. "Love you, bye."

"Love you too," he replied and realized it was the loneliest sounding statement he'd made in a long time. He quickly hung up the phone.

Ten minutes up the winding road, the cell phone showed No Service and he sighed. *This divorce is going to suck for both of us. Let her have her last fling in Vegas with Darren. She can have his penniless ass forever when I toss her to the curb.*

He rolled the window down and the cool mountain air made him catch his breath for a moment. He grinned and relished the chill it put into his face and hands. It was a cool spring day, but the warmer weather was just around the corner. It was perfect weather for writing.

After he felt fully refreshed from the breeze flowing through the car, he rolled up the window. He caught sight of the sign for Willow Point just ahead. The sign had a willow branch on one side and an arrowhead on the other. Above it all, someone had spray painted a black circle; the paint had run and there were some drips obscuring part of the lower case 'w.'

He frowned at the sign as he passed, but shrugged it off. A few minutes later, he pulled into what had to be downtown Willow Point; it was half a dozen boarded up buildings. The gas station even had plywood on the windows and bars over that. Ed pulled up in front of the lone gas pump and saw that it was an older manual model.

He got out of the car and looked around at the buildings. A door banging shut behind him caused him to whirl around as a man in a beige shirt and jeans stepped out of the gas station building.

"You lost or just passing through?" the older white man asked. Ed studied him for a moment and realized he was your typical redneck gas station attendant. He shouldn't have expected much more from a small mountain town.

"I'm staying in one of the cabins by the lake," Ed replied. "Just for a few weeks."

"You nuts? It's rainy season," the gas station attendant replied.

"Uh, my wife recommended the area. She used to live up here, over in Turnberry."

"Whatever," the man replied. "She must not like you much, sending you up here right now. Why don't you come back in June?"

"I realize it might rain a little," Ed replied. "Look, I just need some gas and maybe a few items from your store. You are open for business, right?"

"Only during the day and only when it ain't raining," the man replied. He pushed the worn red baseball cap back on his head. "How much gas you want?"

"Oh, fill it up? I'll go check out what you got inside," Ed replied.

"Alright, I only take cash" the man replied.

"That's fine," Ed replied as he walked toward the building.

"Don't steal nothin'. I know my inventory."

Ed turned back to say something, but the man had already turned away to work with the old gas pump. Ed shook his head and went inside.

It was like stepping back into the 1940s with the exception of some of the products on the old wooden shelves. The only cold items he could find were kept in a floor freezer that looked like it was straight out of World War Two surplus. He searched the shelves and found some dry food items and fetched a small container of milk from the floor unit he now realized was just for refrigerated items. There weren't any frozen goods at all.

The attendant came back in the store and headed to the cash register.

"That'll be seventeen fifty for six gallons," the man said as he sat down on a stool behind the counter.

"Quaint little place you got here," Ed said as he walked up to the counter.

"Quaint," the man replied with a grunt.

"You don't have any freezer stuff?" Ed asked.

"Grocery across the street opens May fifteenth," the man said. "I can't run much more on my generators than the little fridge."

"You don't have electricity in town?" Ed asked.

"Unreliable," the man replied as Ed set his items on the counter. "No one comes out in the rain to fix a downed power line. I got two generators ready at all times to keep the lights on."

"Two? Well, I'll be," Ed replied. "Say, you got a name?"

"Al," the man said as he looked at the items Ed had picked out to buy. "That'll be thirty-two seventy-five for everything including the gas."

"Sure, sure," Ed said as he took out his wallet. "My name's Ed. Is Al short for Albert?"

Al took his money and opened the cash register to make change.

"Ed short for Edward?" Al replied.

"No, it's short for Edmund."

Al handed him his change.

"Quaint," Al replied and ripped the receipt off the old register. "Stay inside and lock your doors if it's raining. I don't recommend heading out too far at night either. Ranger station is twenty miles away and they won't come until morning and only if it ain't raining."

"What's the deal with the rain anyway?" Ed asked as he took the receipt from Al.

"The dead rise during the rain storms," Al said as he put Ed's items in a paper sack.

"The dead?" Ed asked with a laugh.

"When it rains after dark," Al replied with no hint of humor. "The dead own the night."

"If the place is crawling with the dead, Al," Ed replied with a grin. "Why do you stay here?"

"She might come home," Al said plain as day. "Then I can put her to rest for good."

Ed looked at Al and waited for him to break character. Al simply looked at him with a deadpan face.

"Great talking with you, Al," Ed said as he picked up his bag.

"Pleasures all yours," Al replied and picked up a newspaper from behind the counter. He opened it up and ignored Ed.

Ed shook his head and walked out.

When he reached his car, he opened the back door and opened his messenger bag. He pulled out a spiral notebook and opened it. He retrieved a couple of printed pages tucked into it and put the notebook back in the bag. He got into the car and looked through the pages. One of them had a map of the local area with a road highlighted that led to the lake. On the shore was an X with a circle.

He oriented the map to the direction he was heading and started the car. As he pulled out, Al poked his head out of the store and watched him go. Al shook his head and went back inside.

Ed took a left after the last of the buildings on the main road and pulled onto a one lane gravel road. About a quarter mile past the last building, he drove by a cemetery off to the left surrounded by a thick iron bar fence with iron points all along the fence pointed in toward the graves. Ed blinked his eyes and looked again as he slowed the car to a stop. He looked behind him, but there were no other cars or people anywhere near. He got out of the car.

As he walked to the graveyard, the cool wind picked up and Ed found himself shivering. He continued to the rusty wrought iron fence. He walked around and found a gate, but it was chained and padlocked close. The lock looked worn by the weather and seemed as old as the fence. The fence was above his head and he didn't fancy trying to scale it, so he just went up to the side of the fence and examined the spikes pointing inward. They were all rusty, but some of them had something else caked on them. Ed looked around and found a stick. He poked the residue on the spikes and the stick sunk into what appeared to be a thick, gooey substance. The smell made Ed wrinkle his nose and back away quickly. It smelled like death.

"That's a long way to go for a joke. Halloween must be a dream up here," Ed murmured. He got back in the car and resumed his journey.

The gravel road made the pace slow, so it took another twenty minutes to reach the edge of the lake where the road turned to the right. He stopped at the first cabin along the gravel road. He stepped out and looked out at the lake which was only about twenty yards away and had a little pier jutting out into the calm water. He looked up in the sky and saw the growing cloud cover, darkening and ominous.

Ed reached back into the car and got the printed papers. One of them had the combination to the lock on the rental property. He grabbed his bag from the back seat and went up to the door. As he punched in the combination to retrieve the key, his eyes passed along the front of the cabin and noticed the bars on windows that were board up with painted plywood. He hadn't noticed it before. He just assumed the entire wall had no windows since it didn't face the lake where the real view was.

Vandals this far out?

He unlocked the door and stepped inside. The furniture inside was all covered like no one had been expecting to rent the cabin out. He checked the number on the rental agreement and double-checked the address on the cabin. They were both number nine. His mind instantly traveled back to one of the more recent romances he'd written about a numerologist.

Nine could mean completion, conclusion or compassion.

He laughed. He didn't believe in numerology, but that main character certainly did. She chose her partner strictly based on numerology and it hadn't worked out. That was when the guy who was totally wrong for her swept her off her feet and they fell madly in love. His mind wandered to Tina.

Maybe our numbers were never compatible. The universe works in strange ways.

He shook his head. "Let's go with completion, meaning I'm going to complete this manuscript."

He pulled one of the sheets off a dining room table and waved away the dust. He set his things down on the table and tossed the sheet behind the couch. He flicked one of the wall switches and the lights came on inside the house. Now that he could see, he realized the building had not been made ready in any way for rental.

"This isn't going to help your rating, anonymous lazy landlord. But at least there's electricity."

He went out to retrieve the rest of his things.

As Ed settled in and cleaned up the house, he was relieved to find the building had been stocked for business with non-perishable goods and supplies. He didn't need to use leaves for toilet paper. There was also running water, so he didn't have to bath in the lake much to the neighbors' relief, he was sure. Not that he'd seen any neighbors.

Upon closer inspection, he noticed the plywood on the windows was on runners, so he was able to slide the ones covering the window overlooking the lake out of the way. After he was done cleaning everything, he retrieved one of the beers he'd purchased at Al's store from the fridge. It was sufficiently cooled to be refreshing. He sat down on the couch and watched the rain come down outside. It made a soothing splashing pattern on the lake and the wind would send it sheeting in waves across the surface.

That's about the time he started to see things moving in the lake. They appeared to be branches or sticks emerging from the water and then submerging again. He stood up and walked closer to the window and squinted at the water's surface which was rapidly becoming harder to see with the dying sunlight. Just for a moment, he thought he saw a hairy skull rising from the surface before it dipped below out of sight. It caused him to jump back.

Then the rain stopped and the surface of the darkening

lake became calm again.

Ed stood at the window staring out at the lake until it became so dark, he couldn't see anything beyond the pool of light coming from inside the cabin. He rubbed his eyes and drained the last of the beer.

"Too much time on the road," he said. He walked to the master bedroom of the cabin, stripped off his clothes and climbed into bed. The cool sheets had a calming effect on him and he drifted off to sleep.

The pounding rain on the roof of the cabin woke him up deep in the middle of the night. He sat up with a start and then sighed.

It's just the rain.

The sound of breaking glass made him turn his head toward the open door of the bedroom. It came again and again. Ed quickly slid on his slacks and shoes. He looked around the room, but couldn't see much from the light coming in through the door. He'd left the lights on out there.

He poked his head out and looked toward the window facing the lake. Half a dozen rotting arms poked through the broken window. Guttural moans wet with mucus drifted in through the shattered portal. He quickly pulled his head back into the room.

What the hell?

He got dressed quickly and edged his way out of the bedroom. The arms still reached through the window, but they didn't seem to making much more progress than that. Ed realized the bars must be stopping their progress. Water from the rain trickled in, bringing with it a dark ooze from the bodies trying to get through.

He went to the front door but as he was about to open it,

he heard wed thuds against the wooden structure from all around. He made sure the front door was locked.

There was a bang and a flash of light from behind him. Ed turned quickly to see the fading light of the lightning bolt illuminating the lake and what had to be dozens of dead people in various states of decay traveling towards his cabin from the lake.

Then, they began to climb on top of each other, cling to the metal bars on the window. An undulating mass of decaying flesh reached toward him through the increasingly compromised window, getting higher as the bodies piled higher and higher on top of each other. Then Ed heard a loud pop and the mass of bodies disappeared on one side temporarily.

"The bars are giving way," Ed whispered. He looked around wildly and grabbed his cell phone. He turned it on and saw he had no signal.

"Shit!"

A body fell through the window with a wet plop on the floor. In a panic, Ed ran into the bedroom and shut the door. He turned the light on and pushed the bed against the door with great effort. He sat down on the bed and put his head in his hands. He could hear the rain pounding on the roof and the dull thud of undead fists beating on the outside of the cabin trying to gain entry. He raised his head and spotted the side table near the boarded up bedroom window. He ran to it and opened the drawer. There was nothing in it besides a small framed photograph... of his wife, Tina.

"You bitch!" he screamed.

The slow drumming of wet, dead fists on the bedroom door caused him to turn around to see the door begin to buckle under the sheer weight of the dead.

may

Motherly Love
Angela Faro

Mother's Day, 2022

In the hot and stuffy attic, Debra—a downtrodden looking woman with long, wild silver hair and pale blue eyes that were once bright but had dulled over the passing years—sits surrounded by dusty boxes full of old photo albums, yellowing with age. She reaches for a familiar album. "Aha, there you are!" She has been searching for some time for this particular album, photos of her daughter Allie growing up through the years.

As she opens the book of memories she feels a sudden frosty cool breeze out of nowhere and, startled, she hastily slams it back shut. She shivers. "Where on earth did that come from?!" Debra is hit by an uneasy feeling like she is being watched and begins glancing around furtively but, seeing nothing out of the ordinary, she shakes off the nervous vibes and returns her focus to the album.

Cradling the book in her arms like a baby she sadly stares at the cover then gently traces the writing emblazoned across it with her index finger. "Allie," she reads it out loud. You can hear the sorrow and regret in her voice. Suddenly she fumbles and drops the album and a colorful folded paper falls out of the pages down to the ground. She sees the paper lying there on the floor and her eyes glaze over, brimming with tears. She stares off into the distance for a moment, remembering.

Mother's Day, 1999

An adorable spunky five year old brown haired and big old blue eyed girl in uneven pigtails and a frilly and well worn pink dress with stains across the front held out a handmade card to her incoherent mother. "Mommy look what I made in school!" The little girl proudly held the card out eagerly awaiting her mother's reaction to the folded, cut, colored, and crafted bits of paper she had worked so hard on in class.

Her mother lay half in a daze on the couch, in her own world, oblivious to anything around her including her own child, who was clearly starving for affection.

The girl tried one more time to get her mother's attention, this time getting right up close to her face. "Mommy?!" she urgently cried, worried that she might have to see her being taken away in an ambulance again. This time she got a reaction however, albeit not the one she was hoping for.

"What, Allie? What the hell do you want from me?!" Debra snapped at the poor frightened girl.

Allie immediately broke down into tears and threw the card at her mother, before running away to her room shouting behind her, in between her sorrowful sobs, "I made that for you Mommy! You're supposed to say thank you."

Debra could hear her daughter's bedroom door slam shut but she simply sat and stared emotionless at the cluttered room around her, relieved that the closed door muffled Allie's sobs to no more than a dull murmur so she could go back to dwelling on her much more important adult problems—like where was she going to get her next fix?

Mother's Day, 2022

Debra snaps out of her daze and her eyes go back to the folded paper card her daughter had made for her so long ago. At some point way back when in a rare moment she was alert enough to see straight, she had opened the card to see what Allie had made and it brought tears to her eyes. She never told her daughter she had read it, though, out of shame for not thanking her for it in the first place when she had so proudly offered it that day. She didn't mean to be a neglectful mother. She had no desire to purposely hurt her daughter's feelings. It wasn't the way she wanted it to be but she just couldn't cope with her life without those mind-altering drugs. Ever since Allie's father had passed away it was all she could do to just barely exist day to day. It had been a long time since she had been brave enough to travel down this memory lane and this was the first time she'd done it completely sober.

She leans down to the ground to pick up the old familiar makeshift card. It is shaped as a heart and multicolored, uneven and imperfect yet you could see it was made with love and care, as best as a five year old could be expected to do. Slowly and carefully she opens it up and on the inside is a stick figure little girl handing her stick figure mother a bouquet of flowers with the words 'i luv u mom' scrawled below, barely legible. Debra stares somberly for a moment before carefully folding the card back up and sliding it back between the pages of the album where it belongs when suddenly another cold gust of air bellows through the attic. Debra can feel the hair on her arms standing up as she breaks out into goosebumps. "Again with the cool breeze. I'd better check the thermostat up here," Debra states to the otherwise empty room.

Debra shakes off the chill and leafs through the album looking at old photos and keepsakes long since forgotten and packed away so as not to be an unfriendly reminder of the unfortunate events that had occurred. She had to make herself do this though, her therapist told her it was imperative to her recovery that she comes to terms with her past. It might be too late to apologize to her daughter but it is never too late to make amends with oneself as long as one is still breathing. That is what they had told her anyway, so here she is. So many locked away and forgotten memories to unpack.

She thought of the countless times Allie begged her to just be present and at least pretend to care one iota about her but Debra just couldn't be bothered, she was either too wasted or just counting down the hours to her next fix. Since she didn't pay attention she didn't notice when Allie was crying out for help. The girl didn't really have any friends and kept to herself at school and Debra had been all but banished from the rest of her family so Allie wasn't in contact with them either. It was a lonely life and as an angsty teenager she just couldn't handle it at home anymore, so she ran away.

Debra turned the pages of the album, recounting the many memories from times long past and on the second to the last page there was a note, handwritten by Allie. A goodbye letter and the last contact she had ever received from her daughter.

I always tried so hard to be as good as I could be. I thought maybe if I did enough extra chores or if I did good enough in school that you might actually one day be proud of me. But of course it turns out it was all in vain. All a huge waste of time. Because you aren't even in there any more. And you don't give a shit about me. You never have and now you'll never get that chance again. The things you put me through, I don't know how you can live with yourself. All I know is that there must be something better out there than this, so I'm leaving. Maybe I'll find my better life or maybe I'll just take the easy way out like Dad did, which I can't honestly say I blame him. He must have felt so lonely with you just like I always have. Goodbye.

Debra was brought back in time in that moment to when she first found the farewell note. The feeling of the hurt caused by her daughter's harsh words and then the panic setting in as she tried calling Allie's cell phone and no answer. Again and again she called but nothing. Eventually she reported her daughter missing but it was too late. She was long gone, another missing person they searched for to no avail for years. Debra can feel the tears pricking at the corners of her eyes threatening to spill all over the note so she folds it back up and carefully put it safely in the protective page of the album, closing it calmly and carefully.

Another gust of wind rushes through the attic as Debra's cell phone buzzes with a text message alert. She ignores her phone at first, lost in her thoughts but then it goes off again vibrating urgently to alert her of the message so she opened up her phone screen to see a message from Allie's old number.

Happy Mother's Day, Debra

She stares in stunned silence at her phone for what seems like the longest time before mustering up the ability to respond.

Is this some kind of sick joke? This can't be my Allie.

All of a sudden the biggest gust of wind yet blows through the attic making the room into some sort of violent wind tunnel, Debra's long silver hair blowing messily to and fro around her. Her cell phone buzzes with a new message as the wind seems to call her name, wailing painfully. *"Debbbbbraaaaaa!"* Terrified she opens the text message to read it.

Turn around, Debra

Panic setting in, she can hardly control her body movements. She tries to fight it but she is somehow forced to turn around as if someone else were controlling her and when she does her jaw drops in shock and fear as she sees a ghostly vision of Allie before her. The girl looks angry and vengeful, the wounds of her self inflicted death boldly apparent and she is slowly and freakishly approaching her mother. Debra tries to speak but it is as if her vocal chords are frozen. With pleading eyes she stares at Allie's ghost, wanting to apologize but no sound will come out of her mouth no matter how hard she tries. Suddenly Allie rushes forward fast and fierce pushing Debra and knocking her to the ground near the photo album which suddenly flies open in her face with the pages blowing back and forth, the wind turning the pages until the final page of the photo book is open to reveal one final keepsake—newspaper clippings revealing an article about the discovery of Allie's remains years and years after she had first gone missing, and an obituary taken out in the paper by Debra.

The ghostly Allie suddenly turns her head and stares at the obituary written with love by her mother. Love that she was never shown and that she never knew. Love that she was so desperate to feel. For a moment the look of anger and vengeance leaves her face and in that moment Debra is able to speak once again. She pleads with her ghostly daughter, "Allie, I'm so sorry I mistreated you and I'd do anything to go back and change things! Please forgive me!"

Allie stares sadly, pondering her mother's words and in that moment it seems as though this apology has quieted her rage for good and she speaks calmly but woefully to Debra. "I forgive you, Mother, but we can never go back."

Allie reaches out to her mother, arms spread wide to embrace her. Debra eagerly opens up for a hug from her long lost daughter, relieved to have this opportunity to make amends but as her daughter puts her arms around her. Before she realizes what is happening she is enclosed into a much too tight embrace.

"You have made your bed Debra, and now it's time for you to lay in it!" The vengeful spirit now speaks in a terrifying voice unrecognizable to Debra while slowly squeezing the life out of her like some kind of boa constrictor crushing its prey. Allie then whispers in her ear as Debra wheezes her final breath and the wind immediately stops, "It's time to come home, mother."

Mother's Day, 2025

As a young mother with her bright and bubbly four year old girl are viewing a possible new home to purchase, the girl is roaming around the rooms of the house and her mom can hear her mischievous giggling.

The mother calls out, "What's so funny kiddo? You sound like you are up to no good."

The little girl runs back to her mom, excitedly jabbering and jumping up and down while tugging on her mother's arm. She begs her mother adorably mispronouncing all of her 'L' sounds with 'W' sounds. "I wike this pwace, can we wive here pretty pwease, Mommy?"

Amused her mother chuckles, "Oh yeah? What sold you on this place, my silly goose?"

The little girl, smiling cheerfully, says, "I'm not a goose, Mommy, but there's another family that lives here and they have a little girl too! She's my new best friend!"

The mother shakes her head good-naturedly. "Ah, I see." Sheepishly, she turns to the realtor who is showing them the house. "Kids sure say the darndest things don't they?"

The realtor laughs and nods in agreement, grinning widely

at the girl. This isn't the first he's heard about this mysterious family but he sure isn't letting on to it. "Imaginary friends, pretty normal thing. My daughter had one too at that age."

They finish up the tour of the home and the real estate agent shows them back out to their car, waving amicably to them both and wishing a Happy Mother's Day to the young woman.

The girl and her mother are waving back when the mother's attention is suddenly drawn up to the attic where she could swear she sees a little girl in uneven pigtails and a frilly pink dress staring out the window and waving at them with what appears to be her mother standing lovingly behind her, looking on. Her daughter once again giggles delightfully in the backseat and waves enthusiastically at her new friend up in the attic.

JUNE

Plato's Allegory

Pauline Ugalde

June 1st, 202X

again, another day of frenzied, internal theorizing, barely dammed by the slightest semblance of nervousness, shyness, or shame. All at once, he yearns for the wait to end, and to never end. If the wait ends, he may at last compare his theories with the creator's intent. If the wait never ends, he may refine his opinions endlessly, and craft the perfect theory. If the novel—film—game—releases, the story will finalize. He will see if his analysis of the developer's mind was accurate. If that occurred, then he'd have no reason to talk about the game anymore.

Without his theories, he was no one.

It'll be fine. There can't be an update today. We haven't received anything in so long. What are the odds... .

Sigma
@Summationdev
Everything's going so well. I'm so grateful for
the team putting up with me.
I want to thank each of you for your support.
Please keep doing what you're doing. Without
you, we couldn't MANIFEST my vision at all.
June 1, 202X, 9:51 PM

"Aw! They really do care! Even about a random nobody like me."

His smile is sweet, but short-lived. *Wait.*

He reads the tweet again: '*MANIFEST my vision.*'

Why did you say that? Why would you phrase it like that? Why would you call the development process... 'manifesting?'

Is dread welling up from within him, or is it excitement? "Holy shit. Sigma actually did it. They acknowledged it!"

He doesn't care that he's shouting, alone in his apartment at night. He must message Sam on Entropy. Alex can't wait. "I've been saying this for years! And there's finally proof! I have to—"

Alex is too eager to think straight. He has to tell someone! He has to know! Now!

Wordstroke
Today at 9:55 pm
sigma tweeted! i checked the twitter cuz i was bored and they tweeted just now!
Scattershot
Today at 9:55 PM
Wow you're excited. You can't even type good!

9:55 PM

Usually I'm the one textspeaking at you!

9:55 PM

Isn't it late where Sigma is?

Wordstroke

Today at 9:55 PM

no one knows where they live some say it's the east coast but i think they just stay up

Scattershot

Today at 9:56 PM

... FUCK.

9:56 PM

I just read it.

9:56 PM

Why'd they phrase it like that?

Wordstroke

Today at 9:57 pm

YES!

9:57 PM

that's what i'm saying! we have a lot to discuss tonight.

Scattershot

Today at 9:58 pm

Talk with you soon. And please take a bit to calm down first. Don't have a heart attack over there.

Wordstroke

Today at 9:58 pm

I won't. I have to check my notes. Cuz the wording of this tweet. IT MEANS THINGS!!!

Scattershot

Today at 9:59 PM

That's more leik it

June 2nd, 202X

Sam's feet hang partway off the edge of his bed as he awakes, arms flailing. "Ah! holy crap!"

Frantically, he mentally gropes for an explanation: *No I didn't drink last night—it's Tuesday—that'd be stupid. Not unwelcome, but stupid.*

Untangling from his sheets, Sam blinks at the sunlight already streaming through the tiny sliver in his curtains. *There's only one explanation, then.*

Stumbling to his desk, Sam fidgets, as his computer boots up. As soon as it allows, he opens Entropy and a word processor, each in a separate tab.

Scattershot

Today at 7:01 AM

I had a dream last night. Have to get ready for work but will post the dream journal later.

7:01 AM

But I'm blaming you for it.

7:01 AM

Alex? If you're gonna talk about cosmic horror do it before midnight from now on okay?

7:01 AM

Once he closes Entropy, the enormity of what he promised to do hits him: "Why..." he murmurs. "Why did that happen?"

Slowly, he types the date and time at the top and saves the file, in his dedicated Dream Journal folder. "I can't. I don't understand. Think, Sam." He face palms. "Think!"

Words dribble out of him and onto the page. Sam pecks at the keys, deletes the results, and undoes those deletions many times, never content with his prose. Eventually, however, he does write something down.

Scattershot

Today at 5:00 PM

I worked on this on and off today. I couldn't get the words out. Nothing felt right. But here it is.

5:01 PM

Written 06/02, 7:00 AM-4:30 PM

I don't remember much anymore and I hate that I don't. It must've been bad—I woke up hanging off my bed this morning. My legs hanging off the side. I thought I overslept but I didn't.

I don't remember much anymore but I was scared.

But it wasn't a chase dream like what yours usually are. I don't remember any people in it or places.

I only remember the feeling. The feeling of hands holding mine. Not in a bad way. Sitting? Standing? in a crowd. A huge one. We were all there for the same reason. Waiting for something. We were all looking at the same place, waiting for something to come out. Hoping something would. Willing something would.

Like how you always say. Like you said last night.

We were waiting for something to *manifest*.

I don't know if you were there but I bet you were. The dream was *your* fault after all.

Scattershot

today at 5:03 PM

Legit I'm not mad but I think I'm gonna take a break for a while. Will stay off Discord for a few days till I feel better.

5:04 PM

I'm so happy for Sigma you KNOW a game's good when it's invaded your dreams and you don't automatically think you're crazy. But damn I don't like this.

5:05 PM

You should probly take a break too, Alex. It's only been a day and you were already no chill like the early days of Summation's release schedule.

5:06 PM

I know you hate waiting but we can't do anything else at this point. No matter how much you want it to come out, Summation won't come out sooner just cuz you want it to.

5:06 PM

Take care of yourself man.

5:06 PM

Oh one last thing when are we getting groceries again? Don't think I didn't see you eat that peanut butter sandwich before class last night.

5:06 PM

I can make my stuff last a couple more days but...

5:07 PM

So let's hit up Costco this Friday okay?

Sam jerks; the microwave's done. *Damn you Alex! You made me realize that sounds like something from the game!*

Sam sighs in relief, plate in hand. *I hope he's not mad. I don't wanna leave him when he's so excited but it's so much. I was almost happy we stopped getting regular development updates...*

If nothing else so Alex wouldn't dump ten pages of theories into Entropy every few days and get pissed when I wouldn't read them all before we talked.

Phone on his lap, bluetooth monitor glowing brightly on the living room wall in front of him, Sam cracks his joints and hits play on his phone, starting the YouTube video he searched for earlier. Laughing, he turns the volume up on his phone, the monitor's speakers responding in kind. "Look what you've done to me, Alex," he snarks. "'I'm gonna take a break,' I said. And look at me!"

A swig from his glass, perched on a nearby towel, then a remark toward the video's narrator, as if he's sitting across from Sam: "Yeah yeah—go on about 159 Summation Facts I Probably Didn't Know. Even I know at least half of these already, and I still have a sense of shame.

"Somehow."

June 3rd, 202X

Yeah, I know doing this so early in the morning before work will just make things worse, but I'll be thinking about it all day anyway, so I might as well... .

Alex hovers his mouse cursor over Entropy: He already saw that he received messages last night on his phone, but not their contents. It takes Alex only a few seconds to read Sam's posts, but much longer to process them. He sighs. *He's right. I... I'm such a handful aren't I?*

He begins to type a response: 'I know I can be a bitch—'

'You're right. I need a—'

'I shouldn't have gotten so excited... .'

Drafting again and again, Alex finally settles on a message. It still doesn't flow well, and it's blunt, but he's happy that he even wrote something at all, let alone sent it.

Wordstroke

Today at 7:10 AM

I'm sorry. I know it's so hard to deal with my bullshit. I get excited so easily and I know you can't keep up.

7:10 AM

Even if you want to.

7:11 AM

you've always been more cautious than me. And more

7:12 AM

skeptical.

7:12 AM

You're right man. I need to pull myself together.

7:13 AM

We don't even know why Sigma's tweeting again. For all we know they might not be online again for another month.

7:13 AM

Or more.

7:14 AM

So you're right. Let's take things slow for a while.

7:14 AM

Let's voice chat only once a week for now.

7:15 AM

Summation's not going anywhere. We've waited years for the full release. What's a few more weeks or months gonna do?

7:15 AM

Good luck today.

7:16 AM

Talk to you soon.

7:17 AM

Oh and Costco sounds great. We'll drive over together after school.

Alex sits back, the tension in his body already fading away. *I can wait a week. If it's this hard for me to not explode from excitement, I can't imagine what Sigma is feeling right now! They've had to keep it all to themselves for who knows how long?*

Smiling to himself, Alex wanders out of his room into the rest of his one-bedroom apartment. Nostalgia welling up within him, as he gazes at every piece of fan art from his most beloved franchises on every available surface, Summation included, Alex prepares breakfast.

"Crap! I forgot about my dream..." he recalls, catching a banana midfall as he swipes it off the countertop. "But it's okay." He shrugs. "I have all day to write it down. No need to freak out over it.

"But I will tell Sam that I got the banana."

Even later that evening, as Alex sits down on the floor for his own dinner, he only posts brief Entropy messages about his dream.

Wordstroke

Today at 7:00 PM

I forgot to write this earlier but I had another dream last night.

7:00 PM

Not sure what it was anymore but I think it was like yours.

7:00 PM

But there was a screen? We were watching it but there was nothing on yet. But ehh as long as no one dies in my dreams I'm not worried.

7:01 PM
Have a good night, dude.
7:03 PM
And an update on my food stash. I broke into the peanut butter for breakfast again. But at least I got the banana.

Tired but satisfied, Alex lies in bed later that night, wrapping up browsing on his phone. In his mind's eye, he envisions lists of videos he plans to share, during his next talk with Sam, even recalling the faces and voices of their creators. Internally, he strikes off some that are too long, crazy, trivial, or all three. Even those mental images fade, as he begins to drift off to sleep.

        At least, until his phone emits a rising, bright, three-tone chime next to him. Reflexively, Alex unlocks his phone and enters the message display screen, containing a string of texts, all sent at the same time.

Thursday June 4, 202X

000-000-0000, Thank you for bringing
your dream out of the
SHADOWS., 12:00 AM

He deserves to see every
DIMENSION
of your findings., 12:00 AM

Strip him of his
DELUSIONS
however you can., 12:00 AM

You must
EMERGE
into the
LIGHT
together., 12:00 AM

This is where
I
Shall
MANIFEST., 12:00 AM

Tuesday June 10th, 202X

Sam's hands shake as he perches his phone on its stand on the floor. The ice cubes in his drink clack as he pokes at Entropy's home screen. With one hand, Sam initiates the video call with Alex, and with the other, he takes a swig.

Scattershot started a call, today at 7:00 PM

(Alex barely registers Sam's face before spotting the drink.)

Alex: "It's only *Wednesday*! What's with the drink!? Did our eggs from Costco go bad early again?"

(Sam swigs again and focuses the camera on his drink properly. He grins.)

Sam: "Ya know how when things don't go your way, you always say to ignore your problems and drink heavily?"

(Alex gives a nearly imperceptible nod.)

Sam: "Well I'm taking your advice. Eight days too late."

(Initially confused, Alex leans toward the camera, scanning his friend's face. It takes him several moments to respond.)

Alex: "Well that's good. At least I'm not the only one."

(He presents a mug of hot chocolate. Sam squints at it.)

Sam: "It's not a frothy mug of water though."

(Alex laughs.)

Alex: "There's vanilla vodka for taste."

(Sam mimes high-fiving the screen. Alex sips his drink once before setting it down, and returning the gesture. Once he does, his brow furrows.)

Sam: "I was wondering what was *taking* you so long. And why you didn't take me to the most deserted part of Costco to tell me."

(Alex nods. His composure shatters. He's almost about to cry.)

Alex: "It was *so* hard, Sam."

(He holds his phone in front of his laptop's camera.)

Alex (choked out): "It's been…"

(Phone still visible, he takes and posts a screen shot of his messages, from 000-000-0000. Sam glances at the screenshot once before nodding. He raises his glass to the camera, as if in a toast.)

Sam: "*That'd* get you to weekday drink."

Alex (tearfully): "Uh-huh."

(Sam posts a link in Entropy, to a YouTube video called 'All Summation Text Messages', posted the prior Sunday, the seventh, by a YouTuber named Nirh.)

Alex: "I...

"I wanted to watch that with *you*."

(Sam shakes his head and looks down. He opens Nirh's video in a new tab and finds the timestamp where his own texts appear on screen, his name and phone number redacted. He screenshots it and posts it in Entropy. Alex's laptop emits Entropy's electronic, two-tone chirp, but he doesn't even look away from eating dinner, off a plate to one side of his laptop. He relaxes.)

Alex: "Good. I couldn't figure out how to break the news to you, that you weren't alone. Even after a week."

(He quotes the pair of messages, sent at midnight, on June fourth, staring intensely into space.)

Alex: You stare into the same *shadows* as he does, Sam. But you *delude* him into *obsessively* rationalizing what he sees.
(Sam nods.)

Sam: "Is it too late to apologize for calling you crazy?"

(Alex laughs, and Sam flinches at its loudness.)

Alex: "We have bigger things to worry about. Are you gonna send any more texts in for Nirh's next video?"

(Sam shakes his head.)

Sam: "I can't, man. I never asked for this! Why would Sigma—"

(He shakes his head again, harder this time.)

Sam: "No. Why are they letting someone use their game to scare us!?"

(Alex shrugs, but otherwise doesn't respond. In a new tab, he opens a document called Summation Theory Dump and scrolls to a page titled 'Why manifesting?' The latest batch of notes was from that morning, at 8 AM.)

Sam: "Someone's stalking us. So many of us!"

(Alex nods slightly.)

Sam: "But what the hell do they want? Why use Summation fandom to get to us? Why don't they—"

(Sam's phone emits a bright, three-tone chime, twice successively: the incoming text message notification noise. He freezes and gapes at the lock screen.)

Messages
Now, from 000-000-0000
Your money is useless to me, Sam.
Messages
Now, from 000-000-0000,
Your WORDS, your STORIES
Are ALL I Need.

(Sam goes pale. Alex raises an eyebrow. Sam places his phone face down on the floor and motions to slam his laptop lid shut, but he restrains himself, closing it quickly, but silently instead. As he does, Alex glances down at his own phone, squinting at the Do Not Disturb icon in one corner.

(Sprinting to his room, Sam grabs a piece of scratch paper and a pen and writes, 'Do not Disturb is on,', backward and mirrored. The Os are zeros, the Is are ones, and the Ss are twos. He walks back to the video call, sits down, flips up the screen, and puts a finger to his lips. Alex leans in, as Sam holds up the piece of paper. Maintaining eye contact with Sam, Alex rises, mutes himself and drapes a black T-shirt over his laptop's camera. He repositions his laptop so his bedroom's wall mirror is directly behind him to read the now unmirrored message. While Alex's back is turned, Sam crumples up the paper. Sitting down again, Alex unmutes himself and removes the shirt.)

Alex: "Sorry I had to step away. As I was gonna say, before I forget? I have some study aids if you want them. I know you don't wanna admit it but we both know you damn well need them."

(Sam's face maintains its composure, but just barely. His voice remains even.)

Sam: "Which class?"

Alex: "Ya know, Multicultural Folktales and Storytelling! So you won't flunk our final."

(Sam nods.)

Sam: "Of course. What are you gonna give me?"

(Alex shrugs.)

Alex: "Just enough so the final isn't a complete nightmare."

(Sam laughs. Drink in one hand, he mimes clawing at his chest with his free hand. He takes a large swig.)

Sam: "Are you gonna bring caffeine pills too?"

(Alex shakes his head.)

Alex: "No. It'll be something new. Just hang in there a bit till I come over. I know you're exhausted, but I'll be over sometime after eight."

(Sam nods. Off screen, he gives a thumbs-up.)

Sam: "So I better stay up late."

(Alex laughs.)

Alex: "Eight isn't late but sure—whatever you say...

"See you soon."

(They smile at each other and end the Entropy video call, eighteen minutes past seven.)

Sam swigs from his drink again and opens YouTube: he has just under forty-five minutes to wait. "I swear if any more stuff like this happens," he quips, "I'll never sleep again…"

Serious now, Sam briefly returns to his desktop, hovering his cursor over Entropy's icon. Inhaling sharply, he right-clicks on it, scrolls up twice, and clicks the 'Delete' option in the menu.

He barely looks, as prompts appear, asking him to confirm this change. He mashes the left mouse button, the cursor hovering over 'Yes' or 'Confirm' in each dialogue box, until the app is gone.

Tuesday June 17, 202X

Usually, laughing hysterically in the shower only occurs after you just finished stabbing someone to death.

The dichotomy of this fact only makes Alex laugh harder, as he recalls the past week, specifically the past twenty-four hours. "Oh man he loved that part so much!" Alex howls. "That version of the theme song was so good! Sam was… Hehhehhehhehhehh!"

Towel wrapped around him, and comb in hand, Alex stands before the mirror, humming and bobbing his head to the song Sam recently discovered and subsequently grew to love immediately. He can't hold in his laughter, as he makes sharp strokes of the comb through his dark hair. "He's not coming for you," he imitates Sam, "he's coming for your show!

Hehhehhehhehhehh!"

Ready at last, Alex emerges from his bathroom, strutting to his room to pick up a backpack. Filling it with items he readied around his house, Alex leaves his apartment at the time agreed on by himself and Sam, but not before he rereads Sam's live-messaging session of his newly-discovered favorite film. As he finishes rereading Sam's last batch of texts, he pauses. A convertible? A red and green convertible, that wasn't painted in those colors a week ago?

A newly painted convertible drives up, its roof folded back. Sam waves at him. "Which high school did you get that from?" He indicates the vertically-striped, red and green t-shirt.

Alex lets out an energetic laugh, as he slips into the passenger seat. "Where'd you get that forkin' ugly paint job?"

"Answer the question, Mr. Anderson," Sam jokes in a stern tone, putting an index finger to Alex's temple, as if poised to shoot him.

Alex pretends to capitulate. "It's just Wes-t of here."
Sam remains stoic until he turns off the street containing Alex's apartment building. He grins. "Seriously. Who'd you get that shirt from!?"

Alex allows himself a devious smile. At the next red light, he gives Sam an intense stare. "Sam?

"You know who."

Sam nods enthusiastically. "Did that janitor put up a fight?"

He hasn't said a word in response yet, but Sam is already on the verge of laughter. "You know how!"

If anyone else had heard him laugh, they definitely would've assumed he was not only confessing to murder, but enjoying the retelling of it. "I waited till he was asleep."

Sam guffaws. "Did you gut him like a fish?"

Alex shakes his head, as Sam stops at his own apartment building. "No. But I had to lug his buckets of blood downstairs."

Sam simultaneously shudders and laughs again. Alex jabs at Sam's arm, as they enter the building. "But you already know that! You must have killed his twin to get that shirt!"

Sam's smile turns sweet. "I legit didn't think Etsy would have this, but… ."

Alex shrugs, as Sam leads his friend to a door at the end of a hallway, on the first floor. Unlocking it, he sweeps his arm around the combination kitchen and living room. "I didn't just want us to have matching shirts to celebrate finals ending. I was craving pie—"

"That's not pie," Alex tries to interject. "Those are quiches—"

"So I made these! The extras are for you to take home!" Sam continues talking, as if he didn't hear Alex's correction, but at the end, he smirks at him.

Alex grins, strides to the countertop, and, in one smooth motion, pulls a curved knife from the knife block and slices open the nearest quiche. Sam watches as Alex begins laughing again, recognition crossing his face. "When did you get this!? After getting that forkin' ugly paint job?"

Sam winks. "What!? I want my own personal knife! We both know personal knives are a thing!"

In unison: "Thanks, Sigma."

Sam approaches, hand outstretched. Alex passes the knife to him, hilt first, winking as he notices the Greek letter Sigma carved into the hilt. Sam acquires his own share of the quiche. Once they take turns using the same knife to acquire slices of the actual pie, they sit on the floor, in front of the Bluetooth-enabled monitor. Below it, Alex spots Sam's phone and laptop, their batteries under a clear dome. The gutted electronics lie face-down on a bed of soundproof foam. Alex removes his own electronics from his backpack, prepared identically to Sam's, and sets them down.

"So," Sam asks, not bothering to interrupt enjoying the quiche to talk, "why didn't you tell me to watch that sooner?"

Swallowing, Alex begins to answer, but Sam cuts him off. "and don't tell me it's because you thought your theory was too crazy. When your friendship's founded on making your prospective friend watch all the Saw movies, nothing," he jabs at the unplugged Bluetooth monitor, black fabric fastened over it, "is crazy anymore."

Alex nods in affirmation, setting his quiche down. "I thought you saw—"

Sam shakes his head. "I did. But I wanted to read it with you."

Sam rises and picks a DVD case off the counter. Alex smiles. "Perfect."

Sam lets out a short burst of laughter and sets the DVD case on the floor in front of him. "I know why you picked this movie, Alex. But I wanna hear you say it. Why…"

Sam gulps, glancing at the partially dismantled electronics nearby. "Why the one stalking us, and so many fans like us, is copying this movie."

In contrast to Sam's tense demeanor, and his own energetic behavior until now, Alex is unusually serene. "That's exactly what I explained."

He reaches over Sam's lap and opens the case. "But don't think just because our final is over, that you're not studying anymore. After you read this once? Destroy it.

"Where I," Alex mimes striking a match and slashing something with a knife, "Can see."

It's only eight PM, but Alex is already sleepy. Content, but sleepy. Entering his apartment building as Sam drives away, he takes his time walking up to the third floor apartment. Electronics restored to normal working order, he sets his laptop on his desk, and his phone on his pillow. Already in pajamas, Alex pads to the kitchen and fills first a water bottle at the sink, then a travel mug with hot chocolate and a shot of vanilla vodka. Straw and lid in hand as well, he enters his bedroom, he closes the door, setting his drinks down next to his bed. Phone in hand, Alex lies down, smiling softly to himself. "I hope Sam will be okay."

He directs his self-talk toward his phone, as if in a call. "Burning that letter must have scared him really bad. But we had to. If not... ."

Alex finds a suitably-long YouTube video; It's nearly an hour. "Why did your neighbors not say anything? They didn't even care that the smoke alarm went off! They were so close to calling the cops when I brought you that wall tapestry for our friendship anniversary. They thought I was a Zodiac Killer disciple or something... ."

Alex sips from his hot chocolate, listening to, rather than watching, the video. He stops looking at the time.

The knock at the door, just past ten PM, doesn't even phase Alex; Sam has come by that late before. He gives a warm and inebriated, smile, to the mail carrier. "Sorry to keep you up so late," he tries to console her. "I know you can't keep your eyes open. Just like me."

She nods slowly, rubbing at her eyes. "It's okay. I got this to you and that's all that matters."

She steps closer, handing him an envelope. Apologetically,

Alex opens his door wider. The mail carrier obliges, and removes her baseball hat as she enters. Wobbling, but persistent, Alex crosses the room to retrieve and fill a glass of water, followed by retrieving precut slices of quiche and pie from the fridge. Cradling all three items close to his chest, Alex makes the return trip, and the mail carrier accepts the meal gratefully. Unphased by the lack of a plate or utensils. She remarks, "If you're this sensible when you're drunk you must be a stick in the mud when you're sober. The name's Chris. Chris Cypher"

Alex giggles, but quickly takes it back, as Chris sits next to one wall, barely stopping to breathe between bites. "Sorry—it's just funny—it's the same as a character in a game I like."

Chris gives a thumbs-up. He sits next to her and slits open the envelope, removing a folded sheet of paper.

He only sees one word, before he begins to shake.

Multicultural Folktales and Storytelling Study Guide
1. Humans: The NARRATIVE Species
2. Storytelling Methods: From Bards to BRANCHING PATHS
3. The Power of Stories: Morals MadeMANIFEST

As he watches, his hurried handwriting, the color of the ink, and even the paper itself, morph before his eyes. Chris drops her glass. Shaking, Alex opens the paper fully. Both he and Chris hyperventilate, as he reads the single paragraph of text on the inside aloud.

"It's not captured, Sam. Wess is wrong. This entity in Summation that communicates through the game? It's not being held captive and it's not the story ending that'll set it free. It's us. It's not using Summation to cross into our reality. It's using us. We are its congregation, not just Sigma's fans. It needs us writing about it on the wall and whispering about it in the classroom. Without those things it is nothing. I couldn't keep this theory to myself, Sam. And even if I did it wouldn't matter. Even if I didn't download Summation—even if you didn't—that doesn't matter. As long as someone did... as long as this thing knows this theory..."

Chris takes the envelope from Alex. The envelope, and each line of Alex's address change color, until they collectively mimic the background and font color, and formatting quirks, as Summation's text. The same font Sigma used in their videos.

The same formatting that now adorns the document Alex hid in the DVD case for Wes Craven's New Nightmare.

The same 'study guide' Alex watched Sam read, learn verbatim, burn, scoop the ashes into a bag, drive to a nearby park, and bury.

Alex lays back, still, chill and clammy, staring vacantly. Chris examines the back of the envelope, quickly locating a Σ, in place of a return address. She takes out her phone and photographs the envelope's text and contents.

Even as she gently pulls the paper out of Alex's hand, he doesn't react.

Chris gathers as much of the broken glass as she can in her jacket, which she ties off and places on the counter. She layers towels atop of the site of the broken glass she fails to retrieve. She shrugs. "Sorry," she apologizes.

Alex doesn't react.

"Thanks for letting me in." With a pen on the counter, she scrawls her phone number on a napkin and cautiously perches it on Alex's chest.

He doesn't react.

As Chris leaves, still looking over her shoulder, the

napkin's color changes to match the envelope, and Chris' note also transforms, to match Summation's formatting. Even the S in her name turns into a Σ.

Tuesday June 24, 202X

"Thanks," Sam calls through his front door to the delivery woman. Through the keyhole, he sees her smiling. She gives a thumbs up and walks away, while adjusting her baseball hat with one hand, and her black hair with the other.

When she's out of sight, Sam opens the door just wide enough to grab his food, before slamming it shut. Takeout container on the floor, Sam unlocks his phone and logs into his remaining social media platforms, checking first his privacy settings, then his messages. Nothing seems amiss, until he checks his texts.

Just after eight AM this morning, Alex sent a flurry of them. Sam barely registers that the first contains an image, before he sprints to the bathroom, enlarges the image, and reads it in the mirror.

Alex Anderson: .ebiuǫ ybuts ym saH ʞɿoweɟiɿqƧ, 8:08 AM

'Spritework has my study guide.'

Sam's stomach drops. His phone tinkles against the tiled floor, as he lunges toward the toilet and vomits.

He doesn't realize that he's collapsed backward, arms splayed to either side, left hand inches from his phone, till he notices the aching in his back. Poised to smash it against the floor, Sam slides his phone toward him instead. Sam pulls a notepad and pen out of his sweat pants pocket, copies Alex's untranslated note, then deletes his text.

Still weak, Sam crawls back to the living room. Shutting his phone off, and securing it on its soundproof foam pad, he boots up his laptop, lying on his stomach in front of it. Opening a browser tab, he affirms that no one can track his history, place cookies on his device, show him ads, read his communications, or learn his location. Once slightly reassured by his security measures, pecking at the keys, he finds Spritework's top news story that day: an article with a video thumbnail underneath the headline. Sighing in relief, he clicks into the article and locates the video transcript. *If I watched anything now I'd puke again... .*

Infinite Sequences, Definitive Conclusions

By: Brian Lee Screye

Updated 9:58 a.m., EST

Update: this story initially broke on June 24, 202X, at 9:18 a.m. Check back for developments.

On Wednesday morning, the Spritework headquarters received a package: a silver, metal box, with a hinged lid in the top, like double doors. it bore no return address. The Greek letter Σ was carved into one side, filled in black, and a three-dial padlock, surrounded by two black, raised, conjoined circles, secured it shut.

Carved on the front, and also filled in black, were the numbers 1, 0.8, 0.64, and 0.512, each smaller than the last. Beyond 0.512, they were too small to read with the naked eye.

The mail carrier stayed to watch, as I fumbled with my phone's calculator. "The numbers are 20 percent less than each other," I said to my colleagues. "If you multiply 1 by 0.8, you get 0.8. And 0.64 is 80 percent of 0.8."

I took the padlock in both hands, but fail to find a decimal point on any dials. Repositioning the box front side-up, I looked at the numbers through my phone's magnifier, but beyond 0.512, they became illegible.

The scribbles stretched into infinity.

My colleagues, and the mailman, nearly had a collective heart attack, as I jumped up, phone in hand. "It's an infinite series!" I shouted.

As everyone stared at me, I researched the term, confirming that high school math never truly left me. "'An infinite, geometric series has a common ratio, the number relating the terms, less than 1,'" I quote. "'The formula to calculate the sum of an infinite geometric series is A/(1-R), where A is the first term.'"

I pointed at the carved numbers. "1 is the first term. And 0.8 is the common ratio!"

"How can an infinite series have a 'sum' if it goes on forever?" someone sitting in the back I couldn't see asked.

I ignored them.

I confirmed one last fact, the mathematical symbol for infinity.

It looks like a sideways eight," I explain. "It's a line that doesn't have a beginning or end. Like the symbol around the combination lock. And hell, even the lock shape itself."

When asked if he found the package suspicious, the mailman, who wishes to remain anonymous, answered, "No. I thought a game or console was inside. But give me a sec. I want to check something."

I placed the box combination side-up and entered 888. It popped open, the doors swinging outward to either side. As they did, the mailman returned. "I checked my records for today's scheduled deliveries," he said. "This one isn't recorded anywhere, But I..."

He trailed off before continuing, "Why did anyone let this

get on my truck? Why did I give this to you. Why did I let you open it? Why didn't I think anything was wrong?"

The mailman then broke into tears. Two of my colleagues, who also wish to remain anonymous, accompanied him to an empty office to rest. As of initially posting this story, he is still there.

Black envelopes, closed with a black, infinity-shaped seal, crowded the box. All bore Σ as a return address, and contained at least one sheet of paper. When observed, each envelope's contents appeared handwritten, but when exposed to light, they changed, to match the indie video game Summation's typographical style. Each paper also included a residential address.

As of initially posting this, I have read every letter and intend to cover as much of their contents as I can. However, I will first contact each address, to secure permission from the authors.

What I can currently disclose, is that collectively, the letters discuss theories about Summation's plot. Created by a developer only known as Sigma, Summation has released gradually over the years. Based on remarks earlier this month, development on the last release is going well. Spritework will attempt to reach Sigma for comment.

Sam frantically scrolls through the article, squinting at the pictures of the box and its contents. Queasy once more, he retrieves his phone and checks Alex's texts again. His first text is not the first image Alex sent him.

There are more.

Alex Anderson: I got my study guide in the mail., 8:08 AM
Alex Anderson: it was xactly the sme as wht u got, 8:08 AM

Alex Anderson: but the font changed 2 S's as me & the mail lady watched., 8:08 AM
Alex Anderson: the envelope too., 8:08 AM
Alex Anderson: no 8 symbol., 8:08 AM

On the verge of panic, Sam performs a whirlwind search of domestic and international gaming journalism outlets. As he feared, every outlet he checks received a similar package on the twenty-fourth, at the earliest time possible for their local mail delivery service. Every box used the same locking mechanism. Their contents consisted of envelopes, from domestic and international addresses. All materials were translated into not only the gaming journalism outlet's primary language, but several others, as proficiently as if translated by a native speaker.

Every mail-carrier reacted with varying levels of surprise, fear, and panic, as each confirmed their post office or equivalent lacked any records of receiving the package. However, none of the interviewed personnel saw the boxes as suspicious, until gazing upon their contents, alongside people who understood it.

Sam slams his laptop shut and forces it to shut down. He replies to Alex using voice-to-text.

Sam Switch: Where is she?, 8:18 AM
Alex Anderson: here, 8:18 AM
Alex Anderson: she knows her phone number changed, 8:18 AM
Alex Anderson: came this morning, 8:18 AM

It'll upset her, and we'll look crazy for doing it, but she has to know.

Sam replies at once, even as dread, and an unseasonal chill, grows within him.

Sam Switch: I'm coming when the light is running low., 8:18 AM

Once Sam confirms Alex has read all his messages, he copies them down, then deletes the digital versions. About to exit the ap, Sam considers, staring around at his disheveled living room and abandoned takeout container.

Sam Switch: You want breakfast? My treat. Sorry it won't be fresh. Haven't gotten groceries in days., 8:19 AM
Alex Anderson: endless pancakes. x2., 8:19 AM

Sam laughs. Fear abated for now, he shovels his breakfast bowl into his mouth with one hand, and orders endless pancakes with the other. When finished, he sets an alarm for two minutes to midnight.

June 26, 202X

Sam coming over, on the twenty-fifth, is the first, and only, time Alex has ever felt relief, at hearing someone sing outside his front door at midnight.

After letting Sam in, he informs him about the new living arrangement: Chris, Sam, and himself will sleep in the same room, and alternate watches. No one leaves the house, "except if any of us does something stupid enough to set the house on fire." Further, Alex explains that before Sam's arrival, Alex and Chris deleted all unnecessary apps from their phones and computers, and ensured they left a minimal digital footprint when they did use them. They agreed to carry their analogue records on their person at all times. "And no reading Latin aloud!" Alex reiterates, at one in the morning, after Sam takes Alex's demanded digital privacy precautions, that he did not implement already.

Whether due to exhaustion or ridiculousness, Chris and Sam both laugh. At least, until Sam watches Alex take a notebook from a cupboard. "Is that human skin?" he asks.

Alex doesn't answer.

"How haven't I seen that yet?" Sam persists, still receiving no reply.

"It's awesome!" he finally exclaims.

Alex giggles, and Chris shudders. "Hehhehhehhehh!

"I meant to give it to you as an early Christmas gift, the year we first met, after you watched the movie the Necronomicon came from. So you could keep your notes in here and no one would look."

Chris peers at the empty notebook. "Well you're right—because I sure as hell wouldn't have thought to look in it. Because there's no way I would've realized it was fake human skin."

Sam copies all of his texts with Alex, and Alex's with Chris, into the replica Necronomicon's pages. Alex follows suit, using Sam's notepad, and Chris borrows one of Alex's remedial college math notebooks.

Now adequately prepared, they begin their main order of business. "You can stop whenever you want," Sam assures Chris, as she sits in front of Alex's computer. "This is a hard game. Especially if you're—wait are you—"

Chris shakes her head vehemently. "No! Not at all!"

Sam continues. "You're not a gamer. But this game is meant for people who are video game-literate so there will be lots you won't get the first time."

Alex sets the replica Necronomicon beside Chris. "I wrote down some stuff Sigma's said during interviews and on their Twitter. Development notes. Inspiration for stuff. Shoutouts to things. I'll tell you when to look at it."

Chris nods, nestling her hands on the keyboard. "Do I need to retake high school math first?" she asks, only partially joking. "Or a cryptography class?"

Alex glances at Sam, who holds his gaze. Neither of them responds.

As instructed by Alex's first note in the replica Necronomicon, she reads the first excerpt from Sigma's Twitter, with annotations by Alex, before proceeding. Partway through, she hits Enter on Summation's desktop shortcut: a miniature version of its signature letter.

"You're in good hands." Sam motions to squeeze Chris' hand.

She nods, and he does so. "Alex has no fucking chill but he's not stupid. If he's going all Snowdin, he has good reason to."

Chris nods rapidly, but doesn't look up from the replica Necronomicon. Sam chuckles. "Yeah—he gets you engrossed real quick. And yes: we both know he's probably a cult leader in an alternate timeline."

Chris laughs softly and nods again, but still doesn't stop reading. I'd know. He's charismatic, no matter how much he plays it down... ."

Chris, at last, stops reading and looks up. She begins to wrap an arm around Sam's shoulders. "That's fine. We'll be paranoid tinfoil hat friends for the next few days—"

"Or more—" Alex calls from the bathroom.

"Or more," Sam amends.

"Or if this is as serious as it seems?" Chris contemplates, "Until the world ends."

Sam nods. "If we can't give normalcy hugs we might as well not be together."

Alex emerges, fresh from the shower, fully dressed, as if to go out. He sits on the living room floor next to Chris, who occupies his desk, now pushed up against one wall. "Where are you?" he inquires, peering at the screen.

Chris considers before answering: "Yes, I'm there," She says to the screen, not seeming to acknowledge Alex.

The dialogue slowly continues appearing. "And yes, mysterious voice who can't turn caps-lock off.

"I'm. Connected?"

"Hehhehhehhehhehh!"

Now lying on the floor behind Alex and Chris, Sam Turns his head to face them grinning. "Excellent," he quotes the game, as Chris continues onward. "Good luck you two. I'm gonna get some sleep. Wake me up when she starts asking about math."

Alex's intense expression softens momentarily. "Of course! I will."

To Alex's delight, Sam quotes the emerging on-screen dialogue, without even looking at it. "Truly, excellent."

Staying up all night to play Summation isn't the difficult part. Alex can't help but cry with joy, once Chris begins to theorize on her own. Repeatedly, he resists the urge to take video of her experience. *I can't leave a trace of this*, he reminds himself, again and again.

Spending all of the twenty-fifth replaying the game, and, as Chris correctly predicted, brushing up on high school math, isn't difficult either. Especially regarding arithmetic and geometric sequences.

Helping Chris prepare to call her boss, on the morning of the twenty-sixth, however, goes unexpectedly smoothly, but is no less heartbreaking. Sam and Alex listen to his reaction, miming hugging the air periodically, as Chris details everything about her situation. "You got through COVID better than anyone I know," he notes. "So if you think you're in that much danger? I won't argue."

Chris' new friends don't hold back their tears, as Chris' boss openly cries over the phone. Even so, when Chris tells him to check her mail daily, keep her essential mail in a safe place, and destroy the rest, he agrees to do so. "And," Chris emphasizes, as he sniffles, "make sure however you destroy it, that no personally identifiable information can be gathered from it once it's been destroyed. And make sure you're alone. And that no one could reasonably get audio or video of you destroying it."

Her boss barely chokes out an "Okay," but he eventually does. "I'd give you the best customer service award later this year," he attempts to joke, "but then I'd have to explain why."

Alex, Sam, and Chris laugh a little. "Stay safe, Chris," he concludes the call. "I'll alert our other drivers about these letters. And how to deal with them."

Chris nods, before bursting out laughing. "Sorry—I nodded but we're—"

Alex pokes the video call button. Flustered, her boss laughs too and waves at the trio, even while he continues to cry. "Thanks for everything, Grant." Chris concludes the call.

Grant nods once as she hangs up, and the three of them stare long and hard at each other. "Who's on watch now?" Sam asks.

"I'll do it," Chris volunteers. "It's not like I could go to sleep anyway."

The boys nod, and make soft, agreeing sounds. The two of them lie down, in Sam's spot. Chris sets an alarm for two hours from now, seven past ten. On her haunches now, she picks up a piece of scratch paper and begins to doodle, interlocking, geometric shapes. Before he drifts off to sleep, Alex smiles tenderly, as he watches her draw, intimately familiar with her expression: That of beautiful sequences floating before her mind's eye.

It's not the call from Alex's phone, only a minute after he wakes up, that scares everyone.

It's not the voice on the other end: "Hello? This is Brian Lee Screye from Spritework. Is this the Anderson residence?"

The interview is only difficult because Brian asks Alex to slow down, multiple times, and he barely manages to comply.

What makes everyone's blood run cold, even Brian's, happens midway through the interview. As Alex speaks to the game journalist, completely occupied, Sam and Chris check their social media feeds.

Chris sees it first, even before Brian: "Sigma tweeted."

Mid-question, Brian goes silent. Chris elaborates, "Well technically it's that thing where you can make a post longer than two hundred-eighty characters and link it to a tweet—but they tweeted. It was just now."

Brian, Alex, and Sam remain silent. Speedreading, Chris stops midway through the linked post and takes Alex's phone from his now-sweaty grip.

Everyone who's said I haven't been involved in these incidents is right. I've also received identical boxes with the same infinity symbol. It was my first idea for my Internet username. But I changed it because it was overused. Until today only I knew this.

Everyone sits completely still, as Brian takes notes on his end of the call. "Please continue, um... Coefficient," he catches himself, before he says Chris' real name.

Chris obliges. No one has time to breathe a sigh of relief, as she shudders, reading shakily.

> What's happening to me's worse than being cyberattacked or stalked. Even with all my security the boxes always appear at my work desk. My computer always says 'YOU MANIFESTED ME' in Summation's font. Even when it's off.

Brian's hyperventilation eclipses Alex and Sam's, even over the phone. In spite of their reactions, Chris concludes her reading.

> My game's the reason those letters exist but whatever's sending them's not related to Summation. SO when it fully releases on the thirtieth, please support the team by buying it. But don't play it. Don't open it. Please don't ask what the shadows, flitting across our cave wall, truly are. Please, stay in the dark.

June 29, 202X

The next three days are a modern spy thriller, in a suspense-driven horror film's setting, blanketed by existential dread.

Somehow, the existential dread is the most comforting part of Coefficient's stay at Axis' house. As she says with her new friends many, many times after she arrived at Axis' door on the twenty-fourth, "We survived a zombie movie. Or are still surviving one, depending on who you ask.

"But there's no guns or arguing about whether to hide in

the basement or the ground floor. Just the loneliness."

Creating a new email address, on an encrypted server, installing fake name, address, and credit card number generators, and putting her phone in a lead box when she slept? These acts become, if not natural, then logical, to her. Recalling and sharing her fragmented dreams with the boys, and recording them in the replica Necronomicon, eases just enough of her stress, so she can function during what little of their daily lives remain. Worrying if someone tampered with the shower water, or hid a bug in the bathroom light, only occurs periodically: not constantly.

Eventually, she even stops fearing random sounds in the middle of the night. "Either it's the janitor," Axis summarizes, the evening of the twenty-eighth, "or it's not. It's okay that you're scared."

Coefficient, for the first time, shakes her head. "That's the thing. I'm not."

Their group's increased precautions, and confiding in Mr. Screye, finally pay off. On the evening of the twenty-eighth, Coefficient, Step, and Axis, go out on the town. "I'll never make fun of people who thought 1999 was the end of the world ever again," Step remarks wryly over dinner.

"I never thought I'd actually wanna go out. Or party," Axis agrees, between sips of his drink.

"Have you guys ever watched any end of the world movies together?" Coefficient asks, plucking a French fry from their communal platter.

The boys shake their heads. "What's the point? Even people who don't nitpick stuff as much as I do know none of them are as good as the real thing now."

Everyone continues eating in silence. *I found his limit. For a guy who learned to code just to encrypt his documents I didn't think that'd be where he draws the line...*

It's late, but the restaurant, the second the trio goes to that night, is still open. As promised, they see him enter, seemingly immersed in whatever is on his phone, and swaying slightly, from what onlookers would assume was prior alcohol consumption.

Step gets up from his seat and meets him near the front door: "Man are you okay?" Only some of his slurred speech is fake.

Mr. Screye shakes his head exaggeratedly. "After what I've been through these past nine? Ten days? I'll never sleep again."

Step grins and, after an affirming nod, hugs him, before leading him over to the table. Coefficient and Axis look up from their food just long enough to wink at him, before the Spritework journalist begins helping himself to the communal French fries.

It's nearly midnight when the four of them return to Axis' apartment. Mr. Screye, who refuses to use a pseudonym, but insists on the group calling him Brian, already prepared his devices and analogue notetaking setup before he left New York City. "This will be the first and last time I use company funds to rent a chauffeur and private jet," he snarks, as he unrolls his sleeping bag.

Coefficient, then the other Anderson apartment residents, nod. "I'm surprised you wanted to travel at all," she observes.

Brian shrugs and rises off the floor, entering the kitchen and grabbing a bag of popcorn colonels. In silence, the four of them wait for Brian to finish preparing the stovetop popcorn, add it to the largest sealable container in the house, shake thoroughly to distribute the pepper, cheese, and butter, and place it in the middle of the group. At last, Step hooks up his laptop to his

Bluetooth monitor, at its new home on Axis' wall. He doesn't even make his usual gripe about buying a DVD player adapter for Axis' sake, as he inserts the DVD, and hits play.

Coefficient doesn't even bat an eye, as she turns to Axis. "I was wondering when you'd make me and Brian watch this."

The analysis of Wes Craven's New Nightmare comes the next morning, on the twenty-ninth. The four of them give short, well thought-out remarks about the story, concluded by Brian delivering breaking news, in the span of one sentence.

"The article went up eight past eight this morning."

He initially looks away, but he changes his mind, hands grasping for support as tears begin trickling, then pouring, down his face. "I wanted you guys to sleep in. I thought we all deserved the first full night's rest we've had in a long time. And our last one ever."

Without saying a word, Brian leads the group in a reading of his article, containing his interview with Axis three days prior, titled 'Plato's Allegory.'

Coefficient doesn't even flinch, as she listens to Brian read Alex's last interview responses aloud.

Axis: Summation's plot reminded me of the allegory of the cave, from Plato. A group of guys lives in a cave, facing a wall, with a fire behind them. But they can't turn around. So all they see are the shadows of what's behind them. They wonder what they are, until one man leaves the cave and sees the sun outside.

He's blinded at first, but he grows to love the sunshine and the things he sees. But when he comes back to the cave to tell his friends, he's not used to seeing in the dark anymore.

So they make fun of him.

Brian: So these texts you received, about shadows and shattering

Step's delusions were references to this.

Axis: Yes.

Brian: So you've known all along how hopeless things were. But never told Step. Not till he knew what you knew.

Brian can't compose himself enough to read Axis' answer. Through his tears, he, at last manages to repeat, "Yes."

Coefficient leans forward, all of her attention focused on Brian. She saves what little comfort she can give for after she recounts Brian's comments, however. *He was brave enough to come, and continue reporting, in spite of his fear. I want to honor that, in my own small way.*

Brian: So it doesn't matter if no one downloads Summation's full release or if no one plays it. The story was good enough to... to manifest this thing. And destroying every piece of content about Summation won't help either. Because the fandom's overwhelming support for its initial release sealed our fate.

Unlike Axis' real-world response on the phone, Brian doesn't agree verbally: He only nods. His last news story now complete, Brian closes the Spritework page and looks up at the clock. The others follow: Twelve hours on the dot, until release time.

Their last phone calls, in spite of their best intentions, end in tears, but not necessarily entirely sad ones. Brian phones his coworkers, commentating what he sees online, and how he feels in the moment, regardless of profanity and imprecise language. Chris phones Grant, who, somehow, decides to stay on the line, up until the very end. "Even after what I learned I wanna do this," he justifies, between ragged breaths. "I wish I could be there, Chris. Because I want to share my... My playthrough... With someone. Even if they won't have much time to savor it."

Alex and Sam take turns speaking to their Multicultural Folktales and Storytelling professor. "We loved you so much." Sam speaks the sentence between multiple breaths. "Or still do, I guess. You might damn well be the last person we think of before... ."

Alex, however, remains uncharacteristically serene. He takes the phone gently. "Know that whatever happens wasn't your fault," he reassures his professor, who makes nearly inaudible, active listening noises on her end. "People tell stories for so many reasons. It just so happened, this one became so much more than the sum of its parts."

As Sam and Alex say their goodbyes, Brian taps each of them on the shoulder, and takes each of their hands. He indicates Sam's Bluetooth monitor, displaying Twitter, using his head, Chris slips into the knot of watchers seamlessly.

Not a moment too soon, every sigma on every piece of art on Alex's walls, transforms, ink and thread swirling and morphing into new colors and shapes. The black infinity symbol, against a white background, replaces them all.

No one reacts, as the same symbol tattoos itself on their palms and the backs of their hands.

No one reacts, as the Sigma in all of the game developer's tweets, profile picture, banners, and every piece of digital material they have open in other tabs, impossibly transforms into the infinity symbol, as organically as inscribing it with an ink and quill.

No one reacts, as a tweet notification chirps out of their phones, heedless of their security measures and lack of battery power.

The text of the tweet appears on each wall, the ceiling

and floor, as if projected, before at last, floating in midair in front of the screen, like a hologram.

@

Jun 30, 202X, 12:00 AM

JULY

The Georgia Peach Revolution
Jennifer DiMarco

Daddy always called me his Georgia Peach. Nevermind we moved away from Georgia when I was six; we were never stationed anywhere for longer than three years. I didn't correct him because part of me wanted it to be that simple. I wanted him to live out his Southern dreams and raise his only daughter to be the Belle of the Ball. He'd already served two tours in Iraq where his troop found shelter in bombed out ruins infested with black widows and six-inch camel spiders, where their patrols were so lousy with scorpions they had to pick them out of their boot treads. He'd survived those dry, ugly years only to be sitting on his front porch in the Everglades when the summertime night sky lit up with streaks of teal, chartreuse, pumpkin orange and three shades of blue. Lacking the stony-iron yellow of common meteorites, this comparatively prismatic light show was happening all over the world, heralded by some as the 'New Promise' of peace on Earth.

But Skyfall wasn't the rainbow after the flood. It *was* the flood. Just nobody knew it yet.

Mama had refused the cancer vaccine years ago so it was just me and Daddy by then. I was taking a gap year trying to figure out if I wanted to enlist or pursue a degree in environmental science like my high school guidance counselor had urged. I'd been volunteering with the Everglade Preservation Society begging for pennies from rich soft-tech entrepreneurs who didn't know a sawfish from a Mayan cichlid; it was thankless work that nonetheless felt important. And I wanted so badly to feel important.

When I came down for breakfast the next morning, Daddy was perched in front of the old flat screen with the live news captions turned on and the sound turned off. The sync was delayed but I stopped and stared anyway.

"'Space plants?'"

He half-swiveled toward me without taking his eyes off the broadcast. "Yeah, Peach," he confirmed, lost in reading. "I didn't want to wake you."

I sank down on the old pleather ottoman and reached for the remote, thumbing up the volume.

"—FEMA and National Guardsmen were deployed to all known fall sites as of oh-nine-hundred this morning. While samples have been sent to the CDC and national labs, biologists have not confirmed what appearances seem to suggest: Earth has been seeded. When—"

Daddy snorted. "They estimate about a million pods." He turned to the big picture window that looked out over the lagoon. "Doesn't sound like a 'seeding' to me." He stood and walked to the glass, putting one hand on the pane. "Sounds more like a bombardment."

I watched him standing there and felt cold seep into my bones. His body was wiry and worn from years of survival, decades of memories relived every night. I knew what haunted looked like and the darkness in his eyes when he turned to look at me was unmistakable.

"Our time is done, Peach." His hand was still pressed to the glass. I couldn't look away. "Our time is done."

The sound of distant thunder. An incoming triad or quad of airboats, easily breaking a hundred decibels, pervaded our morning and almost drowned out the news anchor; our first responders were clearly running late.

"—which some are already calling roots. Growth of these tendrils appears to be accelerated in areas of temperate rainforest and tropical wetlands where the soil has a high concentration of—"

"I should have gone out there," Daddy said so softly I wouldn't have heard him except he was still staring at me. "Why didn't I?"

I opened my mouth but no words came.

He whispered, "I should have taken my ole Glock and—"

Red and white FEMA airboats cut through the wetlands no more than a hundred yards from the front porch. The window shook. The walls shook. Sound bounced off every surface of the room and made the photos on the mantel chatter like skeleton teeth. There were four boats, each with six-foot aircraft-style propeller fans, the blades a blur of motion further obscured by my unshed tears.

Didn't he have enough nightmares? Didn't we all?

We killed some on accident. We killed some on purpose. But no one was saying 'killed' at all in the beginning. They were as sentient as ferns or redwoods... so not at all because humans were ignorant and ultrasonic response wasn't a checksum on the test for sentience. No one wanted to know that their house plants scream when they don't get enough water.

Averaging forty pounds and ovaloid, beyond the glossy fused crust of entry, the pods had the unmistakable internal composition of *fauna*—ninety-nine percent oxygen, hydrogen, nitrogen, carbon, calcium, and phosphorus just as their vapor trails across the sky had indicated and just like the human body. But what emerged from the fissures in their diamond-hard shells were thread-like ringlets that were definitively *flora*—zinc, boron, iron, copper, and molybdenum. However, their internal slurry, their heat-harden crusts and their coiling tendrils contained no gold. Not even the point-two milligrams that humans carry from birth. Gold facilitates the hundred billion electrical signals our brains send our bodies every single day and they had none.

"They're eating BPA and polyethylene," Daddy told me two months after Skyfall. I'd already gone back to school but was studying remote for the quarter because the university dorms had been commandeered to house grow beds for the pods. We were still calling them seeds and pods back then.

He'd lost weight. He barely ever left the living room and plates of untouched sandwiches I'd made him were scattered across the horizontal surfaces. The one night I'd stormed in and rolled up the flat screen, demanding he spend the evening with me, he'd walked out of the room with, "It's not your house... yet."

He took a six-pack from the fridge and a new bottle of Jamison from the cupboard. He sat alone on the front porch and watched the remote lights of the portable lab erected around the Everglade Six; that's what they called the sextant of pods that had landed in the lagoon. It was my twenty-third birthday but what does that even mean when your planet has been invaded?

They ate microplastics and shat nitrogen-rich soil with an 6.2 pH and two parts per million... of gold. They were cosmic alchemists, mysterious flora/fauna hybrids that converted our phthalate fallout into treasure.

Yes, I was studying environmental science… but I changed my major after the Hunger.

"You want us to coexist," he mumbled without opening his bloodshot eyes when I covered him with a blanket hours later. The lights of the military lab still bled grow-light violet across the inky black of the wetlands. The light on the water didn't quite reach us and for some reason I found that a comfort.

"We can't, Peach," he added, his words even more grumbled as he fell into intoxicated sleep. "We just can't."

The next morning, I woke to a quick claim deed on the kitchen table signing the house over to me. Daddy's keys—on the enamel alligator keychain—sat on the paperwork with a single yellow sticky note: Happy birthday, Amanda.

I'd always hated my name.

After twenty-four hours, I called the police. After a week, I realized they weren't going to do anything. He was a grown man, a veteran, healthy and without any reported SMI. The fact that he'd taken no clothes, left his wallet and his SUV, didn't seem as worthy of resources when you had space plants shitting gold in the middle of the Everglades. It was like the whole damn world was holding its breath.

For a while I stayed angry. I even considered dropping out of school. Instead, I made up an elaborate lie about a bogus hypothesis involving the velocity of ultrasonic sound propagation and what it might reveal about the pods. My research proposal was accepted; it just shows how desperate they were for ideas that they let a freshman into the dorms.

A uniformed soldier slid a black metallic card through a

reader, scanned his retina, then entered a long alphanumeric code and the main entrance opened. What once had welcomed countless students to flood its wide halls, the double doors had been retrofitted with a steel lock at least a foot thick. Fort Lauderdale's NovaSci University had become the Isengard of the American Southeast; these dorms housed nine hundred ninety-six pods in various states of growth from undetectable hibernation to rapid hydroponic rooting. Plus four partially dissected remains that were being allowed to decompose.

There were other teams of researchers throughout the building, each assigned to a group of six pods in states that fit the teams' queries. I was to report to the resident botanist who would have the equipment to carry out my prospective tests but the doors swung slowly closed behind me and the echo of the bolts as thick as my arms sliding back into place left me standing there in the empty corridor.

I forced myself to move forward.

The dorm room doors had been painted and not carefully. Drips of blue and green splattered the off-white linoleum at regular intervals and strokes of paint washed up over door frames and onto adjoining walls as if the workmen weren't willing—or allowed—to open the doors to paint them properly. Like patient records in a hospital, digital clipboards hung from hooks beside each room. Some were left on and I leaned in to read their secrets without touching them.

Pods in blue rooms were classified as 'cold seeds' that had never sprouted roots. A green demarcation were 'active seeds' that boasted anywhere from one to four hundred ringlet tendrils.

I thought I saw movement to my right and wondered how many other students and researchers were wandering these halls of horror. That's when I saw them: A small hallway that dead-ended in a blank wall. Just four rooms but all of their doors were painted red. The floor there appeared splattered with—

"It's not blood."

The unfamiliar voice in the quiet made me jump a little and I looked over my shoulder down another corridor. A woman older than me—perhaps a graduate student?—stood with her hand on an open blue door, the 'patient's' clipboard tucked under her arm.

I looked away from her down the short hallway. The floors were soiled with paint, of course, mimicking nothing so much as crime scene blood spray patterns in the haste to mark the doors.

"Right, sure," I agreed as I turned back to her but she was gone, the blue door closed behind her.

I stepped into the red-speckled hallway.

These had not been dorm rooms. Maybe offices? Each door had a square glass window and while the larger windows within all the rooms had been boarded over when the dorms had first been requisitioned, these interior portals had been left clear of everything other than the expected hasty overabundance of red.

Above my head, the florescent lights buzzed and crackled and I considered that the bulbs hadn't been changed because so few people walked here. I stepped up to the first door and looked in.

A metal examine table stood in the center of the room with a single cool white bulb illuminating what looked like nothing more than a space rock. There were no visible fissures in the oval and though some of the fusion crust had crumbled away, leaving a dusting of blackened soot on the silver surface of the table, seeing my first pod like this was anticlimactic. Seeing the cooled pāhoehoe lava fields in Hawaii had been far more spectacular. I moved on to the next red door.

All the original furniture had also been removed from this room and replaced with a standard examine table with a clip-on light. The pod here, however, was deformed, not oval but elongated and folded in the center as if the forces of entry had discovered a weak point in the pod's crust and tried to collapse it into itself. I looked at the clipboard but it was powered off and a tap of my hand just prompted me for a password I didn't have.

It was hard to stay angry at rocks. I considered leaving the red corridor and maybe leaving the building all together. What had I expected to find? Retribution? Explanation? My father?

"What am I doing here…?" But even as I asked my question aloud, I was already walking to the third door. The completionist in me, I guess.

The clipboard was powered on. I took it in my hand like I was invited and read:

Seed Number 141,937
Skyfall 47.48135° North, 122.57098° West
Retrieved by JBLM
Slice electrophysiology performed by PfiMerck

I stared at the word 'electrophysiology' for a long time. I knew what that was. I'd seen thin filets of human brain suspended in aCSF and exposed to electro pulses introduced to the incubation fluid to test effective response. The result of this test according to the clipboard record: Nothing. The test had been useless.

I looked up from the file.

The pod lay like a loaf of sliced bread. At the ends, the 'heels' had been laid bare or had toppled over and the next several wedges leaned against those so filets of the pod fanned out at both points. It was almost artful, almost an abstract sculpture, a study in geometry and form. Except for the hand.

There, near the center of one slab of pod, marred with the striations of whatever wicked tool cut through the alien stone, still curled in on itself like the tender end of a fiddle fern, was a toddler's tiny hand… but not a human toddler. The skin was soft green, the fingers thinner and without a pinkie. This unborn creature had lost its life, ceased development, when its gestational cocoon had been subdivided, cleaved, shaved into slivers.

The clip-on light wasn't on or had burned out but the ambient flickers from the fluorescents above me in the hallway revealed enough of the slices to tell an unsettling story of dissection and waste. *Learning nothing is still something,* I heard some random professor justify in my head, but I wasn't passing judgment on the scientists, I was readjusting my entire perspective on the universe. *This* pod *had* taught us something. And yet….

But that wasn't all. I kept staring. I kept discovering.

The pale golden Florida sunlight had found a way into the fourth red room. A thin shaft shone through a knot hole in the plywood sheet fixed over the exterior window. I thought I could even see the errant plug of a branch lying on the window sill where some final vibration from a nail gun or drill had jarred it loose. My gaze followed the sun's arrow to where it glanced off the top of one almost entirely vertical slice of yet another eviscerated pod.

Embedded in the segment was a bright white sphere the size of a shooter marble, about an inch in diameter. Half the sphere was still held firm in the solid grip of the stony pod but staring, sightless from the outside edge of the slice, it was very clear what I was looking at: The gray-blue iris; the eggshell sclera, and the onyx-black pupil peppered with gold dust like a monk stone filled with silica and copper.

The eye was human.

A video surfaced two days after my discovery in the NovaSci dorms. It went viral before ethics authorities could take it down and even when they did, others took its place from all over the world. The 'seeds' were eating and not just microplastics.

Those coiling root ringlets proved too strong to cut once they wrapped around prey and the entry crust shuddered and fell away like dry mud when the catch was secure. A maw opened—impossibly small—but even under a rein of bullets an adult man could be crushed by entrapping threads and pulverized so thoroughly that the bag of skin that had been a human being could be drawn into the loamy maw that unfolded from nowhere. A single pod, once it began to eat, was impervious to all known weaponry—even, China found, a nuclear blast—and could no longer be approached without causalities. It would eat until it had what it needed: The strength to hatch.

Two hundred thousand people died over two days.

Every red door pod was destroyed. Every blue door pod was destroyed. Half the green door pods were destroyed and the other half fought back. Another hundred thousand human causalities.

We called their awakening the Hunger and our response the Harvest. Aggressive, reactive words that tried to erase the screams, the terror, and the realization that we had all underestimated and miscalculated the arrival of our first alien visitors.

Yet still... we called them visitors.

Not conquerors.

My father's wedding ring was found in the ruins of the lab at the center of the lagoon. I was lucky; if it had been gold, they would have eaten that, too.

"We come in peace," the first one to speak told us. They grew to adulthood in a year and towered over us by then: Eight feet easily, flexible as water reeds, stronger than iron. They had their own language but it sounded like a cicada speaking Mandarin or a cricket reacting to a Theremin. They could easily mimic any Earth language but context and sincerity were in doubt.

After all, how peaceful were you when you ate the species you wanted to live beside?

I changed my major to linguistics and early childhood education.

Coexistence was our only hope.

Seed of Hope Day Center was a mixed preschool with a brave new world philosophy and an on-the-nose name. I applied the week before graduation and was handed the headmaster job without question. After all, I was one of only a thousand or so Americans who had accepted the neuro-implant that allowed me to parse seedlin vocabulary… a little. I could even manage a few mangled but understandable words.

"To be honest," admitted the site manager with the button nose and lilac curls. "You're the only one who applied."

"It's a fantastic center." I motioned to the open concept environment around us. It had regions of sensory experiences: Soft, hard, wet, warm, colorful, musical, and more. Everything young learners—human and seedlin alike—would thrive in. I shifted nervously in the ergonomic chair shaped like a lotus. "As long as I'm not the only teacher."

"One teacher for eighteen students?" The site manager stood up abruptly and gathered her digital paperwork with my biosignature emblazoned across two dozen forms. "That would be danger—ridiculous! See you Monday morning." She never met my gaze and left without shaking my hand.

On Monday, under the careful eye of thirty-eight motion tracking security cameras that sent live feeds to both the American government and the Seedlin Provisional Council, I was the only instructor for six four-day-old seedlin and twelve four-year-old humans. Other than daily periods of photosynthesis, seedlin stopped eating as soon as they could speak so as the human children filed into the center handing me their vaccination passports for entrance, every young seedlin met me at the door with the same safe words: "We come in peace."

But, of course, they hadn't.

"Free play until ten," I told the impressionable young minds. "*Wyn'wvv*," I repeated for the seedlin. *Free time.*

I heard one of the seedlin repeat my poor pronunciation and correct it, "*Whyn'wav.*" But they knew what I meant.

I took in the situation and found I wasn't really surprised to find myself here. There would always be parents willing to risk their children to get them out of the house. Those who saw their children as, ultimately, replaceable. Parents who believed the vital importance of socialization trumped the threat of active shooters, deadly viruses, and carnivorous aliens. Gracious forbid a child should be awkward or nonconforming; what had Abraham Lincoln or Elon Musk done for humanity, after all?

The twelve human students were barely more than toddlers, yet all of them were already wary of the seedlin. A few of them had even clustered at the front window, watching their parents drive away and clearly wondering what they'd done to be abandoned; two little boys had started to cry.

The seedlin's green-tinted skin and absence of hair or gender-identifying genitalia was on full display as the aliens had not agreed to clothe their young. They had no parents or individual familial units so decisions were made unanimously with cold logic; clothes were unnecessary. Like flora, they adapted to the weather or died. No seedlin lived anywhere below fifty degrees Fahrenheit (which, with global warming, didn't leave much land seedlin-free).

The four-year-old humans were about the same size as the seedlin young though the seedlin were far thinner, faster, and willowy strong in a bend-don't-break way. They watched the human children with an intense, curious yearning in their large eyes and often rubbed their own bald heads like cats nervously grooming. Their ears were just small openings on the sides of their heads, their noses like mice without the whiskers and their mouths thin with narrow, deep green lips.

"Jeremy, would you like to come have a juice box?" I coaxed one blonde human boy who was producing enough tears and snot for all eighteen students combined. "I have apple and pomegranate."

Jeremy shook his head so adamantly that mucus hit the window.

"We'll have story time soon," I assured him, remembering that he'd come in with a book in his hands.

Jeremy just stared at the small gaggle of seedlin who stood in the rainforest play zone being lightly misted by warm water and bouncing on red and orange rubber balls patterned with flower petals.

I knelt down to the little boy's height. "They won't hurt you, Jeremy," I gently assured him. I sounded very convincing.

Jeremy turned his head as if in slow motion like he was an animatronic with pulleys and gears or under hypothesis. His pupils had almost swallowed his blue irises in fear. "They ate my daddy," he told me.

In my peripheral vision, I noticed two then three then all six of the seedlin react to this. I opened my mouth and almost answered: *They ate my daddy, too,* but one small, green creature stepped up to us.

"We didn't eat your daddy," the seedlin insisted with sincerity so clear and simple it reminded me it was truly a child. "None of *us* did."

The seedlin glanced behind it at the other five standing in perfect triangular formation; the precision didn't help paint a picture of innocence.

Jeremy hoovered snot back into his nose and swallowed. "Who *did* you eat?"

Shots fired, little buddy. I looked at the seedlin with morbid fascination. They had *not* taught us how to navigate *this* at NovaSci.

The seedlin youth tilted its head to one side as if considering then rattled off, "Derrick Moore. Kitty Moore. Hank Thompson. Gerald—"

"Okay!" I cut off the recitation and stood with a smile so forced I thought I'd sprained a cheek muscle. "No one here ate anybody's daddy." All eyes were on me and my mind raced.

Set a good example. Be the change, I told myself. I took Jeremy's snot-slimy hand in one of my own and the seedlin's hand in my other. Its hand felt incredibly fragile at first then it squeezed back, locking onto my longer fingers with alarming strength.

"So…." I was sweating and I felt like every one of those thirty-eight cameras were trained on me. "Let's have circle time!"

I sat criss-cross applesauce and wasn't sure how only an hour had gone by since the center doors had opened on this very first day. Time apparently had no meaning and had slowed to an impossible creep that allowed me to think, re-think and over-think every word I uttered and every motion I made. Seedlin vocabulary and short, friendly phrases kept escaping me so I struggled to get through even basic sing-alongs or group games.

We all sat together now… or as together as was to be expected, I assume. The circle was Jeremy to my right with the eleven other human children curling around to the six seedlin with the outspoken seedlin directly to my left. There was a small gap between the twelfth child and the first seedlin but not even enough space to fit another lily pad pillow so I considered that a win.

"Does anyone have a story to share?" I asked, my voice steady despite the real plea. "Did anyone do anything fun over the weekend?"

No one spoke up. No one raised their hand.

I knew tag was out of the question. The seedlin were too fast. Nothing too physical actually; the seedlin were too strong. Nothing too vested in language; this was a bilingual classroom with very little (no) crossover. It wasn't time yet for a snack or a nap. Would the seedlin do either? Or would they just stand in the sunshine near the front window?

I have to admit I was amazed how quiet and still those eighteen children watched and waited. I knew seedlin rarely questioned authority and teachers were seen as such but this brave new world—where plants ate your parents then you went to school with them—was cultivating very different four-year-olds.

"Jeremy!" The boy jumped and I felt bad for my sudden exclamation. I smiled an apology and tousled his hair. "You brought a book with you today. Would you like to do show-and-tell?"

A ripple of interest washed through the students... all of them! Even the seedlin were all looking at one another with some kind of... excitement? Several of the security cameras started whirring which I found very distracting and I made a mental note to ask the site manager what my options were.

"Would everyone like that?" I asked the class as a whole and their quick chorus of *yeses* was exactly the encouragement I needed. I looked down at the little point-man seedlin to my left. "Does that sound good?"

It just looked at me. It blinked its third eyelid, the nictitating membrane sliding across its eyes toward the center of its face then receding again. "*Shoo'entil?*"

It was my turn to correct: "Show-and-tell."

The seedlin kept looking at me then looked at its fellows who stayed silent.

Finally it was Jeremy who spoke, "Come on! It'll be fun!"

The seedlin tilted its bald green head to one side and finally nodded, a human gesture quickly learned.

"Wonderful!" I actually clapped my hands. Maybe this day would work out after all. "Who would like to go first?"

Jeremy opened his mouth but the seedlin beside me stood up. "I will be first," it announced without room for argument.

The cameras were so loud as they swiveled that I assumed we were making history. I remembered the site manager saying something about how other centers could watch each other's feeds. I hoped I was teaching everyone that coexistence was possible.

"Okay then," I nodded my head for familiarity. "What would you like to—"

"*Shoo'entil*," said the seedlin and it exploded with a wet pop like a water balloon filled with hot aloe vera. Patches of green skin slapped into the walls and the other children even as another seedlin stood up.

"*Shoo'entil*," said the second seedlin and it, too, exploded as the human children began to scream and scramble and run.

"*Shoo'entil*," said the third and the fourth seedlin and all the four-year-olds were huddled together crying in the birds' nest play zone periodically screaming and calling for their parents and trying to burrow deeper into the fluffy nests and hide beneath the plush jungle fowl.

And there I sat. Criss-cross applesauce. Covered in hot green blood and alien entrails. Slapped with wet patches of alien skin.

"*Shoo'entil*," said the fifth seedlin without reservation and I just sat and watched, our eyes locked until its little head burst open like overripe fruit.

The cameras were still now but there were lights blinking off, blinking on, transmitting and not. Who was seeing this? Who was hearing this? Was *shoo'entil* a self-destruct? A command to disperse?

When the sixth and final seedlin stood up in my preschool classroom, I could hear gunfire, mortars and sirens in the distance. There was something in the air. Spores, I think, and I lifted my chin and watched them be sucked up into the HVAC system that scrubbed for viruses and sanitized the air. Nothing emerged from those filters.

"*Shoo'entil*," said the sixth seedlin and as I sat there on my lily pad pillow, it blew itself into half a million parts, into particles of iron and sodium, phosphorous and carbon, as it released oxygen and hydrogen, as it dropped milligrams of Earth gold across the preschool pink, shag carpet ruined by blobs of green gore.

I wiped seedlin from my face and looked up at the nearest camera. "*Shoo'entil*," I repeated clearly, strongly, loudly. "We are *not* done."

That was the first day of the revolution.

August

Alternate Route 93

J.W. Capek

Jessica always hated this stretch of highway across Nevada and this trip was even more miserable. Necessitated by her mother's final stages of cancer, she had left behind yet another argument with her husband, Eric. Adding to the anger, her biggest real estate package was failing and she couldn't devise a way to retrieve it. All she could do was watch the dry heat vapors rising from the asphalt. The little red light blinking on the dashboard was a warning of some sort. Was it another of those electronic glitches cars sent out to confuse their drivers or a dire warning the motor was dying in the middle of the desert? For Jessica, it could be the warning light of her mood bordering between rage and depression.

Jessica watched the speed posting zip by. On this part of the interstate, traffic speed was determined by the current availability of gasoline, the boredom of the flat divided highway, the weather, and the current Nevada laws. At eighty miles per hour, Jessica was the legal limit, but trucks and cars passed her easily. Even the big RV's swept by, their tailwinds buffeting her Mercedes S Class.

Driving from California to the little town in Idaho and been a quick decision to get to Jessica's mother before her emergency surgery. Jessica just wanted to be on her way after the disconcerting phone call about the cancer in critical mode. There weren't many flights to the small local airport, a car rental would have been necessary to complete the trip. She decided to throw a few things into her car and take the Interstate east. Over the Sierra Mountains with their cool forests, into Nevada with stretches of desert, high plateaus, and endless staring at the road ahead.

Finally, a rest stop was noted, just two miles. Then, one mile. Next Exit, the sign read. Jessica pulled off to join the other travelers pausing by the few trees, restrooms, and picnic tables. Easing into a parking place next to a car filled with noisy children, Jessica sat for a moment. The children were irritating as they reminded her of the frequent argument she had with her husband. Eric did not want children. Jessica wanted both—a family and a career as an upscale real estate broker. She felt exhausted, as if the seat belt was all that held her together.

Annoyed by the children screaming in the next car, Jessica released her seat belt, stood and stretched. Grabbing her keys, she walked up the path to the Women's rest room. Inside the darkened room, there was an odor of antiseptic and wet concrete. Evidently, the highway crew had recently cleaned the facility. There was graffiti on the metal stalls, the metal mirror was cracked in its hazy reflections. Touching as little as possible, Jessica finished by trying to wash her hands. The water only drizzled out and there were no paper towels. She pressed her elbow to the dryer on the wall and a weak flow of air streamed out.

Hating to get on the road again, Jessica walked about the grounds. Her long brown hair blew in her face as she thought about the past months. She had tried to get her mother to move to Sacramento when the Cancer diagnosis was first made. Her mother insisted on staying in Idaho. Now they were reaching the last stages and Jessica felt anger. Why had her mother waited so long to seek medical help? Why hadn't her mother come to California where she could get better care and had a daughter to care for her? Why didn't Eric take leave to accompany her on this trip? Why was she so angry?

The heat cut the walking short and Jessica returned to her vehicle. It was dusty from the drive. She bumped her head getting into the driver's seat and her glasses fell onto the floor. "Shit!" she exclaimed as she retrieved them and the temple piece fell off. Her vision was very good but she depended on the prisms in her prescription to avoid double vision. It was hereditary but the lenses corrected her to perfect singular images. As always, she had a new back up pair with prism strength and they would suffice until she could get to an Optometrist. Taking them from her near-by purse, she put them on for now, clipping on her sunglasses.

While stopped, Jessica touched her dashboard display. She still marveled at the way her traffic directions appeared onscreen. No paper maps for her, the route was all mapped out from her home driveway to her mother's street.

Her car started right up but the mysterious red light was still blinking. The thermometer said the outside temperature was one hundred-thirteen degrees. She turned up the air conditioning to cool the car. Used to the rushed driving on California freeways, Jessica knew she would have to accelerate up the return ramp. She would have to enter at a higher speed than the traffic still zipping past.

Slowly following the exit route, Jessica passed a truck with a massive trailer revving up. It followed her to the on ramp.

Jessica speeded up the ramp, looking for a break to fit in. She demanded all the vehicle could give as it gunned past eighty, eighty-seven, ninety-three, ninety- seven miles per hour. Years of freeway driving pumped the adrenaline into her body as she watched her luxury car bleed it's guts accelerating to the red line. Suddenly, on the freeway, another huge tractor pulling three trailers changed directly into her lane. It barreled down on her. She started to brake but the tractor trailer following up the ramp frantically beat its airhorn. The speedometer hit one hundred miles per hour as she looked back and forth at the oncoming truck and the road ahead, going faster than she had ever driven a car. A glimpse in the left mirror showed a fuel tanker truck pressuring the three trailer truck into her lane and all she could see was a truck's grill aimed for her back window. The pounding beats of her heart resounded in her ears. She forced the accelerator into the floorboard, within inches she pulled ahead of the three trailer. One hundred and one miles per hour! All she could see was enormous grill work looming in the mirror. Behind her she heard air horns and brakes squealing but she couldn't look back—her eyes were glued to the asphalt ahead!

The other roadway lanes disappeared! Highway lines crossed each other to multiple directions—to the shoulder or midline to traffic in the opposite direction. The asphalt folded in waves! Jessica couldn't scream. She could only hold the leather steering wheel in a death grip, trying to sort and focus the stripes ahead. The white lines of the Interstate multiplied, crossed each other and separated in a maelstrom of directions with sets going north and the others south! The road was split, the lines crisscrossing with advisory signs multiplied.

Whether she released her foot from the gas or it responded to inner fear she didn't know as she tensed for impact.

She held her breath for the collision from that truck smashing her from behind. A spare thought raced through her brain. *I hope the flashing red light wasn't the airbag.*

The crash never came. In shock, the woman could only hold onto the steering wheel and edge to the right side of the roadway. *Stay to the right, get on the shoulder, slow down, slow down, hit flashers, stop!* Jessica recited instructions to herself.

When the auto finally coasted to a stop, Jessica's whole body trembled violently. Looking out the rear-view mirrors, there were no trucks, fuel tanks, or trailers. Frantic and trembling, Jessica looked back and forth. There were no vehicles to be seen in her mirrors or the directional camera screen on her dashboard. The highway was strangely vacant from only a few moments earlier. Sobbing, she released her belt and clamored out of the car to vomit on the deserted road. The wind drowned out the sound of her dry heaves.

Whether it was the blood pumping through her brain or the result of the tremors, the highway looked different from the advantage of the shoulder. When able to re-enter the sedan, she clenched the steering wheel to stop her hands from shaking and started to move the car slowly forward on the shoulder.

The landscape had changed, it was still Nevada but in the burst of green instead of the dry brown grass. A sign next to the shoulder announced "Arty's Bar-B-Que, Next Exit" and thankfully she followed the ramp to a frontage road for a small truck stop. It was surrounded by leafy green trees with an artesian well in the front. Inside the cozy bar, the air conditioner created a welcome respite from the glaring sun and heat.

"Hello there! Glad you stopped by," said the friendliest man Jessica had ever seen. He looked like a model restaurateur standing behind the bar. Whether it was her frazzled condition, or he really had such a great smile, Jessica was just glad to see him.

"I'm… just a bit shaken. Had a near miss on the freeway and I need something cold to drink." She adjusted her purse on a barstool and sat next to it.

Accommodating her, Bartender Supreme asked, "How about a brew?"

"Oh, I don't think I need anything alcoholic. Not now! How about some iced tea?"

"Or a tall lemonade?" he urged her, and she answered with a nod.

Fingering the frosty glass, Jessica asked tentatively, "Has there been a truck—a three trailer—here today?"

"Not around here. We don't allow three trailers on the Eisenhower Highway anymore. Used to. Let me get you another lemonade." Again, he smiled. Not a leering grin, it was genuine. A smile.

"No thank you, I've got a way to go." She paused, unwilling to try her legs. Gradually, her eye caught the directions to the Rest Rooms where she walked in and washed her face. She willed herself to calm down. She saw only a brown haired woman with stylish long wavy hair looking back from the mirror.

Finally, she walked steadily to the bar. She paid for her drink, nodded to the bartender, and returned to her waiting car. Somehow, it didn't look so dirty sitting beneath the parking lot trees. Perhaps a breeze had blown away a few layers of dust.

It was only a few miles to the Wells junction with the route north to Idaho. Jessica stayed in the right lane all the way. Surprisingly, the traffic seemed lighter and other cars were also following the speed limit. At the highway intersection with State 93, Jessica exited, stopped at the sign then turned left towards Idaho.

She drove a steady speed on the two lane highway until checking in at the Nevada Stateline casino for the night. Walking through the slots area on the way to the elevators, she noticed the upbeat attitude of all the players. They stood staring at the bulky machines in front of them and pulled large handles to twirl digits, pictures, and various icons. There were sounds of clanging, grinding levers, and bells ringing. *A lot of jackpots*, she thought but was too tired to participate. She hardly made it to her room and collapsed on the bed. She was too exhausted to even have nightmares about the afternoon.

The next morning drive north into Idaho was uneventful and the car hummed quietly. Jessica tried to locate her satellite radio but the reception was only static. A random FM station was broadcasting and she recognized some favorite songs. Idaho slipped by and soon she was in her hometown.

Using her spare key, Jessica opened her mother's door and called out, "Mom! It's me, Jessica, are you here?" She cautiously entered the foyer, not wanting to startle her mother. She was preparing to go upstairs to see her mother in bed.

"Oh, Jessie, what a surprise!" said the mature blond woman stepping into the hall from the living area. "Why didn't you tell me you were coming? Come here and give me a hug," Helen said enveloping Jessica and her amazed expression. "I love it when you come! Where's Mitch and the kids. I miss those grandkids. The latest pictures just amaze me, how they keep growing.!" She moved quickly to the door and looked at the empty sedan. "Are you here by yourself, did you drive all the way alone?" Before Jessica could answer Helen, her mother continued, "Oh, yes, this was the week they were going camping! Come on, come on in and sit down. How long can you stay?"

With her arm around Jessie's waist, the energetic woman guided her daughter to a chair. She went to a thick cabinet in the corner and turned a dial to turn off the television. Again, she laughed and said, "What a surprise! What brings you here? How was your trip to Sacramento for the big real estate event?"

Jessica was too astonished to speak. Driving frantically to be by her mother's deathbed, Jessica had steeled herself to find a parent wasted by years of fighting cancer. She was already in mourning for the death to come. Instead, she was greeted by a healthy and loving mother who fussed about with a smile and the pleasure of greeting her daughter—who lived in the area.

Jessica hesitated and spoke carefully. "Mom, I was worried about you... I thought you were ill. I guess I just wanted to see if you were all right!"

Helen looked confused, "Of course I'm all right! There's nothing wrong with me that a good night of Bingo at church won't cure." Distracted, she went on, "I'll have to call Betty and tell her you're here! You could come to Bingo with us tonight!"

"No, Mom, I'm really tired, you go ahead, you had plans." Jessica could not process what was occurring. She welcomed a chance to sort things out. To change the subject, Jessica said, "Idaho certainly looks green and beautiful this year. With the Western states' drought, I didn't expect such lushness here. In California everything was brown, dead or on fire."

"What drought? We're having a healthy rainfall; the mountains have a record snowpack." Helen looked puzzled by Jessie's words.

After dinner, greeting and hugs, Helen and her friend left for Bingo. Jessica wandered about the house that was no longer home. It was more than different paint replacing wallpaper. The curtains weren't new, just a different color. The kitchen was a mixture of avocado appliances. There was a noticeable absence of a microwave. The clock on the wall was analog. Next to it, hung an avocado colored plastic telephone. A paper calendar was displayed near the doorway with the current month and year on it. Today's monthly calendar. Jessica pulled her phone out of her pocket to confirm the day, but the screen was blank. *I'll need to charge it tonight*, she thought.

Doors opened to strange rooms, there were fewer steps up to the landing, but most of all there were the photos in the hallway upstairs. Helen's wedding picture was there but the groom was not the father she remembered. This smiling newlywed had luxurious red hair! Helen only came to his shoulder, while Jessica remembered them as equal in height. There was a framed graduation portrait of Jessica in cap and gown. Her name card was tucked in the corner, but it was not the Jessica she recognized in her morning mirror. Not even a younger version. This graduate had Jessica's face with wildly curly hair—ginger red hair Jessica never had in her life. She also failed to recognize a multitude of children at different ages. Their framed school pictures detailed their academic progress. One large family portrait was obviously taken at a studio. The woman was a current version of the graduate Jessica, three children sat around her, and a husband stood protectively behind. She didn't know the children at all. The pater familias was a handsome man, he just wasn't her husband, Eric.

More confused than ever, Jessica went into the bathroom to brush her teeth and prepare for bed. Standing at the sink, her reflection looked back at her—a younger woman with curly red hair.

Moving through the days in the small Idaho town, Jessie could find no explanation for her change in perspective. Her mother was a vigorous senior in excellent health with solid friendships and support from her church community. It was so refreshing to see her mother this way, as she remembered her Mom from her own childhood. Jessie evidently had matured and now lived in the area with her husband, Mitchell, and three children whose names totally escaped her. Oh, yes, her mother corrected her about the climate. The western United States were not having a drought. Maybe global warming was over.

Driving around to see how the "hometown" had changed, the navigational screen was blank. Remembering the town, Jessie pulled into the high school parking lot. Mostly deserted now because of the summer, over on the field she could see teams skirmishing for sports practice. She wondered if they were as young as she felt old. Another car pulled in, parked a few spaces away, and a handsome man in shorts and tee shirt stepped out. He pulled some boxes from the back of the car and Jessie thought she recognized him.

"Mr. Davis? Hello!" she called out from her opened window. Surprised, the man with graying hair at the temples looked puzzled, set his boxes aside, and walked over to her car.

"Hello," he answered. His smile was inviting. "Do I know you?" He seemed familiar with strangers knowing his name. Years of teaching produced numerous students who delighted teasing their old teacher.

"Don't you remember me?" she asked as many students had before her.

"Well, maybe," he answered waiting for the next statement.

"I'm Jessie Hollister from your history class. I'm Jessica Logan now.

"Of course you are!" he laughed and asked, "What brings you here?" It was a routine teachers used to remind themselves who this mature person was, and why they were different from the gawky teen in his classroom.

"I'm visiting my mother. Just thought I'd stop my old school." She still hadn't given him a clue to her identity, but they chatted comfortably. "You're looking great," she said honestly. He was athletic and tanned. She remembered him as being slovenly and probably hungover as he stood in front of the social studies class. Students would make fun of him behind his back.

"You came back to teaching after your... sabbatical... ?" She asked with some hesitation. Davis had been fired but the administrators said he was on 'long term sabbatical.'

Mr. Davis looked confused. "Sabbatical? Jessie, I've never been away from the classroom in all the years I've taught here. What about you? It looks like you are doing well." He viewed her Mercedes with approval as he spoke.

"Yes, I'm a real estate broker in Sacramento."

Mr. Davis again looked confused. "Sacramento?"

"I mean, I just got back from business in Sacramento." Jessie recovered the statement. "I mean... a Western Conference. I live... up north now."

Silence followed. Neither could think of an anecdote or funny story to share. She remembered him as a pathetic teacher and he didn't remember her at all. Both of them fidgeted until Mr. Davis laughed and said, "I better get going, I want to get my office organized before this semester starts. Glad to see you, take care of yourself" He escaped further discussion by picking up the boxes from his car and going into the school.

Jessie sighed. Mr. Davis was another person who was totally different from her memories. She needed to talk to someone who could explain all this happening but was fearful some disease was taking over her mind. Nothing was as she remembered or expected. It all started when she crossed the multiple lines on the Interstate Highway. It was as if she had crossed into another dimension. *That was it! Jessica told herself. Something happened. Logically, people drove through Nevada all the time without going crazy. Time. Maybe it had something to do with time. Wasn't time always a factor in Science Fiction events? Did dimensional time have a geographical shape or limit?*

While Helen fixed dinner that evening, Jessie sat at the dining area with her laptop trying to find an explanation. There was none. The machine wouldn't even re-boot. Like her smartphone, it was completely dead. Wi-fi was probably non-existent. Jessie now found mental ideas from countless movies and books all coalescing to focus at her event on the highway. Closing the laptop, she went up to her room to peruse old books. She found science fiction favorites from her teens. Thumbing through them, she was intrigued by the possibilities. *Time. Place. Heat. Speed. Mental Trauma. Somehow, they all contributed to her being in the present now.*

Not able to access the Internet, Jessie went to the small library in town the next day. Walking through the foyer, it was as she remembered. There were vintage photos on the wall, maps of the state, and a cork bulletin board for announcements. One antique map was centered around Wells. There were no highways detailed. Someone had drawn irregular circle around the little desert town. A different pen color extended the amoeba. Finger like projections were traced on the map extending the area to include territory north to Canada. The date of the map appeared to be the nineteenth century.

"Can I help you?" a librarian asked.

"This map is interesting. Why are the concentric circles drawn on it?"

"It's just something we found in the archives. No one seems to know who drew it or why. The glass protects it from further sketching although sometimes we find patrons trying to scribble on it." She quickly ushered Jessie towards the main desk. "Now, are you familiar with our library? Let me know if you need assistance." She dismissed Jessie and pushed a cart of books toward the bookcases.

Jessie hesitated to enlist the aid of the librarian who couldn't quite understand her confusing questions. With words like dimension, parallel universe, or alternate reality, she didn't understand the definitions well enough to clarify them. Thumbing through a cabinet drawer of index cards, Jessie found complicated names dealing with quantum mechanics, sub-atomic particles and astral projection. Frustrated, Jessie acknowledged she was a real estate broker, not a quantum physicist. As Jessie was leaving the building, the librarian asked her cautiously, "Your questions are unusual. Did you say you drove through Wells to get here?"

"I didn't say, but yes, I drove in from Sacramento. I took the Alternate 93 route just before Wells. Why?"

"Oh, nothing." The woman bit her lower lip, then went on. "I also came through Wells on my way from Ohio." She looked directly at Jessie then quickly hid her expression behind a book she was refiling. "I was just thinking it was an interesting place." Her eyes blinked, then she quickly looked away, and murmured, "An interesting place."

"Yes, interesting." Jessie added the question, "Have you

been here long?"

"A few years, long enough to want to stay. A person can be a librarian almost anywhere, any time." Her voice sounded as if it were repeating instructions.

Jessie paused, but as the woman retreated to the bookstacks, the conversation ceased.

Driving home to Helen's, at a four way stop, Jessie glanced to her left and right. She could not grasp what she saw coming towards her at the intersection! It was a knight in chain mail, full mounted regalia, holding a lance, leisurely riding a horse. The visor was up as the knight crossed in front of her and a smiling face grinned and nodded to her. The plume atop the helmet blew gently with movement of the steed. The lance was dipped lightly as if to acknowledge her stopping. Hearing the clopping sounds of the metal horseshoes on the asphalt, Jessie whispered out loud, "What am I seeing?" Her eyes followed the knight in wonder.

Looking down the street to the City Park at its end, Jessie saw tents and flags. People were milling about in various costumes from Court Jesters to peasants to Crowned royalty. Slowly, Jessie turned and pulled slowly behind the knight, following towards the park. There she could read the banner, "Renaissance Faire." It made her laugh at the scenario she had created in a few seconds of surprise. Not a displaced time, it was a small town re-enactment. She was not a quantum physicist or an historian or a peasant woman hawking wares at a jousting match! Jessie wasn't sure who or where or when she was. She began to wonder if she could go back to wherever she was before.

With hugs and promises to hurry back and bring Mitch and the kids, Jessie pulled away from her mother's home. The car had been checked, the blinking red light dismissed, the tank filled with fuel. The drive south through Idaho was even more picturesque than before. While obeying the posted speed, Jessie was aware of the other vehicles also following the limit, even the trucks. At the last Rest Stop in Idaho, Jessie pulled into a parking spot under a tree for shade and noticed a highway worker trimming the rich lawn. The women's rest room was impeccable: Fresh towels, filled soap dispensers by the clean sink. Hot water. Painted a soft pastel, there were no vulgar sayings or graffiti on the stalls. Jessie relaxed even more and returned to her car.

She stopped again at the Stateline Casino to stay overnight. She wanted to be fresh for the next day's drive back to Sacramento. Checking in for the night, she was surprised at the holiday atmosphere brought on by the players. It was the same in the room for blackjack, roulette, and poker tables. Even the obvious losers were enjoying the festive atmosphere. There was something strange about the environment and she realized there wasn't any cigarette smoke. In all her adult life she had never seen a casino without smokers or stagnant gamers sitting like zombies in front of slot machines. Not being a gambler herself, she considered the possibilities, then went to her room instead. A restless night replaced the hope for solid slumber. In the morning, she could hardly eat for nervousness, but the waitress was so friendly, Jessie felt more comfortable. She thought to herself. *The confusion of the last days eliminated my anger felt on my initial trip. Maybe… maybe… oh, maybe there was a lesson in this confusion.*

Driving the sixty miles in the morning sunshine, Jessica exited the US 93 and turned right onto the ramp entering onto the I-80 west bound. Going west, the road grasses were dried. She stayed in the right lane looking for a highway marker or sign. It should only be a few miles after the interchange—a few miles closer to the scene of terror. On the shoulder of the west bound lanes, she finally saw it. "Arty's Bar-B-Que, Next Exit." The road sign appeared old and rusty. She slowed down, she watched carefully but there was no exit. None at all. She slowed even more, desperately eyeing the side of the highway. Other cars started to crowd hers, to pass her, honking! As they sped down the lanes the horrible terror came back. She was caught in a pack of speeding cars and trucks, RV's and horse trailers, fuel trucks, sports cars, motorcycles.

Jessica maintained the traffic speed up to the next exit. It wasn't the Bar-B-Que! Jessica pulled into a parking area and braked, but kept the motor, and the air conditioning, running. No Bar-B-Que. Instead, separate Rest Stops flanked the interstate. At a glance, it seemed ordinary, not fearful, but dry and dusty. The outside temperature on her drive panel said one hundred thirteen degrees outside. The red panel light had started blinking again as the car pointed towards Sacramento.

Her eyes searched the parked cars and people traveling. *What did they know that she didn't?* Jessica asked herself, trying to make a decision. *Why was she returning West? Why had she even thought of returning to her California life? Was it even possible? There was a lot of real estate she could manage in Idaho. The librarian had found a place here, Jessie was already established. As for the ready-made family, it was hers without the bloating pregnancy, birthing, diapers, and sleepless nights. From what Helen had said about the children in the portrait, they were model kids. Without a doubt, Mitchell was far handsomer than Eric and he was a great father. Eric would never have taken children camping just so Jessica could spend time with her mother. Mitchell did.*

Briefly, Jessica thought of the "other Jessie" somewhere in California. *Did she even exist? What had happened to her?* Jessica dismissed the concern. *After all, she was a real estate broker not a dimensional travel agent.*

When her car shuddered from another tractor trailer passing behind her, Jessica saw her life ahead. It was almost double vision of paths leading to the on-ramps to continue going West or re-enter roadway East. Whatever this dimensional time warp phenomenon was, she knew the ramp she would take. If time was indeed a factor, Jessie would cope with it.

Jessie released the brake and started for the exit leading back towards Wells. Briefly, she noted the blinking red light had stopped and gone dark. Following the lanes, she drove beneath the overpass and approached the eastbound ramp towards Alt 93. It was flat, there was no traffic, she accelerated. Ninety-seven, ninety-eight, ninety-nine, one hundred, one hundred-one miles per hour. She continued to accelerate toward the curve of heat waves arching to include the little Wells Interchange further down the express way.

Highway lines starting crisscrossing and separating. Speeding on the empty interstate, Jessie focused on the lines leading to the outside lane. Clutching the steering wheel, she pressed her foot to the accelerator! Sounds of her engine roared over her! Breathing wasn't an option while her body sensed her speed. With a gasp for air, Jessie flinched and over corrected the car. That instant she swerved over the shoulder and above the embankment. The driver's airbag exploded; the seat belt held as the sedan rotated in air. Like a movie stunt, the S Class flew, twirled, and tore into the roadside ditch blasting dirt and debris in all directions!

The drivers of the tow truck called to the accident site from Wells were amazed the crashed vehicle could navigate the freeway shoulder ditch and not be more damaged. Jammed against the highway fence, the luxury car rested until even the wheels had stopped spinning. The truck crane dragged the vehicle out to the road. The driver was nowhere to be found. The Nevada State Police arrived, and the car registration said Jessica Logan, Sacramento, California.

Cars had pulled over and people were standing to watch the crash scene. One driver told the officer he had seen a red-haired woman crawling out the battered car. She limped across the shoulder ditch back to the eastbound lanes. Waving down a recreational vehicle with Idaho license plates, the witness saw her talking to the driver. She was gesturing and speaking excitedly. After a few words, the woman got into the cab and it continued. It was driving in the direction of Alternate Route 93.

September

Vanished

C. M. Kane

One

S ierra...

"Seriously?" Perry asked.

"Oh yeah," I replied.

"I can't believe you asked for this," he said.

We were standing in the dorm room I'd been assigned, and he was just now learning why I wanted to be here.

"How long have you known me?" I asked.

"Since we were three," he said. "But still, I never thought you'd seek this out."

"What do I do all the time?" I asked. "Spooky shit, right?"

"I mean, yeah," he said. "I just didn't think you'd specifically choose this room."

"It's a guaranteed single," I said. "Why wouldn't I?"

"Because it's haunted as fuck," he said.

"Exactly," I replied. "I mean, sure, it's messed up why it's haunted, but still."

"No one's lasted a week in this room," he said. "You know

that, right?"

"I know," I replied. "But I've got a plan. I brought all the things with me to magic this place awesome."

"I don't think a little sage is gonna fix it," he said.

"You're saying you won't stay with me?"

"Not on your life," he replied.

"Guess I better learn to live by myself, then," I said.

"Can you not feel how ick this room is?" he asked. "I mean, it's like it's swirling around and seeping in. I gotta get outta here."

And just like that, he left me alone, the wimp.

"Okay," I said to myself, and whatever entity was in here. "Let's get one thing straight. I'm living here, and we need to learn to coexist, or I'm gonna send you straight to hell. Got it?"

I waited, not really expecting to get a response, but still. I mean, the word around the campus was that this room was more than just haunted. It was a place where no one survived. I was determined to be the exception to that rule, even if I had to nail the window shut and remove all opportunity to end up dead.

"Believe in yourself," I said, then pulled open one of the boxes I'd brought.

Unpacking was an odd thing. I mean, I'd lived at home with my family for my entire eighteen years. Same house, same room, same everything. Okay, not same everything. I'd gotten rid of my princess bed when I was seven, and decided horses were the coolest thing in the world. Then, when I was twelve and so grown up, I decided that punk was the thing that was going to be my identity. My dad wouldn't let me dye my hair pink, but he would let me wear the pink wig I found.

Of course, that only lasted until I met Kevin, and then

everything had to be sports related. I mean, he was the quarterback of the high school team, and I was swooning all over him. Perry tried to tell me what an ass he was, but I wouldn't listen. I just thought Perry was jealous. Turns out, he was right. Found that out when I caught Kevin and Marcia fucking in his car after the game one night. God, how could I have been so dumb?

Perry was there, as he always had been, to help me pick up the pieces. Finally, when he asked me to prom our senior year, I saw him for who he really was. Not just as a friend, but as the person who helped me through everything. How I'd missed it, I couldn't tell you, but now we were absolutely head over heels for each other, and definitely working toward our happily ever after. Not until after school, though. We both decided that we'd work through school and then think about marriage and kids and the whole white picket fence life.

My breath steamed in front of me, and I felt a chill run down my spine. Stopping right as I was putting my sheets on my bed.

"Hello?" I asked the space.

Nothing. Nothing but the cold that surrounded me. I'd always been sensitive to the paranormal, but this felt different somehow. This was something else.

Standing up, I looked around me. Nothing was out of place, everything just where I'd left it. For the first time, I actually wondered whether this was a good idea or not. I mean, how bad could it get? Sure, three other girls who stayed here decided their life wasn't worth living, but that didn't mean I would. Several had simply changed rooms and been just fine. The chill had left me, so I went back to making my bed.

"Come on," I pleaded.

"I'm not going in there," Perry said. "Absolutely not. Even being in the same building is freaking me the fuck out. Can we go now?"

"Fine," I said. "Let me go get my purse, first."

I walked back into my room, snagging my purse off the pegs beside my door, and looked around the place. I'd done a decent job of decorating, but there was something missing. I couldn't quite figure out what. Maybe I'd find what I thought was missing when we got to the street fair we were going to. When I walked out of the room, Perry was gone.

"Perry?" I called, but I couldn't hear anyone. "Perry, this isn't funny."

No one was there. Like, absolutely no one. I walked down the hallway, and a chill seemed to be following me. It was eerily quiet, with no noise coming from anywhere in the building, or outside, for as far as I could tell.

"Hello?" I called, but there was nothing.

By the time I got to the stairs, I was actually starting to freak out. I looked at the corkboard on the wall at the top of the stairs and had to blink.

"No," I whispered, my heart pounding against my chest wall.

Two

Perry...

"Sierra," I called. "This isn't funny. Come on."

She'd gone to grab her purse, but that had been ten minutes ago. I tried to open the door, but it wouldn't budge.

"You need something?" a woman said as she came down the hall.

"I'm just trying to get into my girlfriend's room," I said. "She went in there, but she hasn't come out, and isn't answering me."

"You try the door?"

"Yeah, been trying for a while," I said. "It's been like ten minutes. She wanted this room to prove a point, but now I'm worried something's going on."

"Let me grab my keys," she said, then walked down the hall.

"Fuck," I muttered under my breath. "Sierra. This isn't funny. Open the door."

"Here," the RA said, pushing her key into the lock. "What the..."

The key turned, but the door wouldn't budge. She shoved her shoulder against it, but it was just stuck.

"Here," I said, offering my larger body to put more weight behind it.

Between the two of us, we shoved and shoved, and then finally, we both sort of fell into the room. Sierra wasn't there.

"Sierra," I cried, looking around.

"You sure she was here?"

"Yeah," I said. "She was gonna grab her purse so we could go to the street fair."

"Well," she said. "Looks like she's gone."

"But where?" I asked. "She walked in and now she's gone?"

"No clue," she said, then walked away, leaving me baffled in the room.

"Fuck," I said, moving to the window.

I looked through it and down to the campus below. Her room was on the third floor, so if she'd gone out the window, it would still be open. Plus, she'd still be below, because she was brave and strong, but jumping from this high up was not something she could do. At least, I didn't think she could.

"Where the hell did you go, Sierra?" I asked the space.

A chill raced around my whole body, like a wind swirling in circles. It even fluffed my hair. I shook from the cold, and looked to see if the air was coming from somewhere in the room, but everything was shut tight.

"Sierra," I said, looking around more.

The closet door kind of creaked and I whipped my head around to look at it. Fuck, this room just gave me the heebie jeebies. Walking to the closet, I opened the door.

Three

*S*ierra...

This could not be happening. There was no way I went through some sort of time dimensional shift or whatever it was that landed me here, in the same building, but obviously not the same time.

I ran my hand over the bulletin board on the wall, seeing pictures of the hall's residents. The women were the same age as me, but from a time much earlier than I was even born. It looked like they were from the sixties or so, but I couldn't be sure. Their hair was in that traditional poofy top with the shorter length, and that distinct outward flip. All the pictures were in black and white, but the whole place felt like it was a shadow of reality.

"Hello?" I called out, wondering if I was alone in this strange place.

"Hello?" I heard from behind me. "Who are you?" she asked.

"My name's Sierra," I said.

"Hey," she said as she stepped out of the room I had been occupying. "I'm Victoria."

"Victoria?" I asked, then realized who she was. "Wait, are you Victoria Smith?"

"Yeah," she said. "What's going on? How do you know me?"

I swallowed hard. How do you tell someone that you're from the future and you know what's gonna happen to her. I couldn't tell her, wouldn't. It would hurt her too much."

"I've seen your picture," I said.

"Oh," she said. "It's really quiet here. Where did everyone go?"

"I'm not sure," I answered, because, honestly, I had no idea where the fuck I was. "What year is it?" I asked, hoping it wasn't going to freak her out.

"1952," she answered. "Why? Don't you know?"

"I just forgot," I said.

"What are you wearing?" she asked, looking me up and down.

I probably looked completely out of place, what with my Nirvana tee shirt, distressed jeans, and Converse shoes. Not to mention the threads of red I'd put in my hair when I got here. They stood out quite nicely against the blonde, but Dad would probably freak out when I came home for Thanksgiving. If I could even go home.

"What is this place?" I asked.

"Hello?" I heard, and it was another girl, coming out of the same room.

"What are you doing in my room?" Victoria asked.

"It's my room," the new girl said, and she had the look of someone from later in the sixties, or maybe even early seventies. "It's cold in there, and I was gonna ask about the heater to see if there was something wrong with it."

"What's your name?" I asked.

"Wendy," she said. "What's yours?"

"I'm Sierra," I said. "This is Victoria."

"What are you wearing?" she asked, looking between both of us.

"I think the question is what are you wearing," Victoria

replied. "You guys look like you don't even care who sees you."

Wendy was wearing bell bottom jeans, a white blouse, and a knitted vest sort of thing over it. Everything was muted in color, but if I had to guess, it had bright orange, yellow, and green threaded through it. Victoria, on the other hand, had a nice skirt on that went well below her knees, and a white blouse, buttoned almost all the way up. Her shoes were those black and white ones I remember my mom loving.

"You're one to talk," Wendy said, putting her hands on her hips.

"Wendy," I said, trying to stave off an argument between them. "What year is it?"

"It's 1972," she said. "Why?"

"1952, then 1972," I said to myself. "What's your last name, Wendy?"

"Johnson," she said. "Why?"

"I'm trying to remember," I said. "So, 1992 would be the next one, and that was…"

"Hey," we heard from the room.

A girl walked out, and she was wearing jeans with a high waist, a white tee shirt, and a flannel button down over the top.

"Dude," she said, looking at me. "I love those guys."

"Is your name Sarah?" I asked.

"How did you know?" she asked.

"Damn," I said. "This can't be right."

Four

Perry...

"You okay?" someone asked me, and I had to look back.

When I turned back to the closet, it was just a normal closet, full of Sierra's clothes, her shoes stuffed on the bottom. It was not what I'd seen when I opened it.

"I don't know," I said, backing away from the portal.

"You were screaming," she said, and I recognized her as the RA who helped me open the door. "Seriously," she added. "Are you okay?"

"I gotta get outta here," I said, walking out the door to the warmer hallway.

The RA followed me, closing the door behind her.

"You find your friend?" she asked.

"Was it cold in there?" I asked her.

"What?" she asked. "No. Not that I noticed."

"This is fucking nuts," I said. "I swear Sierra was in there just a little while ago, but now she's gone. And it's freezing in there to me. So why isn't it to you?"

"That room is haunted," she said. "That's probably why it's cold."

"Does that explain the entrance to hell in the closet?" I asked.

"Wait, what?" she said, turning back to the room.

"Yeah," I said. "That's why I was screaming. It's a fucking chasm in there, dark, but with a cold blast of air that feels like it's from the depths of... I don't even know."

"Hell's supposed to be hot," she said.

"Yeah, well, this is cold," I said. "But looking down there, it was fucking terrifying."

She stepped into the room and opened the closet door.

"It's clothes," she said. "Just a closet. Are you sure you're okay?"

"No," I said. "I'm most definitely not okay. We need to find a priest or something to get Sierra back. She must have fallen into that hole."

"There's no hole there," she said.

"Well, there was," I argued. "And she's not here, when she was before. So, if she didn't fall into the hell hole, where the fuck is she?"

"I think you're crazy," she said. "And since you don't live here, I'm gonna have to ask you to leave."

"I'm not leaving without Sierra," I said.

"Well, she's not here," she replied. "And if you don't go, I'm gonna have to call campus security."

"Fine," I said. "But if she comes back, make sure you have her call me."

"Sure thing," she said, and turned away from me.

"Fuck, Sierra, where are you?"

Five

*S*ierra...

"Okay, let me get this straight," Sarah said. "You're from the year 2012."

"Yeah," I say.

"And you're from 1972," she said to Wendy.

"I sure am," she said.

"I'm from 1952," Victoria said.

"Twenty years between each of us," I said. "So that means we're all stuck here."

"I literally just walked out of my room," Victoria said.

"So did I," Wendy echoed.

"Same," Sarah said.

"I did, too," I said.

"So, how do we go back to where we came from?" Sarah asked.

"This makes no sense," Victoria said.

"It's a time slip or something," I explained. "We've each stepped out of our room at the exact right time. That has to be it. What is the actual date?"

"September nineteenth," the other three said, almost at the same time, and we all sort of stared at each other.

"Okay," I said. "So, if we all walked out on the same day, did we walk out at the same time?"

"I walked out at noon," Victoria said.

"Not me," Sarah said. "I was heading to my first class, so I walked out at seven-thirty."

"For me it was three," Wendy said.

"I walked out at ten," I said.

"Well, that means we didn't walk out at the same time," Victoria said.

"Right," I replied. "But it was all on the same day. What were you all doing?"

"Going to class," Sarah said.

"Going to the quad," Victoria said. "I'm meeting my best friend there."

"I was going to lunch," Wendy said.

"Sarah," I said. "Were you meeting someone?"

"Yeah," she said. "My boyfriend was gonna walk me to the first class of my first semester."

"How about you?" I asked Wendy.

"Actually, yeah," she said. "I was meeting my boyfriend, too."

"Victoria," I said, looking at her.

She looked between us, then put her head down.

"It's okay," I said. "Just because it wasn't cool then, doesn't mean we don't think it's fine. Times change, trust me."

"Okay," she said, and when she looked up her cheeks were pink. "My boyfriend was going to meet me and take me to town."

"So," I said. "We were all going to meet our boyfriends, 'cause I was, too."

"What does that prove?" Sarah asked.

"Yeah," Wendy added. "How is that supposed to help us."

"We all know that we left on the same day," I said. "And we were all going to see our boyfriends, or at least meet with them. It has to mean something."

Six

Perry...

I made like I was going to walk down the hall, but as soon as the RA went back into her room, I went into Sierra's.

There had to be something I could find that would lead me to where she was. I just had to look.

There was no way I was gonna open the closet again, even though that seemed to be the most logical place to look. Instead, I went to her bed, sat on it and looked at the door, hoping something would come to me. That she would just somehow walk right back through it.

"Come on, baby," I said. "Just come back. Please don't leave me like this."

Seven

Sierra...

"Think about him," I said to Victoria. "Just think about how much you love him. How much you want to get back to him. Everything you can remember. Concentrate and walk back into your room."

"You're sure this is gonna work?" she asked.

"Not really," I said. "But what choice do we have? If we can't figure this out, we're stuck here. I mean, I don't know about you guys, but I don't want to spend the rest of my life in this in between place."

"I don't, either," Sarah said. "I'll go first if you want me to."

"I think we have to go in order," I said. "But I'm just guessing, so we'll try this first."

"Hey," we heard from down the hall, and we all turned around.

"Holy shit," I said.

"You can't leave," the thing said. "I brought you here to entertain me."

It wasn't very big, maybe four feet tall, but it was ugly. Hair matted on its head, dirty face, clothes that looked like they were covered in mud, and the smell was awful. How we could smell it from as far away as we were, I couldn't say, but it made me gag.

"Go," I said, almost pushing Victoria into the room.

"No," the thing cried, and when I looked in the room, she

was gone.

"Now you," I said to Wendy, and she did the same thing, walking into the room and disappearing.

"Stop," the thing cried as it moved toward us. "You're destroying my world."

"Sarah," I shouted, because for some reason there was an echoing reverberation that was sort of just humming around us.

"You sure?" she asked.

"Yes," I shouted. "Now, go. I'm right behind you."

I didn't take my eyes off the thing at the end of the hall. It lurched and shook, like it was being shaken in a jar or something, like it didn't have control of itself.

"Don't leave me," it cried, but I was ready to be gone.

I turned to the door and Sarah was gone, so I went to step through it, but something grabbed my foot. Looking back, that thing had moved fast to get to me, and had a death grip on my foot. I nearly fell into the room, but was kicking at it, trying to get it to let go. I had to get back to Perry, back to my life, the one I wanted.

Eight

Perry...

"Please come back," I whispered. "I need you. You should be here with me. We have too much left to do."

I heard a crash, then the door opened and Sierra kind of fell through.

"Sierra?"

"Perry?"

"Oh, thank god," I said. "I thought you were gone forever."

She turned to look back at the door, and at her leg, which had something dark coating the bottom of it.

"What the fuck is that?"

I'd barely said the words and she was shoving her pants down, sliding them off without touching the ick that was there.

"Window," she said, but I opened the closet door.

"What are you doing?"

She looked at the closet and saw what I had seen earlier.

"Oh my god," she said, then tossed her pants and shoes and whatever else had the dark ooze on it in, slamming the door behind it.

"Are you okay?" I asked.

"How long was I gone?" she asked.

"I don't know," I said. "Maybe half an hour."

"Gimme your phone," she said, and I did as she asked.

She was punching things into the search engine, looking for something, but I didn't know what.

"Oh, thank god," she said.

"What?" I asked.

"They all made it back," she said.

"What do you mean?"

"Victoria, Wendy, and Sarah," she said, as if it cleared everything up. "They were with me. We all ended up there on the same day, but twenty years apart from each other."

"I don't know what you're talking about," I said.

"Knock, knock," the RA said as she opened the door. "Oh," she said, pulling it shut. "Can't have guests over for that," she called through the door, and I realized it looked like we'd been getting ready to have some fun."

"It's not that," I said, as Sierra snagged another pair of jeans and pulled them on.

"We don't let guys in the dorm with the doors shut," she called through the door. "I know it's your first year, but I wanted to make sure you knew that rule."

"I was just changing," Sierra said. "I spilled something on my other jeans, so I had to change really quick."

"Okay," she said. "Just, next time, make sure he stays outside when you change, okay?"

"Sure," Sierra said.

We walked out of the room together, and she looked back into the space and smiled.

Nine

Sierra...

I could see all three of them when I looked back into my room. They weren't actually there, just taking up the same space I did, but in different times. When I saw them all head for the door, they all looked at me, then at each other, and we all shared a smile. We were back in our own time, our own space, and we were heading out with our boyfriends to just be alive.

When I got to the street fair, I looked around, wondering what I would find that had seemed to be missing in my room.

"Sierra?" someone called.

I turned, and it was Sarah. She was standing in the row of vendors, and she had a little girl with her who was the absolute spitting image of what she'd looked like.

"Sarah?" I asked, walking to her.

"Oh my god, it is you," she said, then pulled me into a hug.

"I can't believe it's you," I said when I moved back. "Have you seen the others?"

"No," she said. "I just felt like I needed to come here today, though."

"Sarah, Sierra," I heard and turned again.

A woman in her forties or so was walking down the walkway between stalls. She had a familiar look, but I couldn't quite place it.

"It's me," she said. "Wendy."

"No way," I said.

"Holy cow," Sarah said. "It's really you."

"Yeah," she said, looking between us.

I reached out and pulled her into a hug, then she went to Sarah for the same thing.

"What are the odds," I said.

"I felt like I had to be here," she said.

"Me, too," Sarah said.

"Excuse me," a woman who looked to be about sixty said, and the three of us turned to look at her.

"It can't be," Wendy said. "Victoria?"

"That's me," she said. "Were you all called here?"

"Yeah," I said just as Wendy said, "Yup," and Sarah said, "I was."

"What do you think it was?" Victoria asked.

"Hey, Sierra," Perry called, and I turned and looked at him. "Look at this."

I walked to him, and felt the other three walk with me. He was holding a small urn of some sort. The kind that you find in those oddity stores that hold scents and such. It was very old looking, like something that had been around since forever ago. The thing was, it sort of gave off this creepy feeling.

"What is it?" I asked, not getting too close.

"Come look," he said, reaching for my hand.

I could feel the evil coming from it, like it had found a way into my life from that other place. I backed up, and could feel the other women's hands on me, helping me get away from it.

"What's wrong?" Perry asked.

"Put it down," I said. "Set that thing down and get away."

But I wasn't quick enough. He just vanished, popped out of existence in an instant. The vase going with him.

"What the fuck?" I asked.

"There was something wrong with that," Victoria said.

"Definitely," Wendy agreed.

"But why would it take him?" I asked.

"Because it couldn't keep us," Sarah said.

Victoria added, "And because you took us away from him.'"

OCtObeR

Bitter

Marshall Miller

arbara Bain was a bitter broad. She was not offended by the term 'broad' referring to her female gender as she saw 'broad' as a term denoting a certain toughness. Most people saw her as tough, and she would be the first to admit events in the last six years had given her some bitterness

Barbara looked at herself in the bedroom mirror and smiled. "This Wonder Woman costume fits me like a glove," she said to the reflection. "This Halloween will be fun!"

Halloween before some six years ago, had been one of her favorite holidays. She and her ex, Jack, and their two children, James and Janet, always had the best costumes and a blast Trick or Treating. As the kids grew older, Jack and Barbara hosted more adult parties at their home after the neighbors and friends finished Trick or Treating. People soon looked forward to the parties as the adults could dress up in more adult costumes, like saloon girls and the such, and role play with sexual innuendos with their spouses and people, not their spouses. Barbara realized the chickens came home to roost due to the festivities six years ago.

Barbara had poured herself into an *I Dream of Jeanie*

costume, a fake diamond in her navel and all. Jack made enough money for a real belly-button jewel to add to their large house as a top-end financial advisor. However, Barbara did not want to risk the chance of losing such an expensive bauble. She should have realized something was amiss when a new office assistant, Carrie Davidson, came to the party in the same costume.

Barbara noticed Carrie looked like a younger twenty-one-year-old version of herself, knock-out blonde hair, curves, and all. As the night progressed and alcohol flowed, Barbara could not help but notice Jack paying excessive attention to Carrie. Barbara lost track of her husband as she played hostess. A half an hour later, Barbara went looking for Jack in the large backyard. Squealing, huffing, and puffing led Barbara to the far end darkened fence line corner. There, she saw Jack, pants around his ankles, giving the high-hard-one doggie style to Carrie.

"You asshole! You cunt!" Barbara followed her screamed insults with a full-out attack.

The resulting catfight became a legend in the neighborhood. Two fit blondes separated by age alone fought and rolled about the yard for ten minutes before anyone tried to break it up. The costumes of both women were shredded as they clawed, bit, hit, and kicked the other. By the time some wives and girlfriends broke it up—what man in his right mind would stop a great catfight?—all the naughty bits of both women were on display. Someone hustled Carrie to her car as Barbara proceeded to kick the crap out of Jack. Luckily, the high school-aged James and Janet were at a friend's party.

Divorce proceedings revealed Carrie and Jack were doing the nasty for some weeks at the office. Jack and Carrie were fired to spare the corporation more embarrassment, and Barbara received a big chunk of Jack's retirement and stock options. Any possible assault charges were quashed as the fewer court actions, the better.

Another firm hired her ex, and he soon married Carrie. Plus, Barbara kept the house. There were no more All Hallows Eve celebrations at the Bain House for six years. This day, with the brother and sister away at college, Barbara decided to end the drought as something had happened.

Jack and Carrie had moved back into the neighborhood with two rugrats. Barbara would show she had got on with her life and rub her still good looks into Jack's face. She even had a teaching position at the local college. However, the fact Jack and Carrie had ruined her favorite holiday for some six years was still a source of bitterness. Thus, the Wonder Woman costume with a lot of candy to hand out to the local children. Barbara had passed out a flyer in the neighborhood telling everyone that her house would be open for candy and drinks for people who wished to visit.

Barbara's immediate neighbor and good friend, Joyce, came over with her husband Mike to share a drink. Joyce gasped a bit at how Barbara seemed to be poured into the Wonder Woman costume. An expensive black wig added to the eroticism.

"How do you do it? You haven't changed in years," the zaftig brunette said as her husband Mike tried not to stare at the bosom and crotch. Barbara laughed.

"Good genes and a lot of sweat." Mike looked away as she spoke and looked him in the eye. Barbara knew Mike always peaked through her bedroom blinds when he had the chance. On one occasion, she had bent over while nude in an attempt to give Mike a heart attack. Men were dogs.

"I'm glad to see the 'ole Barbara is back," said Joyce. "Your humor always livened up the neighborhood."

Barbara hugged and kissed her friend. The one thing

everyone knew was that Barbara was loyal to those she loved. For her ex to have violated that sense of loyalty had been the primary cause of the bitterness.

Other participants in past parties stopped by for a drink and snacks, but they were not ready for any replays. Barbara overheard a couple of wives talking in low tones about The Catfight and wondering if that would ever happen again. Barbara could swear she heard a slight tone of desire in their voices. Some women were downright nasty.

Joyce walked over to her with a concerned look on her face. "I saw Jack and the Bitch walking this way with their rugrats."

"So? I hope they will see I am in good shape. Time to rise from the ashes as they say."

"You're a bigger person than I am, Barbara. I would still want to kick Jack in the balls and punch Carrie in her fake tits."

The two friends laughed, and Barbara obtained a fresh drink for Joyce and a cold glass of beer for herself. She then stationed herself at the front door.

Jack and Carrie were having a conversation on the end of the front door walkway as their two towheaded children sought to pull them up to the front door. Apparently, one of them wanted to chicken out of another meeting. Barbara smirked and opened the front door.

"Hey, kids. Want some candy from Wonder Woman?" Barbara's call caused the two adults to look up as the kids broke free to get candy. There was some muted grumbling as Jack and Carrie saw their hand was forced. They would have to greet Barbara.

"Look, Mom, Dad! Wonder Woman!" the young boy yelled.

Jack undressed Barbara with his eyes as he approached. "You're looking well, Barbara."

"So are you, Jack. And I see Carrie is still attached to the Genie and Barbara Eden look."

"Hello, Barbara," Carrie said icily.

"So, Jack. What are your kids' names."

"Jack Junior and Carol. They are fraternal twins."

"That makes pregnancy easy, two kids all at once. Or do I see a baby bump on Carrie? Are you trying for three or one too many nachos?"

Carrie glared as Barbara gave each of the children a handful of candy.

"Gee, thanks," said little Carol.

"You're welcome."

"So, like your costume Barbara. As one gets older, more zaftig character clothes fit better."

"Hey, Carrie, you're the one with the pooch in front. Thought of some control pantyhose?"

"How are the saggy tits holding up, Barbara? That costume comes with an underwire bra?"

"Now ladies," began Jack, " there are children present—"

"Carrie, your hair looks a little flat and oily. How about a beer shampoo?"

The fight was not as long as the first but just as memorable. Jack and the other nearby adults broke it up and walked Carrie down the street.

"I'll be back to kick your ass, cunt!" Carrie yelled back.

"Anytime, cumbreath!"

Barbara handed out the rest of the candy, said goodbye to the last of her guests, and went to survey the damage of her costume. Her wig had been yanked off and trashed, and there were runs in her nylons, but that was it. She grinned at her reflection.

"I hope she comes back to fight. That would be fun."

No cops were called, so Barbara assumed there would be a Round Three. She and Carrie really disliked each other.

When Barbara went out to lock up, she noticed a Genie lamp set near the door. She picked it up.

"Hey, this is heavy, the real deal. This lamp is not some cheap plastic costume piece."

Barbara figured Carrie had dropped it as they were in a hairpulling contest. Barbara locked up and took the lamp to the kitchen. Under the kitchen light, Barbara examined some odd writing on the lamp.

"Not English, that's for sure," she mumbled. She grabbed a hand towel and began wiping the lamp.

The next second, Barbara was sitting on her ass on the kitchen floor, with the smell of ozone in the air. Then she heard a booming voice.

"Who summons Alka, the Jinn of the Lamp?"

Standing in the middle of her kitchen was a dark-skinned seven-foot male. Barbara could tell he was a defined nude male with substantial genitalia, jet black beard, and pubic hair. Barbara's mouth dropped open. "Is this a dream? Did someone spike my drink?"

The self-proclaimed Jinn Alka glared at Barbara. "Do I look immaterial, like a dream, a ghost?"

In one stride, the male creature towered over Barbara, his phallus inches from her head.

"Okay, okay! You're real. What do you want? And can you take your cock out of my face?"

The Jinn stepped back and grinned. "It is not about my

wishes. It is about yours.”

Barbara slowly stood up. “You’re kidding, right?”

“No, I am not making some jest. Your myths and tales are true. People who help free a Jinn from a lamp or bottle are granted three wishes.”

Barbara paused, thought about pinching herself to see if she was awake, then did not as it may anger this—creature. “So, I get three wishes. What’s the catch?”

“Catch? Oh, you mean limitations. It is just under four hours until midnight of what you call Halloween. At midnight, if you do not use them, the wishes return to my possession, and I may use them at my pleasure.”

“So, why not just stomp me now, prevent me from using the wishes, and you take them back?”

“You think we Jinn have no honor? The Rules of the Three Wishes have existed since the dawn of humankind. I would not sully my honor by forcing you to give up your wishes. So, choose wisely, Barbara Bain.”

“You know my name.”

“Of course. I am a Jinn and exist in a different time frame than you. Thus, I saw images of the past in this house, heard your name.”

Barbara paused a moment more before continuing the conversation. “So you saw my past in this house.”

“Including the history of conflict with the other woman,” Alka said and then grunted. “You former mate was a fool. He could have had both you women with a little planning. Humans are stupid.”

“So, Mister Alka, since I am a stupid human, I must be careful how I use my wishes.”

The Jinn grinned broadly. “Ah, a human a bit smarter than

usual. I may enjoy this night. Your wishes may not be as boring as others have been."

"Like wishing for a room full of gold and then being crushed by the weight or arrested by authorities for theft or money laundering."

Alka's laugh was loud and long. "Yes, this night will be interesting. Now, to the first wish."

'Wait a minute. You still did not tell me why me? Other people must have rubbed that lamp, including Carrie."

"We Jinn can sense when a human desires something, has strong emotion that upsets their balance. That helps to release us from the lamp as your desires, needs, and wishes are so strong. Your bitterness towards your former husband and his current wife reverberate through time and space."

"So my bitterness over the lack of loyalty in the man with who I had two babies is noticeable in your world?"

"And the desires, the wishes created by your bitterness."

"Hmmm. A little while ago, I wished I could yank all of Carrie's hair out by the roots, scalp her—"

"Done!"

A flash of lightning, the smell of Ozone, and a nude Carrie was facing a naked Barbara in some strange room. Both women cried out and tried to cover themselves. Then a harem of women in belly dancing garb encircled them and began yelling "Fight, fight, fight!"

"What did you do, bitch?" screamed Carrie.

"I had nothing to do with this—"

Both women yelped as whips wielded by two harem women smacked their naked rumps.

"Fight or have the flesh whipped from your bones," a voice cried out.

Carrie charged Barbara, and the two women began another clawing-biting catfight. Sometime during the fight, Barbara had two handfuls of Carrie's blonde hair and was yanking it out by the roots as she pressed her foot into the small of Carries back. Jack's new wife had tried to claw Barbara's eyes out, and Barbara had retaliated in a rage. Carrie shrieked as half of her hair was ripped out, scalp and all. Barbara fell backward onto the padded floor.

Then Barbara was back in her kitchen with a bloody scalp in her hand. She screamed and dropped the hair trophy, then cried again when she saw Carrie's bloody head near the kitchen sink. Alka bellowed out a laugh.

"Well done with your first wish, Barbara, " he said with a wide grin.

"I did not wish this. You tricked—"

"Did you not use 'wished' and 'yank Carries hair out' in the same sentence?"

"You sonofabitch!"

"Do not yell insults for your foolish action. Now, you have two more wishes to use. I suggest you think before you speak next time."

Barbara glares at the Jinn as she racks her brain for what to do. She had a dead or near dead rival in her kitchen, a bloody scalp, and the story that a Genie made her do it. Yet she still had two wishes to get her out of this mess. At the same time, Barbara had read too many stories of magic wishes backfiring to know that the Jinn would have an ulterior motive.

"Okay, Alka. May I ask a question about what powers you have?"

"Ask as you like. Just do not express a desire for specific action."

"Could you place Carrie and me back in time to negate the wish I made?"

"Not really. Once a wish is made, the results must be dealt with."

Barbara paused in thought, then spoke. "Okay. Then I have to find a way to get myself out of this mess. You can change the scene now, correct?"

"Yes. I can change the reality as it exists now. I take it you want the body and physical evidence to disappear?"

Barbara almost said 'yes' caught herself. That would use up another wish.

"Let me think as to what I want specifically done. I need to verbalize it as a wish for you to act, correct?"

Alka grinned as he nodded yes.

"Okay, Mister Jinn. I want, that is, I wish all physical evidence of this bloody mess to include Carrie to disappear permanently, no traces for the cops, Jack, or anyone. Got it?"

No sooner did Barbara finish her request than she was sitting at her kitchen table, fully clothed, with an alcoholic drink in her hand. There was a slight smell of Ozone in the air. The kitchen area was pristine, with only a seven-foot-tall Jinn chugging a tall boy malt liquor to upset the Norman Rockwell scene.

"Ah, it is nice to drink spirits after being confined in the lamp for so long."

"How do you fit in that little container?"

"Time and space are different in the lamp."

"Why not a bottle?"

Alka sniffed. "Bottles are for the lesser Jinn, especially the female seducing spirits."

"So you do have a place to live in the confines of your lamp?"

"It is a world unto itself. But it is not freedom. And after so many years, a Jinn becomes lonely. That is how the three wishes began eons ago. Jinns were so glad to be released into the outside world that they granted humans wishes."

"Then why did you return to captivity?"

"That Which Is All-Powerful saw the problems free Jinns were causing. Thus, after the three wishes back into the lamp or bottle."

"So, then, extend the period of the wishes—"

"That is why it ends at Midnight of the day the freedom begins. The All-Powerful refuses to be tricked into allowing Jinns to run free once more."

Barbara glanced at the kitchen clock. It was ten o'clock.

"Two more hours. How about we stretch things out as long as we can before I use the last—"

There was a loud knocking on the front door. Then Barbara heard Jack's bellowing voice.

"Barbara. Is Carrie there? She's missing and was yelling about kicking your ass before disappearing."

"Shit," Barbara said.

Alka grinned and reached for another container of alcohol.

Barbara went and opened the front door. "No, Jack, she is not here. Which you should be glad about as otherwise, she might have had her ass kicked again."

Jack started to walk towards the kitchen. "There is someone in the kitchen. I saw a shadow when I looked through the side window."

"What the hell are you, a Peeping Tom?"

"No look, Barbara—"

"Goddammit, Jack, this is no longer your house. You are

no longer married to me. Now get out of here before I call the Cops for you trespassing!"

Jack stopped trying to barge into the house and glared at his ex-wife. "Well, if Carrie does not appear in fifteen minutes, I will call the Cops for you."

Jack stormed out of the house and towards his car. Barbara slammed the door and stomped back to the kitchen. Alka was helping himself to leftovers in the frig as well as a bottle of wine as Barbara approached him.

"Don't they feed you in the lamp?"

"We have access to traditional foods but not like your American dishes. That is especially true after eons stick in the lamp world."

Barbara grabbed the wine bottle from Alka and gulped some down. "Damn. Now Jack is going to stir up a stink. Why me? Everything was going so nice, and then Jack and Carrie had to show up on Halloween and ruin my new beginning."

Barbara glared at Alka. "And you? Why pick on me?"

"I explained that before, a woman with a short memory. Your bitterness is like a beacon calling for astral assistance."

Barbara found a bottle of whiskey and began to drink with a purpose. "God, just as life was becoming enjoyable again. The kids are in college; I could have male friends over for fun. Then you pop up." Barbara took a swig from the bottle. "How I wish I could be in some nice comfortable vacation place, out of the reach of Jack—"

A bright flash and Barbara was in a room straight out of the Tales of the Arabian Nights. Soft cushions were everywhere, and a ghostly figure moved a colossal hand fan up and down to keep the warm air circulation.

"What–"

Alka popped into existence on a large cushion next to Barbara. "Your wish is my command, Barbara Bain. And it fits in nicely with a desire I have."

Alta reached over and removed one of the Seven Veils from Barbara's body. She soon realized she had no underwear under the silk veils.

"Why? What?" Barbara stammered as she tried to move away from the Jinn.

"It is time for me to start a new harem, Barbara. For my last women companions grew old and died. I think you will find this existence comfortable. I was able to bring a few American food amenities along with you."

The Jinn moved closer as Barbara tried to back away. "Come, get comfortable, my sweet."

Barbara's eyes widened as she noticed the size of Alka's erect male member. This new home in the lamp was *not* going to be comfortable.

november

Nightcapades
Michelle Lee

Chapter One

I had to get my booster shot today, and I needed to pick up my recurring prescriptions. I impatiently tapped my child-sized foot on the ground as I stood in line at the pharmacy for the second time this month. The pharmacy technicians all knew who I was by facial recognition; they saw me multiple times throughout the month.

The one girl, Mallory, usually had my stuff ready for me by the time I got to the counter. I wasn't all that impressed with her aggressive come-ons and unwanted attention. It could be because she hit on me all the time and was trying to impress me, which didn't work, but I appreciated having my meds ready when I got to the counter.

It wasn't her at the counter, not today. It looked like her twin brother, who was every bit as strange as the girl was, though he too knew who I was and greeted me by name when I came in.

Usually, that is.

"Name?" the pharmacy tech, Eric, asked me.

"You know my name," I sighed, the frustration evident in my voice. "Arianna Perez." There was a cold glint in Eric's eye when he stared at me, saying nothing in return. "I'm here to pick up my meds and get my booster shot."

"I know," Eric finally replied. He turned and walked away, making a few of the customers behind me mutter complaints about customer service. A few minutes later, he returned with several boxes of my injections and dropped them on the counter like they were burning his hands.

He fumbled around for the scanning gun and rang them up, typed some things on his computer, and then silently, yet with an attitude, shoved all the boxes into a bag and pushed them across the counter.

"You are lucky you have good insurance, or these would be extremely expensive with as much as you use them," Eric sneered. His tone made it sound like I was a junkie, and I wanted to be on medication for the rest of my life.

I cocked an eyebrow at the inappropriate comment but didn't feed into it. "Where do I go for the booster shot?"

"Take a seat," Eric intoned blandly. "They'll call your name when they are ready."

What is his deal? I wondered as I sat in the two-chair waiting area. I swung my legs impatiently. I was under five feet tall, so my feet didn't reach the floor. I'd been a tiny baby and was now a petite adult. I think some people looked at me and saw someone they could intimidate.

I saw Mallory clipping some papers onto a clipboard, and I cursed silently. She wasn't authorized to give injections, was she? My heart sunk when I saw her wink at me and head in my direction. I guess that meant she was allowed to jab a needle into my arm.

"Hey, Arianna," Mallory purred as she came up to me. "You look good today. Glad you are getting this booster to help protect you."

"Yeah, thanks," I muttered and scrunched my sleeve up my arm. Mallory's tone of voice set me on edge because I knew she was flirting.

"Fill out these top forms and sign on this one where I have the pink flag." Mallory handed me the clipboard and grazed my hand with her fingers.

"Are you guys well-stocked on the booster shot? I think I'll have my boyfriend come and get his shot, too," I asked with an innocent smile. It was a lie. I did have a boyfriend, but he wasn't vaccinated and didn't want to be.

"I'm not sure." Mallory's tone changed slightly, and an edge appeared in her eyes. "Fill that out and I'll be right back with the shot."

I glanced at the clipboard and began the process of filling out my address, phone number, and all the information I didn't want Mallory to have. I was thankful for HIPAA laws. I was sure that the pharmacy didn't want a lawsuit lodged against them.

I waited a few minutes and pulled my vaccination card out, surprised that Mallory hadn't asked for that. A small door to my right opened, and Mallory popped her head out and gestured for me to follow her.

I stood up slowly, hesitating. The other vaccination was completed right here in the waiting area. I figured Mallory didn't want an audience if she tried to ask me out again. Bracing myself, I stepped back into the little room and sat on the chair next to the tray that held the syringe.

"Which arm?" Mallory's tone was all business now.

"Left," I answered, thinking it was evident since that was the sleeve that I bunched up.

Mallory swabbed my arm, and the pungent smell of alcohol filled my nose. She fanned her hand over my arm to dry the spot and then squeezed my bicep a couple of times. More than necessary, in my opinion, and that wasn't because I was annoyed. I was, but not from the bicep squeezing.

"The side effects should be the same as the other shots, but less. You'll have arm tenderness, possibly a headache, and fatigue. Any questions?" Mallory asked as she stuck the needle into a vial and drew some liquid into it.

I found that odd since the other shots were in a vial of their own. Mallory noticed my attention and moved to block my view of the tray. I shook my head no in response to her questions and watched what she was doing.

I sighed at her ridiculous power play and closed my eyes. I should look into finding a new pharmacy.

"You are going to feel a pinch," Mallory told me. Her voice had a note of something I couldn't identify in it.

There was a sharp sting and then a burning sensation as the liquid got pushed into my arm. It felt like fire. My eyes opened when I felt a second prick, but I only saw Mallory pulling out the syringe from my arm. The other two vaccinations hadn't felt this way.

"You need to sit here for fifteen minutes," Mallory ordered me and turned her back. She fussed with something on the tray and then tossed the garbage away and dropped the containers and needle in the sharp's container.

I rolled my eyes but said nothing. I just rested my head against the back of the chair and ignored Mallory as she walked out. I was tired and ready to go home. I wanted to sleep and figured a fifteen-minute power nap wouldn't hurt. I closed my eyes right as a wave of dizziness swamped my brain.

My limbs suddenly felt heavy, and my breathing slowed. I'd never had these reactions before. I felt my mind drift and didn't fight it. I was stuck here for fifteen minutes anyway; I might as well take advantage of the downtime and sleep.

Chapter 2

My power nap became filled with strange voices in the dark. I couldn't make sense of what was happening, and there was a persistent buzzing sound in my head that was annoying me to no end. I wanted to swat it like a fly that needed to get squished.

Someone kept ordering me around and demanding that I do things I didn't want to do. That thought got followed by a pungent smell that had my eyes snapping open and made me sneeze. It was time for me to wake up and put a stop to it.

"Enjoy your nap, princess?" Mallory mocked me. "You can leave now."

She didn't need to tell me twice. I grabbed my purse from the floor and glared at her as I walked out. I didn't say anything, but I wanted to wipe that smirk off her face. I glanced down at my clothes to ensure they were all in place as the door shut behind me.

It honestly wouldn't have surprised me if I had found them out of place. Mallory was the type of person that would feel someone up while they slept or were incapacitated. That was her vibe all the way, at least with me. I had no apparent reason why either.

I locked my car door after I got in. That was a habit of

mine that I'd be fastidious about since the world went crazy—too many people going missing by suspected traffickers. I wasn't being paranoid about it; however, I was careful not to put myself into a position to become one of the statistics either.

My phone dinged with an incoming text message from my mother reminding me to make an offering and prayer for my departed loved ones in honor of the Day of the Dead. I groaned because I forgot and promptly headed to the store to pick up some yellow marigolds. I think I even had a tamale in the freezer I could heat up.

I was too tired to give the holiday the respect I should, and I felt guilty about it. It would pass, my grandma would forgive me. My mom might not, but she wasn't dead, so her opinion didn't count.

I just wanted to be at home. I ran into the store specializing in Mexican cuisine and customs, knowing they would have the flowers I needed. I grabbed a bouquet and, on a whim, picked up a pack of premade tamales and hurried through the checkout line.

My arm started to ache, and my head felt groggy as I got back into my car. I mentally reviewed the side effects I got from the last vaccination and remembered that it had been a lot worse than this, but it took longer to surface.

I shrugged and buckled my seatbelt. I drove home probably faster than I should have and raced into my apartment, dropping my bag on the counter. I couldn't get out of my work clothes quick enough to make me happy. My body sighed in happiness as my legs slid into my favorite pair of sweats.

Feeling better mentally, I walked back into the kitchen and grabbed a tamale and the flowers. On a side table in the living room, I set up a Day of the Dead shrine for my grandma. I used my rosary beads, the flowers, and the tamale as an offering and said a prayer.

Satisfied, I wandered back into the kitchen and ate the rest of the tamales. When I finished putting my dishes in the dishwasher, I was exhausted and didn't even have the energy to play my sim game or call my boyfriend.

I wrapped my blanket around me on the couch and fell fast asleep. My dreams were muddled and left me with a sense of violation and wrongness. I don't know what woke me up, but at some point in the middle of the night, I woke up and dragged myself to bed.

The dreams didn't improve even though my comfort level did. I dreamt that I was a puppet in some crazy marionette show, dancing at the whim of an evil puppet master. I could remember someone talking to me, but not what they said.

When my alarm went off in the morning, I rolled over and felt like I'd fallen off a fourth-floor balcony and landed on rocks. I didn't hesitate to call in sick, then fell into a restless dream-filled sleep. This time, I dreamt my grandma was warning me, but in Mexican, and thanking me for the tamale and flowers simultaneously. It was a little convoluted.

I gingerly rolled out of bed when I woke up and noticed that there was dirt at the foot of my bed between the sheets and that my feet looked like I'd run barefoot through a dirt pile for a solid week without a shower.

Confused, I looked at my floor and saw the dirty footprints that led out into the living room and straight to the front door. My carpet was an off-white color, and the brown stains were easy to spot.

What the hell? I thought. I'd never sleepwalked before.

Instinctively I glanced down at my arm and saw the bruise

from the booster shot and frowned. I didn't recall any side effects in anyone else about sleepwalking. I'd have to do more research, but first, I needed to shower badly.

Chapter 3

It seemed like echelons of dirt washed down the drain as the shower rained down on my feet. It made no sense. I watched the swirling water until it ran clear and then thoroughly washed my toes, getting the dirt out from under my toenails.

I showered quickly after completing that task and dried off. I wiped the steam off the mirror and examined the injection site on my arm. It looked similar to the other vaccinations. Hot to the touch, swollen, and bruised. The typical response for me.

I hung my towel up to dry, walked naked back to my bedroom, and got slowly dressed. The shower helped invigorate me but only to a point. My muscles ached like I'd hiked a mountain yesterday, and I knew that hadn't happened. I'd gone to work, then to get my vaccination, pick up flowers, and went home. This feeling had to be from the booster shot.

I grabbed my phone and saw that I'd missed a call and a few texts from my boyfriend, Rupert. I quickly texted back that I'd called out sick today and made my way to the kitchen.

My socks slid on the floor as I came to a halt, and my mind tried to catch up with what my eyes saw. Propped on the kitchen counter was a picture of me sleeping in the clothes that I had on last night.

I looked frantically all around the apartment with wild eyes, expecting to see someone else in there with me. I was the only one there. Mine were the only set of dirty footprints on the carpet in the living room that led to the front door. There were also a set identical to the others that pointed to the sliding door to my balcony.

It was a sick fascination that made me want to pick that picture up, yet fear kept me from doing it. Half my body leaned forward as if compelled to move toward the photo; my feet rooted to the floor.

My phone vibrating in my hand jarred me out of the trance I was in, and I jumped back a bit. I answered without even looking at the screen.

"H-hello?" I stuttered.

"Ari?" Rupert breathed out. "What's wrong? Why do you sound scared?"

"Did you come over last night while I was sleeping?" I knew he hadn't, but I needed to ask to make sure.

"Babe? That's a weird question. Are you okay?" Rupert's voice dropped. "Did someone break in?"

"I think so," I whispered, still standing in the same place I stopped.

"Call the police. I'm leaving work and will be there as soon as I can." Rupert hung up without another word.

I was still in the exact place as before when Rupert got there. I hadn't called the police. I hadn't done anything. I stared at the offending picture, trying to figure out where it had come from without me knowing.

"Arianna?" Rupert called out, using his key to get in. "What happened?"

I pointed to the picture. I couldn't even form a sentence; my brain wouldn't connect to my tongue. I felt beyond freaked out, thinking that someone had been in here watching me sleep. I shuddered and fought back a wave of nausea.

"What the fuck?" Rupert looked at the picture and then

back at me. He took two steps to cross the distance between us and grasped my arms, forcing me to look at him. "Arianna? What is going on? Who took that, and on the back, why does it say *I love how peaceful you look?*"

Rupert's tone was enough to snap me out of the trance. I shook my head to clear it and verbally vomited my entire night to him; I began to shake as I came to the part of the story where I walked into the kitchen and saw the photo.

Rupert's face went through various transformations as the explanation unfolded and ended on outrage. "Some motherfucker came in here while you were sleeping and watched you?" Rupert seethed. "How? I had to unlock the front door to get in. You didn't leave it unlocked. Does anyone else have a key to get in here?"

I shook my head in response and felt another shiver of violation run through me. "There's writing on the photo?" I whispered.

Rupert stalked to the counter and snatched the photo up, and showed me the back of it. What struck me as odd was that it looked like my handwriting, a little shaky, but mine. He tried to hand it to me, but I shook my head again. I didn't want to touch it.

"What do we do?" I asked my boyfriend.

Rupert stilled his body and gazed at me, his expression blank. He finally shrugged. "Call the cops? I don't know what they can do about it, but we can start a report. I'll change the locks today or get a hold of the building management and have them do it."

I meekly nodded. It was a start. I wasn't sure I could shake the feeling of invasion that plagued me, though taking some sort of action made me feel like we were accomplishing something other than standing here in disbelief.

Rupert raised my hand that held my phone and gently squeezed my palm. "Call the police, Ari. I'm going to go find the maintenance guy."

That puppet feeling came over me again. I nodded, dialed 911, and asked for non-emergency. I relayed the information to the officer that came on the line, and they asked me to stay put and not touch anything. I still hadn't even moved from where I stood. I was okay with that.

Chapter 4

After Rupert supervised the maintenance man installing brand new locks on my door, we waited silently in the living room for the officer to show up. I was cuddled into Rupert's side, drawing comfort from his presence.

He had wrapped my blanket over my legs and surfed the internet on his phone while we sat there. He showed me something he thought would interest me or distract my mind from the situation every few minutes. It didn't work, but I appreciated his efforts.

An hour later, a knock at the door made us both jump. Rupert got up and answered with a worried look at me. He held the door open, and a male and female officer walked in. The woman looked at me while the man let his gaze roam the apartment.

I looked where he did, and I saw a lot of shadows that I had never noticed before. Little places that someone could hide and I wouldn't see them. My skin began to crawl with that thought.

"Why don't you tell us what happened, Ms. Perez," the woman said to me.

I went through the entire story again, and I did when the man asked me to repeat it. My frustration was mounting with each disbelieving scowl the man threw my way. I did my best not to let my temper flare and mouth off to the authority supposed to take my information to help me.

"Do you have a history of sleepwalking?" the male cop asked me.

Rupert put a calming hand on my arm, and I snapped my mouth closed. "She does not. How do you explain her taking a photo of herself while asleep even if she did? That isn't a selfie."

The woman officer shot a glare at the man, stepped in front of him, knelt, and studied the footprints. She snapped a couple of pictures with her cell phone and stood.

"My name is Officer Meadows, Ms. Perez." Officer Meadows nodded politely to me. "Excuse my partner, Officer Richards. We've had a couple of calls like this one today already. You are our third."

"Given that Arianna is your third of these calls, wouldn't it seem unlikely that all three of these people suddenly became sleepwalkers?" Rupert challenged sarcastically.

Officer Meadows nodded slowly in response to Rupert, and I silently cheered them both on. I wasn't a fan of Officer Dick and his attitude.

"Statistically speaking." Officer Richards shrugged. "However, is it a coincidence that all the footprints are approximately the same size as Ms. Perez's feet?"

"Enough," Officer Meadows snapped. "Ms. Perez isn't the only person in this city with those size feet. I did notice that her phone is the same model as the one I have." She waved her phone in front of Officer Richards's face. "Take a look at the quality of this photo, compared to the one left of her sleeping, and you'll notice a drastic difference."

I could tell that the cop had more opinions to voice, though he kept his mouth shut. Officer Meadows went through a litany of questions about my previous day, if anything was missing, or if I had any enemies that I knew of or practical jokers. She covered all bases, filled out a report, and gave me a case number to reference. They left shortly after, and Rupert locked the door behind him.

The damning thing that kept going replaying in my mind was the dirty feet I had this morning and the dirty sheets. Maybe I *had* sleepwalked. Contemplating someone getting in bed with me and me not being aware of it was nightmare-inducing. I felt more comfortable believing I had developed somnambulism.

"I have to work the early shift tomorrow," Rupert told me. "If you don't mind me getting up early, I'll stay here tonight. Do you think you'll go to work tomorrow?"

"I don't know." I thought about it for a few moments and examined how I felt. "My body has those deep muscle aches like you get with the flu. And I'm super exhausted. I have sick leave. I guess it wouldn't hurt to take another day."

"Okay. You lay back on the couch and maybe take a nap," Rupert suggested, dropping a kiss on my forehead. "I'm going to run home and grab that carpet shampooer I have so we can get these footprints washed up. Then we can watch a movie and call it an early night. Sound like a plan?"

It sounded like heaven to me. I nodded and let him tuck me into an Arianna burrito before he left. It wasn't long, and my eyes drifted closed again. I vaguely remember thinking my phone was ringing, but it could have been a dream because I don't recall answering it.

Chapter 5

Life progressed normally the next couple of days. My muscles still felt fatigued, but not that complete ache it had been. The new lock on my door gave me a sense of security, and Rupert staying over helped. Not once did he tell me I'd gotten up and walked around in my sleep.

We'd reached the weekend and slept in later than our typical workdays. Rupert was three steps ahead of me, and I was in the middle of a giant yawn when I crashed into his back.

"What the fuck?" Rupert hissed.

I steadied myself by grabbing onto his waist and then craned my neck around to look around him at whatever had him reacting this way. My brain became a screaming concerto of white noise as my mind processed the scene in front of me.

The walls of my apartment had gotten papered with photos of people I didn't know in various stages of sleep, including pictures of Rupert and me from as recent as last night. A persistent buzzing noise began to drown out the static sound, and the room swam.

Rupert grabbed me as my knees buckled, but he deposited me on the floor as he crossed the apartment to check the locks on the door. His face was a thundercloud.

"Locked! I know we are the only two that have keys to this apartment for a fact, aside from the building manager." Rupert paced back and forth between where I sat and the front door. "I know he didn't do it because that man moves about as quietly as a freight train loaded with rusty metal parts tossed in a boxcar."

I don't understand why I found that so funny, yet a giggle escaped my mouth. Then it cascaded, and I couldn't stop laughing. Rupert was far less amused than I was, but it didn't halt the sound erupting from me. My sanity had snapped like a dry twig on a hot summer day during a drought.

It was evident that Rupert thought I'd lost it too, judging the look on his face. Despite the fear escalating in my bloodstream, I couldn't stop laughing, not even when tears poured down my face.

"Ari?" Rupert knelt before me. "You are scaring me a little, babe; this isn't like you."

"No shit!" I exploded. The laughter and tears suddenly disappeared in a split second. "I can't say I've ever had pictures of sleeping people show up in my apartment either. I don't know what my reactions should be. Tell me, please!"

"There you are. That's my girl." Rupert's face relaxed, and a stupid smile spread across his handsome face to my utter annoyance. It made me want to give him a wet willie or something equally gross and annoying to make the smile disappear.

"I don't want that asshole cop back here," I muttered angrily. "He made me feel like he thought it was my fault that the pictures were happening."

"I have the card for Officer Meadows," Rupert suggested. "Maybe we just call her."

"If they are partners, won't he come with her?" I wondered with a frown.

Rupert shrugged in response and looked back at the collage of sleeping people. He was silent for a few minutes, and I knew that meant he was thinking things through and coming up with a plan.

"If we do nothing and throw it all away, then the police won't ever know the severity of what happened unless one of the other people they had complaints from has one of these in their places, too. I do agree with you that Officer Richards was a douche. What if we get cameras and put some inside to record what's going on?" Rupert offered.

It wasn't an awful solution, but what if someone hacked into them and spied on us? Watched me without me knowing? That creeped me out too. I didn't know the right solution to this problem, and it bothered me. That sense of violation prickled my skin and made me shudder.

Rupert stood and began to take photos of the mess left for us to find. He left the room and came back a few seconds later wearing a pair of latex gloves that he wore when he gave me one of my injections that I had to take for my blood clot disorder. I found that disturbing, though logically, I understood why he did that.

I wrinkled my face in confusion until I saw him start to take down the photos without his skin touching them. He placed them all in a stack on the counter and then put them into an envelope he pulled out of a kitchen drawer.

I felt better not seeing them all staring at me, but I knew they existed and that they had been placed in my residence for me to find. Who would do something like that to me? I didn't have enemies or anyone that disliked me that much. Not that I knew of anyway.

"Come on, Ari." Rupert motioned me to stand. "I'm going to take you out for breakfast and get your mind off this shit."

I wasn't entirely sure that it would be possible. I think the image of all those pictures became seared into my mind for the rest of my life. However, I stood up and allowed Rupert to lead me back into the bedroom and got dressed.

Chapter 6

The following week and a half was a blur of going through the motions, the same routine every day. Get up, go to work, come home, eat, and go to bed. The only variations happened when Rupert spent the night, and those nights were when I got the best sleep. My body still felt sore every morning when I woke up, and I ended up sending a message to my doctor asking if that was a normal reaction to the booster shot I had received.

I also had a sense of false security since no other odd and invasive photos had appeared. I knew it was fake because I had that hovering hunch that the ax was going to fall on my head, or at the least take off a limb when it fell.

There was also that ghost of a feeling that someone watched me. I constantly looked over my shoulder and expected to see someone or something. There never was, but that sensation continued to crawl over my skin, even when I was home. I didn't care for it much.

Midway through the week, I felt exhausted. I played my video game for an hour or so until I felt like my eyelids were too heavy and then shut everything down. Since Rupert was working the night shift for the next two weeks, I decided to go to bed early.

I fell asleep fast. I woke myself up the first time and found myself with my phone clutched in my hand and halfway through my dark living room. I had thought it was a pretty decent sleep. I knew I was sleeping because I kept having weird dreams.

"What is wrong with me?" I asked the empty apartment then headed back to bed.

I plugged my phone in to charge and tried to get settled back into bed, but waking up during sleepwalking had me on edge. My mind raced, and when I fell asleep again, it was restless.

I tossed and turned for a good hour in that state of somewhere between awake and asleep. My eyes were closed, and my brain said I was sleeping, but it also was spinning out of control, and I felt like I was lying there awake with my eyes closed, yet when I tried to open them, they didn't open. It wasn't a restful slumber.

I found myself on my balcony. My actions didn't make sense. For example, why would I use my flower pot as a step to climb up on the wall of my deck? Considering I was barefoot, a chair would have been more beneficial for that movement. I must still be dreaming.

It was preposterous to consider I was capable of this. I wasn't acrobatic, and while I wasn't a weenie, I'd be hardpressed to do a pull-up, and I was little. Yet, I somehow found the courage to jump and grab onto the bottom of the balcony above me, use my feet to help climb up the wall, while I shimmied my hands up the rails to pull myself onto the deck above me.

The dream continued with me doing that until I reached the top of my apartment building, four stories above my apartment. A superhero I was not, so I viewed the entire thing as ridiculous. More so, when I jimmied a window open and began to crawl over the railing and swung my leg through. Then the world went dark.

I woke up feeling hungover when my alarm went off. I hadn't taken anything the night before to make me feel that way, nor had I drank any alcohol. I knew I'd dreamt, but the dreams were fuzzy and unclear. My arms ached, and when I stretched, I noticed more definition to my muscles than had been there before. I couldn't explain it.

I didn't even want to think about it. I didn't want to think, period. I wanted the weekend to be here; Rupert snuggled up next to me, watching a good movie and eating some pumpkin bread. My needs were simple.

I went to work as usual and remembered that I needed to pick up my next two-week supply of medication. I wasn't looking forward to going to the pharmacy. I dreaded it, truthfully. The last time I was there, both of the twins were weirder than usual, and I wasn't feeling in the right frame of mind to deal with either of them.

To top it all off, when I went to the bathroom, I noticed I had a spreading bruise across one of my thighs that concerned me. I knew I hadn't hit anything to make that happen. I was on blood thinners and needed to be careful about that type of thing.

When I got back to my desk, I pulled out the little notebook that I used to keep track of my medications and odd things and noted the bruise, time and date I found it, and the approximate size.

I'd forgotten about it the rest of the day until I got to the pharmacy. I saw a woman in line in front of me with a bruised-up face. Part of me wanted to ask if she was okay and needed help with anything, and the other part of me wanted to keep quiet and not intrude on someone else's business. It was a double-edged sword that so many people mistook for apathy.

I made a lot of assumptions about the poor woman's life when it could have been a medical reason that her face was all bruised. Though, her being in front of me was a fantastic distraction from the weirdness my life had become.

At least until I was next in line for the counter and saw Mallory leering at me around the colorfully faced woman. I almost turned back and left.

"I can help the next person at window two," a different female called out.

I could have cheered. I hid a smile, quickly picked up my

prescriptions, and got out of the store as fast as possible. That was my win for the day, not having to deal with Mallory. I felt like I escaped a death sentence.

It felt wrong for me to think that way about another human, but some people made that instinct to flee come surging out of me like a tidal wave. Whatever, it was what it was, and I put my car into drive and practically sped out of the parking lot headed for home.

My phone rang halfway home, and I picked it up reflexively without looking at the caller ID.

"Hello?" I said through my Bluetooth earpiece.

"Arianna?" a female voice said. "This is Amanda from Dr. Smith's office. Last week, you sent a message about sleepwalking, side-effects of the booster shot, and today another about bruising. Dr. Smith wanted to reach out and see if you'd like to come in for a checkup?"

"Yeah, that would be a good idea," I agreed. "Is there any chance of getting seen this week?"

"We can get you in tomorrow morning, first thing, if you can do that." I heard Amanda clicking on her computer in the background. "Otherwise, Friday."

"I can make tomorrow morning work," I replied, thinking frantically about tomorrow's schedule. "I'll be there. Is first thing seven?"

"You got it. See you at seven. Have a good evening." Amanda hung up before I could respond.

I didn't care. I made a few more phone calls to let work know I'd be late and then pulled into my parking lot. I grabbed my stuff and headed upstairs to my apartment. After unlocking the front door, I almost tripped over my feet when I saw a photo of me sleeping that someone had slid under the door.

Chapter 7

"I haven't been sleeping well, but that mainly started after the booster shot," I explained to Dr. Smith. "I noticed the bruise yesterday. It's the sleepwalking thing that concerns me. I've never done that before. My boyfriend stopped me once, and the first time I had to have made it outside because my feet were filthy."

"I see." Dr. Smith tapped on the computer. "I don't think it's related to the booster shot. It could be from the medication, or perhaps this is a stress reaction to something going on in your life. I think before you leave, we need to get some blood work done. The bruising could be from your medication, which is pretty common if your blood is too thin. It wouldn't take much for a bruise like that to happen."

I nodded because I knew that much about blood thinners. The stress in my life didn't start happening until after I saw the photo montage of sleeping people left in my kitchen. The rest of my life was relatively stress-free, minus the ordinary day-to-day things everyone suffered.

Dr. Smith checked the rest of my vitals, suggested a sleep study if things continued, and then sent me off to the lab to get my blood drawn. She didn't sound overly concerned, which helped me feel a little better and alleviated my concerns about the booster.

I went to work after my appointment and finished out my day without event. I figured I'd hear something back on my blood work the next day. Rupert was going to stop by before he had to go to work. He'd gotten assigned to the night shift for the next couple of weeks, so our schedules would be off, and we wouldn't see much of each other.

With any luck, Rupert would be there before I got there.

I'd told him last night that I was going to the doctor today, and he'd want to spare me the extra stress. That way, if there were any surprises, he'd see them first and remove them so I wouldn't be upset. Rupert was a good man, and I felt lucky to have him.

That was why once again, I found myself racing for home as soon as I left work. I couldn't wait to see Rupert. That was the last thought I remember having until I pulled into my parking lot two hours later. That couldn't be right. Yet the sky was dark, and it had been light when I'd left work.

I glanced down at my phone and saw where I'd texted Rupert that I got stuck in bad traffic. Why wouldn't I remember that? I'd never had blackouts before, and believing that I'd had one while driving was terrifying.

What was happening to me? Sleepwalking and blackouts? The bruising was easy to write off as a medication issue, same with the feeling of being hungover because if my blood counts were off, that would account for that. But it wouldn't be the case for sleepwalking or blackouts.

I got out of my car with shaking legs and slowly made my way to my apartment. I wasn't sure I wanted to tell Rupert about this. Not yet anyway. I wanted my blood test results first. Maybe there was something to be found that would explain everything. I knew it was a long shot, but that was my hope. Everything else was too plain scary to contemplate.

I felt paranoid, and I hated that feeling. Visions of brain tumors, strokes, aneurysms, things of that nature filled my mind to overflowing, and I rushed up the stairs as if I could outrun my thoughts. I slammed my door closed behind me and sent a quick text to Rupert to let him know I was home.

I closed all my blinds and kept the lights off. I was acting ridiculous, and I knew it. I didn't care; this was my home, and it was supposed to be my safe place, yet it felt dangerous. I felt watched, exposed, and like a ticking time bomb. Was I losing my mind?

I didn't think I was. Someone was screwing with me, and I couldn't figure out how who, or why. All my instincts tell me it wasn't Rupert. I began to pace as I thought about what possible motive someone might have to do this to me. I wasn't a mean person; I didn't bully people.

I flopped down on the couch and let out a deep sigh. I slid over and lay down, stretched out, and pulled the blanket over me. I was too tired to worry about this as I had no prospects to investigate. It shouldn't have to be me digging into either; the police should. Yet, I'd heard nothing from them.

I stuffed my throw pillow under my head and huddled under the blanket. An Arianna burrito, as Rupert liked to say. I wished he was here. Well, truthfully, if I wanted something, I wished that none of this was happening at all, that everything was normal.

A single frustrated tear escaped my eye and slid onto the pillow. I stifled the rest because I didn't want to give this situation more of my time and energy than I already was. So I closed my eyes and willed myself to relax. I fell asleep and began another of those strange dreams.

I walked down the sidewalk wearing a backpack towards town but turned the corner to remain in a residential area. I was not super familiar with this one, but I knew the neighborhood as I took shortcuts through there when traffic was terrible.

It was probably what most people would consider low-income, but the way I looked at it was these people were in a house and not paying rent for something they didn't own and couldn't alter how they wanted to.

The streetlights weren't bright, and some of them weren't even working. I noticed that I kept walking under the dark and shadowed ones—seriously atypical behavior for me.

I pushed my way through a row of shrubs into someone's side yard and hugged the wall of the house to remain in the dark. I seemed to have a purpose, an agenda I followed, yet I didn't know what that was.

I walked up to the back screen door and pushed the slider open. Why would someone leave this unlocked, and what was I doing? I didn't break and enter strangers' houses. I didn't break the law at all.

I slunk through the kitchen and peeked down the darkened hallway, taking in the array of family photos that hung on the walls. I couldn't make out the faces, just the faint glimmer of a blue nightlight that reflected off the glass in the frames.

As I walked stealthily down the hallway, I could hear people snoring in one of the rooms. I began to slide the backpack off my shoulders with silent movements. It was impressive that I made so little noise.

A loud ringing started in my ears, and my head swam like I was fighting an upriver current. It was a force that began to push down on me in resistance. My knees quivered, and I was sure I was about to fall.

I woke up when my alarm went off. I was no longer a burrito on the couch. I had sprawled out on the top of my bed in my underwear and shoes. My first question was, why did I put my shoes back on after getting undressed? My next was, why didn't I get under the covers since my skin was pebbled up and cold?

I sat up and looked around my room. Was I having a mental breakdown?

Chapter 8

"Your blood was mostly normal," Dr. Smith told me over the phone. "You had a couple of inflammation markers lit up, which essentially tells me there is inflammation somewhere, though they weren't specific. I wouldn't think there is anything to worry about; you had no signs of fever or infections."

I couldn't argue that because I didn't. I've been to the doctor enough to know what the inflammation markers meant. My muscles were tight and achy; it could simply be that reason. However, I still had no answers for the sleepwalking and now the blackout while driving, other than stress.

"Thanks for getting back to me," I replied in a monotone.

"Consider getting the sleep study done," Dr. Smith softened her tone. "Restless leg syndrome could make your legs tired and cause you to feel like you've exercised when you haven't, especially if it's a lot of movement."

I felt a flash of guilt for not saying anything about the blackout, but it seemed like things would get worse if I gave voice to it. I made a noise of agreement though I committed to nothing. I ended the call with a promise to call back if something else happened or things got worse.

I sent a quick text to Rupert to let him know that my blood work was fine, and I went back to work with a dark cloud hanging over my head. I didn't feel like my life was my own anymore, which was a disturbing thought.

I went through the rest of my day with a chip on my shoulder, though I tried hard not to let it seep through. Given the looks my coworkers gave me, I wasn't successful. Thankfully none of them called me on it, and I left without incidence.

That is how the next day went, and I was grateful that it

was Friday. I planned not to go home and go straight to Rupert's place and spend the night there. When I talked with him, our thoughts were that maybe someone had planted something in my apartment and was watching me or coming in and doing things. We both second-guessed our decision not to put security cameras in the apartment.

Regardless, I was excited to see him and hoped like crazy that I'd finally get some restful sleep. I didn't have any reason to feel paranoid at his place, and he'd be there with me to keep me safe. I'd brought a change of clothes with me since I couldn't remember what clothes I had left there.

The anticipation made the day crawl by, and I was getting impatient to leave. It was probably hard for my coworkers to tell the difference between that mindset and the irritated one I had the past couple of days. It wasn't my intent, and hopefully, they could forgive me.

I was hesitant to share what was going on if they thought I was crazy. If I heard about the things I've experienced from someone else, I'd think they had lost their mind. Even the cops who had responded to the initial break-in had been skeptical. I get why they were, but I wouldn't say I liked it since I lived the situation.

When the clock hit four-thirty, I was out the door. I didn't look back. I was too busy looking forward to being with Rupert. We'd talked about living together, and once our leases were up, we would begin to look for a place to call ours. We made do with the separate living spaces until then, but I missed him in between.

Rupert was waiting outside when I pulled into his parking lot. I didn't even try to hide the grin that split my face when I saw him. I threw the car door open and leaped onto him. I wrapped my legs around his waist and clung to him as he hugged me.

"I'm happy to see you too, babe." Rupert dropped a kiss on my lips and grabbed my bag after letting go. "Did you bring enough clothes for the whole weekend?"

"I have a couple of sets in there. I can't ever remember what I have here, but we'll make do. What should we do for dinner?" I asked, letting him lead me inside.

"I ordered pizza. I wanted a night where we could relax on the couch and watch a movie. Does that sound okay to you?" Rupert shut and locked the door behind me.

"Like I'm going to argue with that." I hugged Rupert again and then took my bag to the bedroom.

"I've got our blanket out here already," Rupert called out to me. "Pizza should be here in about an hour. Long delivery times tonight. If you want to take a bath, go ahead."

I loved that man. I did precisely that. I took a bath, relaxed, got into some comfy clothes, and padded out to the living room right before the food got delivered. We snuggled under the blanket and watched some comedy movie that I fell asleep during about half an hour into it. Moments like these were so perfect that I couldn't imagine anything better.

Rupert woke me up after a while, and we went to bed. He saw my hesitation as I pulled the sheet up over me. He didn't miss much, and I saw the concern crease his handsome face.

"You'll be safe, Ari. I won't let anything happen to you," Rupert promised as he crawled under the sheets with me. "You trust me, right?"

"With my life," I nodded, speaking the truth. "Tell me about your day."

We weren't snugglers when we slept, but that night, I nestled into his side, and he didn't roll away. He filled me in on all the goings-on at his job and the daily issues he faced. He highlighted the funny moments, so I laughed, and the tension bled out of me.

Chapter 9

Rupert woke up when Arianna moved and got out of bed. He didn't overthink it, figuring she was going to the bathroom, but when he heard her walking down the hallway, he followed, instinctually grabbing his phone.

Arianna held her phone to her head and nodded as she walked toward the front door. Rupert hadn't even heard it ring. It was cold outside, and Arianna wouldn't go out without covering her feet. She didn't stop to put shoes on, and that was how Rupert knew she was sleepwalking.

He'd done a little research on sleepwalking and saw where some experts said that it was dangerous to wake them and that it could cause bad reactions like heart attacks or some shit like that. All those thoughts flew through his mind as he watched the woman he loved exit his apartment. She walked out into the parking lot in her pajamas in the middle of the night.

Rupert did the only thing that popped into his head: to use his phone and record what was happening so that she would believe him when he told her. Not one thing that was happening was in character with who Arianna was as a person.

He followed behind her, not concerned in the slightest that he'd left his apartment open. He was more worried about Arianna and keeping her safe.

Arianna lowered her arm that held the phone and went to her car—where the trunk had already opened—she must have hit the key fob before leaving the apartment. She grabbed a backpack out and slid it over her shoulders, and set off at a brisk walk toward the sidewalk and the street.

Rupert rushed over, shut the trunk, and followed, still recording the episode. Her movements made no sense, and he hoped he was close enough to keep her from wandering into the street and getting hit by a passing car.

It didn't look like she was aware of anything around her. She acted like she was in a trance, which Rupert guessed Arianna was if she was sleepwalking. Even then, her behavior should be what she typically was, not these jerky movements that she made every few feet as if she were fighting herself internally.

Arianna turned down a residential street and picked up her pace; she stopped outside a house with no lights on. Of course, there were no lights on, it was the middle of the night, and most people were sleeping. Rupert shook his head.

Arianna was in the process of removing the backpack and taking something out of it. To his utter amazement, she was setting up a tripod. Rupert made sure his phone was still recording as he watched his girlfriend mount a camera on the tripod and carry it over to a window as if she knew what she would find inside.

Rupert stepped closer and remained hidden behind a large tree just inside the yard. Arianna began to silently pull the screen off the window and slide it open. Once again, the love of his life shocked him with her actions. She pulled herself up and over the windowsill and leaned back out to pull in the tripod without a sound.

Rupert snuck closer, keeping his phone trained on the open window where Arianna had disappeared. He got up close and glanced inside. After a few seconds of his eyes adjusting to the dark, he saw Arianna snapping photos of the people sleeping.

Rupert understood that Arianna was behind the entire

thing in a blinding flash of clarity. With no room in his mind for doubt, he also knew that there was no way that this situation was something that Arianna dreamed up on her own or would even carry out if she felt so inclined. She wasn't a sneaky person by nature and not aggressive in the slightest. If someone were blackmailing her into doing this, Rupert felt sure that Arianna would have told him about it.

There was more to this story, and he intended to figure it out before something terrible happened to Arianna on one of these midnight excursions. Aside from that, her shock and fear at finding the photos in her apartment were genuine. It couldn't easily get faked by anyone other than a professional actor.

Rupert's mind was furiously trying to put together the puzzle as he continued to record Arianna and watched while she quietly repacked the camera and tripod back into her backpack. He crept away from the open window so he wasn't visible to her and held his breath while she climbed back out the window and replaced the screen.

Shaking his head, he followed, not sure where she headed next, but he hoped that it would shed some light on the situation. The direction she walked was not toward his place but still the opposite way. She had a good pace going for as small as she was, and her strides were much longer than they usually were.

She turned a couple of random corners and wound up on a side street that was far darker than he liked for his girlfriend to be walking around in her pajamas and barefoot. There was a towering apartment building to his left with one of those old rickety iron fire escapes that sported more rust than was safe.

Rupert knew that was where she was going before the thought even hit the active part of his mind. He didn't know where she got the skills to climb up the dumpster, hoist herself up to the lowest rung, and ninja herself up the ladder. He only knew he needed to follow.

Rupert waited until she was three floors up before he reached up and climbed the ladder behind her. Given the nature of the fire escape, it wasn't quiet, but she also didn't seem to notice him, so intent she was on her task. He felt relatively safe until she stopped and opened a window to climb in on the fifth floor.

Was Arianna about to start taking more pictures? Rupert quit recording and sped up. He didn't think he would be able to be on the same ledge that she stopped on without being seen or heard by whoever lived in that apartment. He halted somewhere between floors and strained his ears to listen for any sounds, whether talking or distress.

When Rupert saw the light come on in a window away from the fire escape, he took his chances and slowly climbed to the fifth floor. He saw no one in the immediate vicinity of the fire escape and breathed out a small sigh of relief. Rupert was willing to risk getting spotted, and he stuck his head in the open window and looked around for a sign of Arianna.

Voices floated back to him from the room with the light on, and the sound of a shutting door had him pulling his head back onto the fire escape, where he pushed himself up against the side of the building. If anyone had a craving for a breath of fresh air and looked his way, he'd be screwed. He seemed utterly suspicious.

"She's still under," Rupert heard a female voice say.

"For how long?" a male responded, sounding annoyed.

"Until I give her the keywords and next commands. Stop questioning me and take the camera and go print out these pictures. Hurry up," the female snapped.

"If there is no worry, why do I need to hurry up? Why won't you let us play with her? It's perfect since she's under and can't turn you down this way," the male whined.

Rupert's blood began to boil at the thought of anyone touching Arianna, much less without her permission. Wait. *Arianna turned down the female.* His mind raced; he knew who this was. Those voices were that brother and sister from the pharmacy that constantly harassed her. Mallory, that was that female's voice.

That didn't explain how Arianna was under their control, but now he knew who he was dealing with and who was behind the photos. It also explained why photos existed of him and her sleeping with no evidence of how someone had gotten inside her apartment. Rupert only felt mild relief at knowing that information.

He pulled out his phone and called the female officer, Meadows. It was lucky he'd saved her number in his phone. It took two times for him to call to get her to answer, and when she did, he quietly explained the situation he'd stumbled upon and listened to the disbelief creep in the officer's voice.

"Unbelievable," Officer Meadows breathed out. "Hypnotism, maybe? I'm up. I need to wake my partner up; call this in, and we'll be there. Stay out of it, but record more of the conversation if you can. Just don't get caught."

Rupert nodded, which he knew she couldn't see, but the officer had already hung up. Rupert switched back to record and heard the pharmacy tech goading Arianna.

"Such a silly girl. You are going to forget all about this conversation, go home, place the photo on your countertop and go back to sleep. You will remember nothing of tonight. You will not remember me injecting you with more of this serum, and you will forget my brother and think you were dreaming."

The last pieces of the puzzle clicked into place for Rupert. He had all the proof he needed now to end Arianna's terrorizing at the hands of the diabolical pharmacy technicians. It must have initially happened when Arianna got her booster shot.

Rupert followed the robotic movements of his girlfriend back to her apartment, where she precisely did what Mallory told her to do. He was going to need to find a counselor to deprogram Arianna. Rupert texted Office Meadows where they were and waited.

He fell asleep and didn't wake up when Arianna slid a needle into his arm and then went back to sleep. His phone rang moments later.

december

Chilly Carl

Maxwell DiMarco

'Tis the season, once again. To share good memories with friends. Give thanks to those up in the sky, and reminisce on times gone by. So as we beckon in the year, with caroling and christmas cheer, to all of you now sitting here: Is it so right to dwell on fear?

Sit down, dear children, bundle tight; a jolly story I'll recite. A warm reprieve from frights and sin, this story takes a look within. Of brand new friends, from twinkling ice, to chase away thoughts not so nice.

As snowflakes tumble through the air, here lies no screaming, not a scare. A festive tale, with naught a snarl...

This is: The Tale of Chilly Carl.

"Aannnd? How about you, Mr. Miserable?"

There it was. Mendel's nickname broke through the wordless chatter of his classmates like a knife through butter. The twelve year old boy let out a long sigh under his breath, making a point of not looking over at the extravagantly-dressed girl seated beside him.

"Nothing, probably," he responded bluntly, continuing to watch the frost-bitten evergreens pass by the bus window, their green needles barely visible beyond the falling snow. But as expected, the seventh grade princess wouldn't accept such a *simple* answer as a lead-in to her boasting.

"Oh, *goodness me!* I can see that *someone's* not in the holiday spirit!" Cinder exclaimed, mockingly reeling back in her seat as though Mendel had screamed bloody murder at her. As her smug smile returned almost instantly, she leaned over and jabbed her classmate in the shoulder. "God, come *on*, Miserable! Can't you *try* to not be a grumpy old Scrooge this year? I'm sure Hanukkah Harry doesn't like seeing you like this."

A spike of adrenaline shooting through his chest, Mendel clenched his teeth, squeezing his eyes shut against the urge to slug the blonde *shmendrik* upside the head.

"Like I've *told you.*" His eyes still closed, Mendel *slowly* turned his face towards Cinder, his rage barely restrained as he growled his words through his barred teeth. "My dad... had a rough... year. And my *sister*... was *ill*... for *half* of it. So even if we *did* buy presents... we can barely afford *rent* as it is."

Finally collecting himself enough to open his eyes, Mendel was greeted with the sight of Cinder with a derisive puppy dog pout, miming a tear rolling down her cheek. Several kids chuckled quietly at this; Mendel just glared.

"Well, *my* Christmas week is going to be just *magical!*" Cinder promptly announced, pivoting in her seat to face the rest of the bus. "Since Mommy and Daddy are home for the holidays, and my sweet thirteen is in *just* six months, we've arranged a celebratory Christmas/New Year's family retreat at our villa back in California! Each of my sisters and I will have our own rooms— each with an appropriate theme, the maids will make sure of that—and every dinner will be one of my *favorite* meals, cooked by our family chef. First, we'll *naturally* start off with..."

Realizing that his time in the hot seat was over, Mendel let out another long sigh, his rage bubbling inside him as he looked back out the window. *Absolute materialistic* meshuggeneh, he thought to himself, scowling silently. It never ceased to amaze him how someone two months older than him could unfailingly act as though she was seven *years* younger.

Born to American parents but raised by beleaguered Canadian babysitters, Cinder, full name 'Cinderella'—after the Disney version because, of course, it would be—had been built up all her life to think she was Adonai's gift to humanity. A delusion the other children of Bécancour upheld for the slim chance that being in her good graces would mean a shot at her parents' money. Why Cinder wasn't enrolled in a private Catholic school, Mendel would never know; she certainly wasn't learning to be *humble* by mingling amongst the 'commoners.'

What Mendel *did* know about Cinder was that she craved *perfection.* Everything needed to be about her, at all times, and anything that *wasn't* stuck out like a sore thumb. Like an endless expanse of white, wooden floorboards, with a single protruding black nail that needed to be hammered into place.

So naturally, the moment Cinder noticed the introverted boy from the rural side of town just minding his own business, she had found the *perfect* target to lord her wealth over. And it made no difference where Mendel was, whether running in PE, taking a test for math class, or even reading in the library (an activity the rich girl openly loathed). So long as Mendel was present on the school grounds, Cinder *would* find him, and proceed to blab his damn ear off.

Mendel assumed Cinder saw their relationship as

lighthearted ribbing between social classes. Personally, he saw it more as being nagged by a borderline anti-Semite, whom he wanted nothing more than to take a long walk off a short pier.

So to each their own on that matter.

A few more minutes passed without Cinder nagging at him, and Mendel allowed his simmering anger to fully subside, taking slow, even breaths to calm his nerves. The din of his classmates blending together into the back of his mind, Mendel pulled his worn winter jacket tight around him as he stared out the bus window, watching as the snow flew past on the wind.

As a little kid, Mendel had always adored snow. Even as money came and went, as his family scraped by day to day, the snow could always be relied on to come back each year, and Mendel had felt comforted by that consistency. And sure, maybe it was cliché for a Canadian to appreciate the chillier months of the year. Yet even today, for all the inconveniences Mendel now knew it led to, snow still held a certain serene beauty to him, and was arguably the only benefit of the bitter cold of winter.

Mendel could remember many a late winter night when he'd sit up in bed looking out his window, watching the flakes of white float by through the surrounding darkness. And his mother loved to tell stories of when he was a toddler, when he would wake up to fresh snowfall and *immediately* run into the woods beyond their house, dancing and singing through the trees. Sometimes, Mendel's dad would follow him out, and they would play tag until they were called inside for breakfast. The image of Mendel laughing as he ran through the woods, his dad pretending to be a big, lumbering monster, was one of Mendel's first childhood memories.

As well as one of Mendel's few memories from before his dad had to start working out of town.

Mendel was jolted from his thoughts by the hiss of the bus brakes. Looking out towards the front of the vehicle, Mendel saw that familiar, rickety wooden bus stop, sitting alone in the snow with barely two feet of berm between its bench and the road. He almost chuckled at the sight; it was shocking how much faster these bus trips went, when he wasn't being forced to—

"Hellooo in there!" Cinder called out, waving a hand in front of Mendel's face. "This is your stop, Mr. Miserable!"

Mendel turned to look at her with a tired expression. "Yeah, it is," he acknowledged bluntly.

"Well? Don't let all of *us* get cold from your tardiness!" Cinder barked, scooting out of her seat and indicating the open door with a flourish. "Up and at 'em! Time to be on your Merry-Christmas-Way!"

Mendel felt a vein pop in his head. "Yeah," he growled, wearily pulling on his backpack as he stood up from his seat.

Mendel's boots tramped against the floor as he passed Cinder, the rich girl promptly sitting back down as Mendel made his way towards the door behind the three other kids from his neighborhood. In the bus behind him, Cinder leaned forward over the seat in front of her.

"Hey, Miserable! Don't forget to tell your mom about what I'm doing next week!" she called after Mendel, raising a hand in an exaggerated wave goodbye. "Hope you all have a good dreidel day!"

"Mm-*hm!*" Mendel replied with gritted teeth, his eyes crazed, head down, and hands clenched so tightly he thought his nails would pierce straight through his gloves. The moment the way forward was clear, he practically *sprinted* down the steps out of the bus, not wanting to spend another moment in the same space as the rancid Barbie doll.

His boot came down in the snow with a *crunch*. The bus doors closing behind him, Mendel looked up at the trees, pausing as the cold air rushed over him. His three classmates were a ways ahead of him, but he didn't know any of them personally. So instead of hurrying after them as the school bus pulled away, Mendel instead took a moment for himself.

The burning rage in his chest was cooled as snowflakes settled within his short, black hair, a few landing on the brim of his nose. For the first time that week, Mendel actually allowed himself to smile, turning slowly in place as he took in the particles of white drifting delicately through the air. It was only a few seconds, but in those fleeting moments, Mendel felt like all the stress of the season had been washed away.

And that was when he noticed something... disconcerting.

As Mendel turned to look back down the road, his gaze was drawn to a large, snowy figure in the distance. It stood on the berm facing out towards the road, a large stick lifted in silent greeting, and a crooked carrot nose protruding from its face. It even wore a black, vintage top hat with which to stave off the cold; a snowman in its most classic form.

But what caused Mendel to begin approaching the snowman wasn't its mere existence; what made the air's comforting cold turn into biting chills wasn't its unorthodox placement. The snow on the road *around* the snowman had been almost entirely cleared, trails winding over the frostbitten asphalt like those left behind by a rolling snowball. Whoever had built this snowman hadn't been very cautious of their surroundings... which was why the icy shape lying in the center of the trails left Mendel with a horrible feeling in his stomach.

Breath coming out in quick bursts of mist, Mendel

increased his pace. Now walking against the wind, the falling snowflakes began biting at his eyes. Pulling up his hood against the pelting bits of frost, Mendel raised a hand towards the shape, his voice cracking as he called out, "H-hello? Are you okay?"

The boy wasn't sure what kind of response he wanted... no. He *did* know the response he wanted. He wanted to hear *anything. Some* sign that the shape he was seeing *wasn't* what his gut was telling him it was.

But as soon as he saw the thin trail of blood staining the snow, he was left without any further excuse to deny the reality. It was a *child.* Face down on the road, ice particles glittering on the back of their wooly winter coat. Short, blonde hair stained dark red.

Mendel cleared the remaining space between him and the corpse with his heart beating out of his chest. "Oh no... no, no no...." He repeated over and over, the words straining against his throat as he stepped into the street, kneeling beside the younger child's body as his heart sank ever further.

It was the corpse of a little girl, no older than six at most. A grotesque, fragmented streak of mud and broken leaves ran horizontally across her back, her jacket seeming to dip inwards around it. *Tire tracks.*

Mendel felt ill.

Turning the girl over onto her back, Mendel didn't recognize her face as anyone he'd seen in the neighborhood. The poor kid must have wandered pretty far from home. She was wearing a large, fuzzy pair of earmuffs, and her face, disconcertingly, seemed... happy.

Mendel set his jaw, running a hand across his eyes as they began to sting. He knew he couldn't leave her body here. Summoning his strength, and choking down the sickly feeling brewing in his stomach, he lifted the girl up with shaky arms, walking her over to the berm. Setting her body in the snow beside her snowman, Mendel felt like he'd been stabbed in the chest as he stared at her smiling face.

At *least... at least it seems like it was... instant,* he told himself, trying to find any sort of comfort he could. But that flimsy reassurance was swiftly overridden, as a pang of realization shot through his heart. *Unless she—*

The thought led Mendel to completely forget about keeping his stomach in check. He reeled back and puked into the snow, staining it an acidic yellow. Mendel coughed and sputtered against the burning sensation, his chest feeling like something was trying to eat its way out from inside as his eyes welled over.

"Why... *why?!*" he sputtered, covering his eyes as he fell weakly to his knees. Stinging needles seemed to stab at his arms as he tried to control the racing of his heart to no avail. "Why... what would—"

Mendel looked up at the snowman, still looming above him, and his damp eyes widened. For the first time, he realized that it had no face. A carrot was its *only* discernible facial features as though the girl's life had been taken before it could be completed.

There was no smile. No eyes.

No one there with her when a car ended her life.

In that moment, staring up at the incomplete figure of ice and frost, an overwhelming fury Mendel couldn't explain in words coursed through his veins. Lunging forward with a furious, wordless scream, the boy drove his fist straight through the snowman's torso.

The fabricated human collapsed inwards from the blow, the lower snowballs falling apart around Mendel's arm in a shower of icy dust. Its stick arms swung down limply to its sides as the top-most snowball toppled backwards, crushing the top hat on impact with the ground before splitting in two. Breathing heavily, Mendel didn't move, nor retract his arm from where it hovered over the ruined sculpture. His mind was racing. His arm trembled as a solitary tear ran down his cheek.

But there was nothing he could do.

Wordlessly, Mendel rose to his feet. He brushed the lingering frost particles from his jacket. And then, he ran for home.

Poor Mendel suffered quite a scare. A life ended, without a care. This image he saw, unmistakable; the snow, her death, now inseparable. But back at home, he soon would find, no such reprieve for his worn mind.

"Keep off the roads!" the radio said; in response, Ines hung her head. A snow storm, the reporter told, a warning emphasized in bold. But although it had told them not to roam... her husband, Gabriel, was not yet home.

Ines prayed for her husband, so far, far away, "Oh please, zis lebn... please know not to delay." Sunday was always his only day off; work wasn't excused for a sickness or cough. And their son had been facing such troubles this year; such stories of woe he had spilled to Ines' ear.

How they both wished their home could be whole once again... but a sound from outside brought Ines' thoughts to an end.

"Fuck!"

Ines looked up from the small, handheld radio sitting on the kitchen counter. Her prayer for Gabriel's safe trip home had been interrupted by her son's voice... nay, her son *swearing*, just outside their front door.

"Mendel?" Ines immediately became worried as she rose from where she sat at the counter, quickly crossing the room to get the door.

As she stepped out onto the rickety porch of their mobile home, Ines found her son collapsed just before the stairs, having slipped on the icy path leading up to the house. His face was buried in his arm, and he made no effort to move as Ines carefully stepped down into the yard.

"Oh, my little klutz..." Ines knelt next to her son reassuringly. "Must I remind you not to run up the path *every* winter?" Reaching out to gently grasp her son's arms, Ines began to help lift him to his feet.

But to her surprise, instead of her son managing a weak laugh, or bemoaning the existence of icy sidewalks, Mendel forcefully pushed Ines' hands away from him.

Not looking Ines in the eye, Mendel extended a knee, pushing himself upright with a hiss of pain. "I'm fine," he simply said, before trudging forward up to the porch.

A bit hurt, Ines got to her feet as Mendel stepped inside, flinging his backpack to the side of the door. "Mendel, *bubeleh*... did something happen today?" she called after him, following her son inside and shutting the door behind her.

Mendel didn't reply, walking into the kitchen and opening the fridge without a word. Taking out a pack of sliced turkey and a loaf of bread, he shut the fridge before walking to retrieve a plate from the cupboard. Ines watched him hesitantly, returning to her seat at the counter on the opposite side of the kitchen.

"Mendel? What's wrong?" She addressed her son a second time as he began to assemble a sandwich. And once again, he neglected to acknowledge her presence. Ines rested her head on her hand, giving him a moment to respond... yet he barely acknowledged her presence.

"Mendel... I'm here if you need to talk. You know that you can *always* come to me with your troubles, right?" Ines' eyes narrowed, as she remembered the issues at school her son had told her about in the past. "It's not Mr. Thomas' daughter again, is it? I asked Principal Bergeron to have a talk with her parents about her behavior; has she started harassing you again?"

Mendel finally spoke up, but he only provided his mother with another question. "Dad will be home this weekend." It was more intoned as a statement than an actual question. Mendel's voice was hollow, completely drained of energy.

And naturally, Ines wasn't going to ignore these signs. "*Mendel.* Do not ignore my questions, young man," she stated firmly.

At this, Mendel suddenly spun around. "How about *you* don't ignore *mine!*" he spat, face contorted in anger; the sight made Ines jump a little.

Ines was momentarily lost for words as she stared at her son. Never in her life had she seen him so irate. She stared back at Mendel in tense silence, not knowing how to respond. After a moment, he bitterly turned back to his sandwich.

"He *might* be home, yes," Ines eventually answered Mendel, resting an arm on the counter and leaning on it heavily. "The forecast calls for heavy snow over the next few days, but your father said he'll try to get on the highway home first thing tomorrow morning."

Mendel refused to look back at his mother, only muttering a quiet, "God damn it." in response. But that was all Ines needed to hear. Crossing the kitchen, she took her son firmly by the shoulders, spinning him to face her.

"*Mendel Naftali,* tell me why you are acting like this!" Ines demanded, watching her son's face with fiery intensity. "I did *not* raise a child who uses the name of Adonai in vain!"

"Well, *some* things are beyond your control!" Mendel snapped. He tried to pry Ines' hands from his shoulders, but her powerful grip held firm.

"Mendel, stop this! I cannot help you unless you tell me what's going on!" Ines' tone was firm, but by now she was practically pleading with her baby boy. "I know you are a growing boy, but I'm still your mother! You can *always* come to me, no matter what happens, or how old you are! Please, *bubeleh,* you don't need to push me away!"

"*You* want to help *me?*" Mendel screamed, tears stinging at his eyes. "Nobody was there to help *her!*"

"Mendel, who—"

Ines' voice died on her lips as the sound of distressed crying arose from down the hall; this brief falter was all it took for Mendel to slip out of his mother's grasp, bolting down the hall to his room and slamming the door.

"Mendel, come back!" Ines called out, running desperately after him, but her plea was only answered by the click of a lock.

Ines stood in the hall by her lonesome for a moment, the cries of a baby filling the house. She felt her eyes begin to tingle, and she wiped them on her sleeve, breath hitching slightly. "Oh, Gabriel, *please* make it home this week… our little forest explorer needs his father right now."

Waking further down the narrow hall to her and Gabriel's shared bedroom, she cracked open the door, the cries of her baby girl becoming louder without anything to muffle them. Putting on what she hoped was a comforting face, Ines turned to the small, wooden crib set beside their bed.

Ines always felt a pang of fear as she walked up to Naomi's crib; a nagging fear of what she would find inside. But as always, despite her distress, little Naomi was just fine. She laid on her back, weeping for Ines' attention, her tattered pink baby blanket pushed to the side by her squirming.

"Shhhh... there, there... *ima's* here...." Ines' heart felt heavy as she gently scooped her youngest child into her arms. She had no way of knowing whether it was her and Mendel's argument, or simply a bad dream that caused her girl such distress, but Ines still felt responsible.

Sitting down on the side of her bed, Ines rocked Naomi back and forth in her arms, her daughter burying her face in Ines' long, curly black hair. Keeping her voice soft and slow, Ines began singing in Hebrew, rocking Naomi softly in time with the melody:

> "Avir harim tzalul kayayin
> Vereiach oranim,
> Nisa beru'ach ha'arbayim
> Im kol pa'amonim.

> "Uvetardemat ilan va'even
> Shvuyah bachalomah,
> Ha'ir asher badad yoshevet
> Uvelibah chomah.

> "Yerushalayim shel zahav
> Veshel nechoshet veshel or
> Halo lechol shirayich ani kinor."

Mendel laid in bed, staring up at the ceiling with a heavy heart. Listening to his mother sing to his baby sister, he recognized the song.

Y'rushalayim Shel Zahav, "Jerusalem of Gold." His mother had made a conscious effort to memorize the entirety of the song's Hebrew translation; Ines now sang it to Naomi every time she cried, soothing her to sleep.

Out of all of his family, Ines Naftali was without a doubt the most devoted to upholding the traditions of their people; sometimes, Mendel wondered how such an empathetic mother could have given birth to a kvetch such as he.

It was barely dinner time, yet Mendel's eyes already felt heavy. Placing his right hand over his eyes, he recited the shema with tears drying on his face. "Hear, O Israel: The Lord our God, the Lord is One. Praised is the Lord by day and praised by night, praised when we lie down and praised when we rise up. I place my spirit in His care, when I wake as when I sleep. God is with me, I shall not fear, body and spirit in His keep."

Barely moments after finishing the prayer, Mendel's eyelids drooped shut. Sleep, however, would not come so easily. As he tried to rest his tired, tear-reddened eyes, the all-encompassing darkness was broken by the shape of the girl's corpse. Left broken and bleeding in the road by an uncaring driver. No one out looking for her, no one to call for help... and by the time Mendel found her, there was nothing he could do... but destroy her last expression of joy.

At some point while his mind wandered, Mendel had unknowingly slipped beyond the threshold of consciousness. From there, his dreams would pull him deeper into a spiral of fabricated images and distorted memories, a warped reflection of the day's events. Further and further down, on a violent wind of monstrous visages. Yet for the entire night, Mendel was not even aware he stood within a world of his own creation. Everything that he saw before him felt justified within reality.

For it was all happening because of his own actions.

It was *all* his fault.

The snow tumbled down with such fury that night. Blanketing all in a sea of pure white. For once, the weather reports were not jossed: Each house on the street was soon ladened with frost.

To the peak of their windows, the snow would soon rise; their houses were buried, a perfect disguise. Yet something seeped through, that the snow could not block.

It was not a person... but rather, a thought.

How it spasmed and writhed, through the dark, winter air, and all of the neighbors were never aware. But Mendel Naftali would learn all too soon...

... that his despairing thoughts reached far outside his room.

The gruesome visions collapsed as a low creaking came from the ceiling. Mendel's eyes shot open at the sound, face damp with cold sweat. He lay motionless on his back, his heart racing, until he could fully process that he was back in reality. The early morning sun crept in through his window, chasing away the darkness of his mind's eye.

It was... just a dream. Only a dream, Mendel reassured himself, running a trembling hand over his face. What were once vivid images of his nightmares began to blur together as Mendel's thoughts became his own again.

The room went black one final time as he covered his eyes to recite his morning *shema*. Only once Mendel finished the prayer did he push himself upright. His first observation of the day, was that it was much dimmer than usual for so early in the morning.

Mendel knew he couldn't have slept in, either; even if she hadn't woken him, Mendel would have heard his mother around the house by now, weekend or not. Could he have woken earlier than usual?

Rubbing at his eyes briskly to clear them of any excess sleepiness, Mendel glanced over at the window quizzically... only to find around three quarters of it covered by a layer of snow.

The sun illuminated a foggy silhouette just beyond the snowy window, which quickly dropped out of sight below the windowpane.

Any drowsiness Mendel had departed *immediately*. Not even bothering to change out of his pajamas, he sprinted out of his room and down the hall, barging into his mother's room in a panic.

"Mom. *Mom!*" Mendel hissed, hoping he could wake her without waking Naomi. Ines groaned in response, rolling onto her side.

"Mendel... what is it...?" Ines muttered groggily, sitting up to look at her son through barely-open eyes.

"I don't know," Mendel answered bluntly, looking over his shoulder in panic. "I saw something outside my window."

"What?!" Ines started, eyes widening; Mendel's prior caution not to wake his sister was for naught. Poor Naomi began bawling as her nighttime dreams went up in smoke. "Naomi, it's okay, it's okay...." Ines leaned over the crib to comfort Naomi, but her shaky voice betrayed the uncertainty of her reassurance. Turning back to Mendel, she tried to get to the bottom of things. "What... did this thing look like? Why couldn't you tell what it was?"

"We had heavy snow last night... as you told me we would," Mendel explained, memories of how he acted the night before filling him with shame. "But I saw some kind of silhouette through the snow. The sun was shining so that I could see it. And I could tell it was watching me; it *only* moved once I looked directly at it."

"Okay." Ines tried to keep her voice steady, lifting Naomi protectively into her arms. "Mendel, take your sister into the bathroom and lock the door. I'll call the police on the house phone and wait for them in the kitchen; I'll come get you two when it's safe to come out."

Mendel was in no place to object. Taking a still-crying Naomi from his mother, the three left the bedroom together. Ines continued on down the hall to the kitchen while Mendel slipped into the small bathroom across the hall from his own room, shutting the door tight behind him. Naomi squirmed around in Mendel's arms, reaching blindly for her mother to comfort her, as he took a seat on the tile floor.

"I'm so sorry, *achot*..." Mendel quietly hushed, trying his best to imitate their mother's comforting vocabulary. "*Ahki* is here, please don't cry...." But of course, Mendel was not their mother, and so Naomi only continued to weep.

Poor Mendel, alone with his sister and tears. If only he'd known he had nothing to fear.

    A new friend was outside, and they wanted to play.
    So glad that they'll meet by the end of the day.

Mendel wasn't sure how long they had been waiting in the bathroom. There was no clock to determine a specific amount of time, beyond the rough estimate in his head. And all Mendel could deduce in that regard was that time was moving at a snail's pace.

Naomi had finally begun to run out of tears to shed as she realized their mother wasn't coming to comfort her. Mendel, meanwhile began pacing the claustrophobic length of the bathroom, rocking his sister in what he hoped was a soothing rhythm. The rest of the house had been dead silent for a long time. The only sound beyond his sister's wordless sorrow was the foreboding creaking of the snow on the roof. Several times now, Mendel had fought back the urge to leave the restroom to join his mother. But he knew that going against her wishes *now* could lead to nothing good. Especially after the night before.

After what seemed like an eternity, Mendel heard the shuffling of snow from the general vicinity of the porch and two voices conversing. A few minutes later, a brisk series of knocks sounded from the front door. Naomi began to cry again, but Mendel's relief that the soul-crushing wait had finally ended left him unable to be bothered by his sister's noise.

Mendel listened as the door was opened, and the voices conversed briefly with his mother. Then, Ines herself knocked on the bathroom door. "Mendel? You can come out now, *bubeleh.*"

Swiftly taking her invitation, Mendel unlocked the door with his free hand, carrying a sniffling Naomi out into the hall, and left to the kitchen, where his mother and two police officers—an older dark-skinned gentleman and a younger, lighter-skinned woman—stood waiting. The older officer gave Mendel a stern salute as he joined them; his companion couldn't help but silently smile at the sight of Naomi.

"Good morning, Mendel," The older officer stated, his tone gruff, but not unfriendly. "I'm Officer Girard; your mother called us about a potential threat to your household. Is it alright if I ask you some questions?"

"Uh... yes, sir," Mendel replied awkwardly. He wasn't entirely sure what the proper way to respond in this situation was. Luckily for him, the police officer didn't mind, simply nodding in response.

"So. Your mother tells us that you saw something outside your window?" Officer Girard questioned.

"Yes, sir," Mendel repeated, mentally bashing himself for using the same clunky response twice. "I couldn't see what it looked like, but when it saw me watching it, it ducked out of sight. I don't really know how it even saw me through the snow on its side, but...."

"Hmm," the officer considered gruffly, turning to Ines. "And your bedroom windows are along the *front* of the house?"

"That's correct, Officer," Ines confirmed, taking Naomi from Mendel and bouncing her comfortingly. "I know it's not easy to see through the snow we got last night, but...."

Officer Girard and his partner looked between one another. "On the contrary, Mrs. Naftali," Officer Girard patiently interrupted, glancing over towards the front door. "What concerns us is that the area you described was quite apparent, and yet there are no signs of anyone having been in the area."

"What?!" Mendel couldn't help but speak up, taking a step forward almost in defiance. "But I *swear* I saw something! Maybe their prints were covered up by the snow?"

At this, the female officer shook her head. "Not quite, little guy. It's been a lil' cloudy, but there hasn't been any new snowfall since an hour before your call. And that snow out there? It's spotless."

Officer Girard nodded solemnly, looking from Mendel back towards Ines. "Officer Ferrell's right, Mrs. Naftali. Please pardon my inquiry, but has your son had any history of hallucinations or poor vision?"

"N-no, never!" Ines stammered, pulling Naomi close to her. "He's never told me about any issues with his vision, and I've never seen any signs that he was—"

"Mom, I would never hide that from you!" Mendel interjected, a bit hurt that his mother would even briefly entertain the concept.

"I know, *bubeleh*, I just…." Ines trailed off. She wasn't sure how to end that sentence without digging herself deeper.

Recognizing the tense situation, Officer Ferrell tried to step in. "Well, uh, it's probably nothing to worry about. Coulda just been your sleepy mind playing tricks on ya, you know?" she half-joked to Mendel.

Unfortunately, the boy wasn't in a very humorous mood, and the cop's half-hearted smile died on her face. "I mean, it's not unheard of…" she reaffirmed, partially to Mendel, partially to herself, "…you come in from making a snowman, you got snow on the mind, then—"

Mendel's heart skipped a beat. " Officer Ferrell, what did you say?"

The officer looked to the boy, slightly confused; her companion and Ines likewise turned to look at Mendel. "Uh… gonna have to be more specific there, bud."

Officer Ferrell's chipper tone did nothing to alleviate the feeling of dread that was coming over Mendel… the same feeling he'd had before finding the body in the road. "About… about a *snowman*," he specified.

A flash of realization came over Officer Ferrell's face. "Wait, you mean that *wasn't* you who made that good lookin' fella out there?"

Mendel and Ines exchanged tense glances. "There wasn't

anything out there when Mendel came home from school yesterday," Ines recounted, shaking her head.

Officer Ferrell was almost beaming. "Ha! I flippin' *knew* I'd crack a case someday!" She whooped, high-fiving Officer Girard's palm as he offered it nonchalantly.

"Contain yourself, Officer Ferrell... but yes, it seems you did," Officer Girard pointedly acknowledged, his partner quickly trying to recollect her dignity. "Even so, it would be rather inane for someone casing a house to leave a *snowman* on their target's lawn. Do any of your neighbors regularly stop by your household, Mrs. Naftali?"

Before Ines could answer, Mendel stepped towards Officer Girard once more, face pale as frost. "Can... can I look at it?" he asked, voice uneven.

The officer gave the boy a quizzical look, but then simply shrugged. "I can see no reason why you couldn't."

Turning to the front door, the officer led the way out onto the porch. Powdered snow was spread across the boards from where the two cops had shoveled away the surrounding mass of sparkling white. Officer Girard retrieved a large snow shovel from where he'd leaned it against the railing before carefully making his way down the steps into the yard.

The whole time, Mendel was craning his neck, trying to see past the looming man to the yard beyond. His heart was racing, and the boy had to use every ounce of his willpower to resist shoving past the officer.

But despite his mind screaming at him, despite his stomach plummeting into a bottomless pit, Mendel simply followed obediently. And sure enough, when he could finally see the yard, it was perfectly clear of any unknown tracks. The only breaks in the spread of white perfection was the pile shoveled out of the way, the prints from the cops' boots leading up to the house, and the tire tracks from their police car, parked just at the edge of the yard with chains wrapped around its wheels. Mendel wasn't sure whether to feel relieved or scream....

What he saw next made him choose the latter.

"No!" Mendel scrambled backwards, knocking into the front of the house and pinning himself against it as though standing on a narrow precipice looking down into an abyss below.

There, in the yard, it stood. The exact same stick arms. The same, now bent top hat. The exact. Same. *Blank. Face.* The snowman stood at the edge of the yard, facing the house; it was positioned almost *perfectly* so that it was staring right at Mendel.

"Mendel?!" Ines exclaimed, moving to her son's side as fast as she safely could with Naomi in her arms. "Mendel, what is it?"

Mendel slid down the house and sank into the snow. He could barely form coherent words as he responded to his mother, "Th-that's th-the... i-it was... i-it *c-couldn't* have—"

"Mrs. Naftali?" Officer Girard addressed Ines worriedly, though the two cops kept their distance. "Is everything alright?"

Mendel froze up. As he looked up from the ground at the face of his mother and the two cops beyond her, something seemed to click in his mind.

I can't tell them about what I saw, Mendel realized. *They'll never believe me. They'll think I killed her.* Mendel subconsciously pressed his back further against the wall of the house, eyes going wide. *I can't... I need to lie.*

Thinking as fast as he could, the words seemed to tumble from Mendel's mouth: "Th-that snowman, it looks just like one I... kicked over yesterday, by the street. It has the same pose, and hat... except it's on our lawn."

Ines' concerned expression turned to one of incredulity. "Mendel? Did you *really* do that?" she asked, Naomi gurgling quietly beneath her hair.

Mendel swallowed hard. "Yeah... I was having a bad day... like you saw... I needed to take out my anger on something."

Ines couldn't help but scoff under her breath. "Mendel Naftali, I can't believe you..." She sighed, shaking her head as she steadily got to her feet. "I'm going to bring Naomi back inside, and then we *are* going to talk about what happened, young man." Behind her, the two cops watched Mendel with more subdued disapproval.

"So, I guess we got a bit of a vengeful prankster here," Officer Ferrell mused, placing her hands on her hips. "And *apparently* a pretty spot-on memory, to get this kind of reaction."

"It seems that way." Officer Girard concurred, though he continued to eye Mendel with mild suspicion; the boy tried not to meet his gaze. "Mrs. Naftali," he addressed Ines as she was about to head back up to the porch. "If it would make you feel more comfortable, we can scout out the surrounding area. Look for any further clues as to the whereabouts of this trespasser."

Ines hesitated for a moment, glancing back at her son, then she simply nodded. "If it wouldn't be too much trouble. Thank you, Officer."

"Of course." Officer Girard nodded in turn. He watched Ines carry Naomi the rest of the way back inside before signaling to Officer Ferrell. "We'll scout the perimeter and do a brief search of the woods. Keep your taser on hand, just in case."

"Understood." Officer Ferrell nodded, following her partner as he strode through the snow around the west side of the house. Briefly turning to Mendel before rounding the corner, she gave him a grin. "Hey, if it'll make ya feel better, I could kick the thing over before we head out."

Mendel's heart was heavy from the lie he'd told but a slight smile crossed his lips despite himself. "Thanks, but it's alright. I was just… surprised…."

With a playful shrug, Ferrell followed Officer Girard to the back of the house. If Mendel could burrow beneath the snow and die on the spot, he would have.

"Oh, god, oh, *god*, what have I *done?*" Clutching his head, Mendel fell onto his side, curling in on himself. The shame washed over him like a tidal wave, tears once more threatening to run down his face. "Why didn't I… I didn't *kill* her, I just… I just *lied* to the *police!* What am I doing?!" His voice was hoarse as he lay in the snow, squeezing his eyes shut against his own thoughts as the cold bit right through his pjs. "It just keeps getting *worse!* First my mom, now *this?* I… I need to tell someone what really happened, or—"

"You could tell me, if you'd like!"

Mendel's eyes shot open. The voice sounded like Officer Girard, but… off. Its cadence was a bit higher, its tone friendlier…

It was his voice, but it was *not* the same person.

Mendel looked towards the corner of the house: No one was there. His eyes fleeted over the surrounding yard: Still no one in sight.

Despite the chill, Mendel felt a drop of sweat run down his face as his eyes continued to dart around towards the neighbor's houses, back towards the porch, and over the snowman, its raised stick arm waving in a greet—

Mendel's mouth fell open in shock. The snowman was *waving* at him.

"Hey, pal, what's the matter? You look like you've seen the ghost of Christmas Past!" Above its carrot nose, two thin slits in the snowball peeled open, revealing reflective, pure black coal eyes. "What, not a caroling kind of person? Never heard of Frosty before?"

"N-no..." Mendel shook his head, eyes wide; he didn't want to blink. "No, *no*, y-you're not—"

"Not Frosty? So you *do* know your seasonal songs after all!" The snowman chuckled, despite its apparent lack of a mouth. Stick arms lowering to the snow, it hefted itself into the air, before placing itself back down slightly closer to the terrified boy. "Really though, it's a shame, Mendel. You'd have a lot more to keep your mind off things if you bought into the holiday spirit!"

Mendel jolted backwards. "Y-you know my—"

"*Course* I do!" The snowman once more cut Mendel off. "I'm your buddy, buddy; I remember *everybody* I've met!" The snowman continued shifting itself towards Mendel as it spoke, its movements almost resembling a bounding animal. "But I suppose we haven't been properly introduced, have we? And no, that little fist bump of yours doesn't count, ho ho ho!"

The snowman laughed merrily, falling down with a *thump* just a few feet away from where Mendel sat, heart threatening to beat right out of his chest.

"You can call me... 'Chilly Carl!' Yeah, that seems like something I'd be named!" the snowman decided. Leaning forward slightly, it extended a twisted, three-fingered stick hand towards Mendel. "Now, what do ya say you get out of the snow? I think we have some loose ends to tie up!"

And indeed, Mendel promptly decided to get out of the snow. As fast as he possibly could.

"*Mom!*" he screamed, scrambling to his feet and sprinting

into the house, slamming the door behind him and practically smashing right into Ines as she left Naomi's room.

"Mendel? What happened?!" Ines gasped, the noise causing Naomi to once more burst into tears in the bedroom beyond her.

"Th-the *sn-snowman*, it was, it was—" Mendel stammered, visibly quaking as the rapid tramping of boots could be heard rounding the house and returning to the porch.

"Mrs. Naftali, are you in there?" Officer Girard called, pounding heavily on the door. "We heard your son scream. Is he inside with you?"

"Yes, he's with me!" Ines responded, kneeling down to look Mendel in the eye. "Mendel, you're making me worried. What's going on?"

"The *snowman spoke to me!*" he practically wailed, distraught tears running down his face. "*M-mom, it was moving around, and it sounded like one of the cops, and—*"

Mendel clung onto his mother and Ines hugged him back. Officers Girard and Ferrell stepped back inside behind them. Ferrell was the first to speak.

"Mrs. Naftali... your son, is he...?" Ferrell spoke in fragmented words. The sight of the poor boy suddenly in distress was truly harrowing to see.

After a moment, Ines looked up at the two officers. Her expression was truly hapless. "My son and I need to talk, Officer Ferrell. Thank you both for your time; I don't think you'll find anything outside."

Even Officer Girard looked saddened by the scene unfolding before him. He raised a hand as if to object but then simply nodded, giving Ines a quick salute. "Very well, Mrs. Naftali. Take care, both of you."

Mendel continued to cry into his mother's shirt as the cops left the house, shutting the door behind them. Mendel tightened his grip on Ines as though she would disappear at any moment.

"M-mom... I'm, I'm scared..." he choked out, Ines' shirt becoming damp with his tears. "What... *why* am I seeing these things...?"

"*Ahuv, ahuv,* it's going to be alright..." Ines whispered, holding back tears of her own. "I... I can talk to your father when he gets home. We'll find someone who'll be able to help you."

"B-but... what if... he *doesn't* come home?" Mendel sniffled, wiping his eyes and soaking the sleeve of his pjs with tears. "What if he got caught in the snow, or he drove off the road... or—"

"Mendel, *haim shelli,* please don't think like that..." Placing a hand on her son's head, Ines began gently running her fingers through his hair. "Even if he was held up by the snow, your father *always* makes time for us. He will be home, safe and sound, and we'll help you, just like we helped your little sister. I promise."

WHUMP.

The two of them jolted as the sound of a heavy impact came from outside. Without thinking, Mendel bolted towards the door.

"*Bubeleh,* wait!" Ines clambered to her feet and tried to stop him but Mendel was already racing out onto the porch and into the yard.

Mendel practically leaped down the stairs, stumbling in the snow upon his landing. He could only fear the worst... but the snowman was back where it had been.

Or, rather, the remnants of its *base snowball* was. The remainder had been reduced to broken pieces of snow, toppled over on the lawn. Just in front of the scene, the cop car was idling, as Officer Ferrell switched it from reverse back into drive. Turning as she noticed Mendel standing at the foot of the porch, she gave him a smile and wave as the car drove away, chains carrying it over the snow-covered road.

Mendel watched the police depart, his body as still as the amateur sculpture their vehicle had just demolished. He wasn't sure whether to laugh, smile, or scream. Behind him, Ines stepped out onto the porch; she craned her neck to see the ruined snowman on the yard.

"Ah," she mused. Much like her son, Ines was conflicted about how to feel about the cops' 'favor.' "Well… I suppose it's better you don't have to look at it anymore." Carefully descending the steps into the snow, Ines placed a hand on the unresponsive Mendel's shoulder. "Come now, *ahava shelli*… no need to stand out in the cold."

But something in Mendel's gut told him not to take his mother's advice. "I need to do something first," he stated blankly.

Ines looked concerned at this. "Bubeleh, I think it would be best if you do not linger around—"

"I need to clear off my window," Mendel insisted. "I need to make sure it doesn't move again."

"Mendel, *stop*. I can check on—" Ines' voice trailed off as Mendel set off through the snow towards his snow-covered bedroom window.

With great reluctance, and recognizing there wasn't anything else she could do, Ines followed her son, outpacing him to his window, and started to clear away the snow. The frost biting at Ines' bare fingers, Mendel watched her work with an unreadable expression.

After a few silent seconds, she turned to him, her eyes

pleading. "I'll take care of it. Go inside, please."

Mendel didn't nod. He didn't speak. He simply turned, and walked back inside.

Sometimes, when you have fallen low, you think of things you cannot know. You reach deep down, and try to find, what could have been inside your mind. A brand new friend, more time to spend?

A way to reach your suffering's end?

When life hands you a golden chance, don't pass it off as circumstance. Reach out, take hold! You can be bold! No need to wait until you're told! Yet far too many never do, and past their fingers, chance falls through.

Poor Mendel lost a chance that day, to meet a friend with whom to play. And now, distraught, he'd always stay.

But friends... friends always find a way.

It had started to snow again. Though, not quite as severely as the night before; from Mendel's view out the window, he could still see the yard through the dark of the night, the snow seeming to glow in the shadows. As well as the remains of Chilly Carl lying, unmoving.

Mendel let himself fall back in bed, his left arm hanging limply off the mattress. He wasn't sure what to think anymore. He'd seen a snowman—one that he had *destroyed,* and then had suddenly *reappeared* on their lawn—*come to life before his eyes!* And it knew his name.

Without a doubt, his mother thought he was seeing things... and as things were, Mendel was inclined to agree.

But now what? Speak to a therapist who'd charge hundreds per session? Add some kind of medication to their laundry list of household bills? All Mendel's life his family didn't have health insurance; the treatment for Naomi nearly cost them their house. How could he go on in good conscience like this?

Lying in bed, Mendel was of two minds. One overflowed with what his apparent condition would mean for his family, and why, all of a sudden, this had started happening with such *disturbing* clarity. But his 'other mind,' in contrast, was completely drained by the events of the past two days. And as much as Mendel felt he needed to consider these issues, at the moment sleep sounded like a temporary reprieve, and he was quickly becoming all too willing to take it.

Placing a hand over his eyes, Mendel began to drowsily recite the *shema*: "Hear, O Israel: The Lord our God, the Lord is One. Praised is the Lord by day and praised by night, praised when we..."

Mendel trailed off. His hand lowered from his face, as he suddenly felt a nagging feeling deep in his gut. His eyes fell on his bedroom window, up on the wall above his bed. Looking out at the snow tumbling through the darkness, Mendel felt himself compelled to sit upright, and look out one last time at the remnants of Carl...

But he found nothing amiss. The snowman remained as just a crumbled pile of snow. Mendel breathed a quiet sigh of relief.

Then the snowman's components rose from the ground, pressing together into a formless tower before reshaping themselves into their original, intact shape. As Mendel watched, overtaken by silent terror, Chilly Carl turned to look directly into Mendel's bedroom window with his shining, black eyes. And then, he began to move closer.

THUMP. THUMP. THUMP.

Mendel *knew* he should have screamed, run for help, or found somewhere to hide. But as the snowman began lumbering towards his window, Mendel realized nothing and no one would be able to save him from the approaching creature.

THUMP. THUMP. THUMP.

Chilly Carl was now right outside the window, peering at Mendel silently through the glass. The two of them were still as statues, neither blinking as they looked at one another... then, Carl raised a crooked, wooden finger to his mouthless face.

Shhhhh.

The sound was muffled by the glass but its intentions were clear; Mendel even noticed that the area of Carl's face where a mouth *should* be did indeed shift with his vocalizations.

The snowman's finger then tilted to the side, jabbing twice towards the front door. It was hard to tell, what with its minimalist features, but Mendel swore it almost looked... playful?

Curiosity killed the cat, as they say. But as Mendel climbed out of bed and grabbed his winter coat from his wardrobe, he felt like he truly had nothing to lose anymore. Quietly tiptoeing out of his room—and making sure to double check that his mother and sister remained asleep—Mendel put on his shoes and pulled his coat over his pajamas before slipping out the front door.

As Mendel descended from the porch to the snowy yard, Carl waved to him cheerily, like a friend waiting by the bus after school.

"Hey there, buddy!" the snowman called out, bounding over and placing itself down just in front of the slightly shivering boy. "Quite a night out, huh? Would you just *look* at this winter wonderland we'll be walking in?"

Now it was Mendel's turn to make a shushing noise. "Can you keep it down?" He hissed, looking over his shoulder at the closed door. "If Mom finds me missing, I don't know what she'll do... especially if she sees me talking to *you!*"

"Ha! And what makes you think anyone can see me at all?" Carl tutted, wagging a finger. "That's why those cops didn't see I'd moved after you ran inside all screamy-like, buddy. It's by my nature that I won't be seen until you *want* me to be seen! And I can promise you, you've got *nothin'* to worry about with me."

Mendel blinked, his face highly quizzical. "Then... what exactly *are* you?"

"You mean you still don't get it?" Carl let out a jolly chuckle, reaching out and ruffling Mendel's hair. "Mendel, pal, I'm surprised! After all, ya little sillyhead: *You're* the brilliant mind who created me!"

Mendel cautiously pushed Carl's hand aside; the rough bark scratched at his hand as he did so. "Like a hallucination?" he questioned, his dread rising.

Carl's enthusiasm promptly dropped. "Oh, *darn,* you lost it," he bemoaned, putting his hands on his hips while letting out an exaggerated huff of disappointment. "No, no, Mendel, don't fret: I'm no vision or dream. I'm a full, frost-and-blood man through and through. Just as real as *you* are. But, hm... As for what I am *beyond* that? Well, let's see, how do I say this in a language you'll understand?" Unconsciously pushing his irreversibly bent hat more upright, the snowman waved a wooden hand in circles contemplatively. "I'm a little something that shows up... when you're feeling *lost.*"

Mendel crossed his arms, indeed still feeling quite a bit lost. "So then, what, like an *angel?*"

Carl glanced over from the corner of his eyes, icy lids narrowing in irritation. "Goddamn, kid, you're asking way too many—" Throwing up his hands, his expression lightened almost instantly. "You know what, *sure!* Why not?! I'm an *angel!* And I'm here tonight to *stop* you from seeing a world where you never existed!"

A stabbing sensation shot through Mendel's body. "Wh-what?" he coughed out; he suddenly had a very, very bad feeling.

"Oh, you poor boy…" Carl shook his head, bending down so his face and Mendel's were level. "You don't really get what you've gotten yourself into, do you?"

Mendel took a step back but Carl held up a hand.

"Now, now! *I'm* not the one who's cross with you, buddy!" he specified, straightening back up with a knowing look. "But *oooh*, people soon will be! *If* you're simply content to waste your mommy's money on a talky doctor, anyway!"

"Okay, *stop!*" Mendel was reaching the end of his rope. "I don't even know what made me come out here, and now I'm only more confused! So start making sense, *now* or else!"

"Hm." Carl tilted his head, eyeing the boy for a moment. "Alright, then, I'll spell it out for you: You lied to the cops, bud. And now, we've got a body to hide."

"Wh-wha—"

"What, what, what?!" Carl parroted, hopping in a circle around the yard. "You heard me just fine, *pal,* and you heard *yourself* say it, too. Today, you dug yourself into a hole deeper than any snow angel. And now, if you want to climb out of it? Well, you're just gonna have to dig another hole."

For a split second, a thin line split open in the snow beneath Carl's carrot nose; Mendel saw the reflective glint of ice just inside. "And I *think* that you know what it's for."

Mendel did know what—or *who*—Carl was referring to. And that realization made his blood go ice cold. Now, he *finally* got it. The full reality of his situation seemed to illuminate in his mind's eye. Carl was right, and Mendel had known it all along: The moment someone came looking for that girl, and learned he didn't report her death? He'd have no excuse.

No, he *had* no excuse. All that he had left was to make sure she wouldn't be found.

Mendel struggled to put his racing thoughts into words. His mouth flapped dumbly, trying to decide what to say. "But... if I go to bury her... w-wouldn't people see my footprints?"

Carl shook his head, bouncing a bit closer to his friend. "Nah, don't worry about that, bud o' mine. Remember how I covered up my trail from checkin' on ya this morning?"

Casually, Carl pointed a finger down towards the snow, directing Mendel's attention to the large imprints left behind by the snowman's hopping around. As if on cue, the snow within the imprints rippled and *rose back up,* leaving a perfect, untouched expanse of snow in its place.

Mendel was awestruck. "Wow...." Walking over to the newly reformed snow, he knelt down and cautiously poked a finger into it. Sure enough, it wasn't an illusion or some kind of hollow covering of frost; his finger was met with a full layer of snow.

Mendel turned his head to look back at Carl, who was looking quite proud of himself. "So, then... we just head out? And nobody will see you with me?"

"Yes indeed!" Carl confirmed, clapping his hands together. "But please, you go on ahead; me lumbering along behind you would just slow you down. I've got a faster way to travel."

Mendel wanted to inquire further about that comment, but decided against it. He didn't want to waste any more time, and it was a pretty cold night. "Alright, then... I guess I'll see you there?"

Carl gave a thumbs up. "Count on it, pal."

Mendel nodded and began to walk down the road, away from the light of home.

Mendel zipped up his coat, as he tread down the street. To locate the corpse would be no easy feat. It had no doubt been buried deep under the snow. At least, he had thought, he knew which way to go.

Just out to the road, then turn left and go straight; he would reach the bus stop before it was too late. And though he felt nervous and scared and alone, Mendel told himself he was not on his own.

Chilly Carl was with him, although out of sight. Keeping watch on his friend, through the cold winter's night. The snowman kept hidden during Mendel's trip, but every so often, his covertness would slip. A slight shifting of snow or a small, moving twig. Just a few simple signs, they weren't all that big. Once, Mendel caught sight of two blinking spots; he was a smart boy, he connected the dots.

A part of him told him he should have turned back. He felt on the verge of a panic attack. Just what was this thing that had coaxed him outside? Was it truly his friend or was it all a lie? Yet as things were, Mendel knew he was stuck. He'd left that girl dead, and was now out of luck.

No grown-up would listen. They'd just know he had lied. At least now, he had someone there by his side.

And so what if Carl was just a bit weird? He certainly wasn't like what Mendel feared. He'd torn off the bandaid, told Mendel the truth. No need to dissect it; there's no need to sleuth. Mendel told himself this, keeping a steady pace.

And that was when his friend jumped out in his face.

"*Aahhh*—" Mendel's scream was promptly stifled by Carl's long, twisted stick fingers clamping down on his face. With a laugh, Carl pushed the boy backwards into the snow.

"Ha! Looks like I beat ya here, slowpoke!" Carl teased, Mendel staring up at him with wide eyes. "Aww, don't gimme that look, Mr. Miserable; friends mess with each other now and then! You'll have to get used to that now that we've met."

Mendel paused just as he was getting to his feet. A strange sense of deja vu had come over him; without thinking, he addressed the matter the bluntest way he could have: "Why do you sound like Cinder all of a sudden?"

Mendel was about to kick himself for assuming Carl would know that name... until he noticed the snowman's knowing expression.

"Well," Carl began, a hint of mischief glinting in his eyes. "You'd know as well as I do, Mendel." Raising his hands over his head and placing them together, the snowman began miming a vague diving gesture. "But hey, no harm in asking for a second opinion!"

Before Mendel could respond, Carl dove straight downwards. Jumping back instinctually, Mendel watched as the snow seemed to absorb Carl's body, carrot, hat and all, his form vanishing beneath the surface with a noticeably... *meaty*... sound. Barely a second later, Carl resurfaced, once more positioned perfectly upright, the frostbitten body of the girl now clasped in his arms.

"So, Girl-Whose-Name-We-Never-Learned," Carl addressed the corpse, Mendel watching with his jaw agape. "You got any ideas why Miserable Mendel says I sound like somebody he knows?"

Mendel wasn't sure how to react to this. But looking at

this girl again, barely visible in the dark of the night, he *did* notice she somewhat resembled Cinder, if much younger. She had the same facial structure, the same shade of blonde hair, the same skin tone... or she most likely had, before it had been tinged a sickly blue by the frost. Mendel's thought process was interrupted.

"'Gee, I dunno, Carl! Wish I could tell you, but I'm super duper dead!'"

Carl had put on a weird, falsetto inflection, moving the girl's jaw up and down in sync with his words. Clearing the remaining foot or two between them, Mendel smacked Carl's hand away from the girl's face.

"That's not funny! Cut it out!" Mendel snapped. "We're here to bury her, not make fun of her!"

Carl simply shrugged his shoulders. "I dunno, pal; I can make *fun* out of anything!"

Mendel simply glowered, crossing his arms disapprovingly. "You know what I meant, you *prostak*. Now where were you thinking we'd hide her?"

"*Prostak.* Another one you heard from Daddy, I take it?" Quips aside, Carl lazily tilted his head back and forth, as though in thought. "Well, we're looking for somewhere we can actually *bury* her. Anywhere that'll keep her hidden once I melt away."

Mendel and Carl looked at each other, speaking in unison. "Deep in the woods."

Carl couldn't help but laugh raucously at this, throwing back his head and inadvertently tossing around the girl in his arms. "Ha! I *knew* we'd get along, buddy! We're more in sync than you thought!"

Mendel managed a shaky laugh. "I guess we are?" Even though he knew it was meant as one, he didn't take it as a compliment.

"Sure are, pal. We sure are," Carl reaffirmed, bouncing in place as he spun to face towards the snow-covered foliage beyond the berm. "And that'll only become truer the longer we hang out together! So come on, follow me. Let's get this girl in the ground then go home for some yummy hot chocolate!"

Carl began pushing straight through the leaves, Mendel following just behind him. Mendel staggered a bit as he stepped off the berm, the snow giving way beneath his shoes. Luckily it wasn't a very deep ditch and thus he was able to find his footing fairly quickly.

As the two trudged along through the snowy night, Carl began humming a cheery tune to himself. Mendel, meanwhile, was doing all he could to stay close behind his frosty companion, and not lose sight of him past the branches smacking him in the face in Carl's wake.

"Do we know how we'll find our way back to the road?" Mendel called out quizzically.

Carl didn't turn around as he replied, "Don't worry about it, bud!"

Shifting the girl into one arm, the snowman waved his free hand around at the drifting snowflakes. "You see these little guys? They'll bring us back where we need to be once this is over and done with." After that, Carl did look back slightly, his tone a bit condescending. "Besides, this was your idea too. I thought you were good at navigating forests in winter?"

"Well, I was, I guess," Mendel reminisced. But that brief lapse in focus caused him to smack right into Carl's back. "Ow!" Mendel exclaimed, stumbling backwards.

Upon reclaiming his balance, Mendel realized Carl had stopped. Mendel stepped to the side, peeking around his snowy companion.

From what he could make out, they were *deep* in the woods; there was no sign of any distant lights, or glimpses of sky between the towering trunks surrounding them. Currently, they were in a small clearing between the trees where three large withered trunks stood directly before them in a vaguely triangular formation. Carl turned around, indicating the area with a tilt of his head.

"So? What do you think?" he questioned casually. "Looks like a pretty good spot to me."

"Yeah, sure," Mendel mumbled. Staring at the girl in Carl's arms, he found he was beginning to have second thoughts about this. "Is this really the only way? Maybe I could—"

"Buddy, look." Carl exhaled slowly, once more shifting the body to one side. "You either bury her now and put this whole thing behind you or you go home and keep dwelling on it until you get thrown in jail." Reaching out, Carl placed a reassuring hand on Mendel's shoulder. "Like I said: You made me. I know what's best for ya. So let me take charge for a sec and help you out. Okay?"

Mendel stared up at Carl without a word. He considered the snowman's words, trying to dissect a hidden meaning from them. But through his jumbled thoughts, all he could gleam was that the matter would finally be out of his hands. He could live his life without worrying about this anymore. So finally, he nodded.

"Okay." Mendel knelt down in the snow, and slowly began to dig. "I trust you, Carl."

Hands dug in the snow, down past dirt, stone and grime. They dug for so long, they lost track of time. Memories burned, needles jabbed Mendel's mind, as against the earth his bare fingers did grind. It could have been hours, for a tight, shallow grave. But it was still more than the car's driver gave.

Between the two of them, Carl did the most. But for once, Mendel found his work came quite close. With a few more quick swipes, the crude burrow was set. Would it fit their cold charge? They would have to see yet.

"On three!" Carl said, holding her by the arm. Together, they pushed, without worry of harm. Her limbs had contorted, her skin had been stretched. But with one final push, they released the poor wretch.

"I think our job is done!" Carl proudly intoned, eying the mishmash of bent skin and bone. "We've nothing to fear; we've ended her hurt. Now all that is left, is replacing the dirt!"

Mendel looked at the girl, compressed into the ground. About to be left, where she'd never be found. "No... I just... this just can't be alright!" He screamed out the words to the surrounding night.

"Oh come now, old buddy!" Carl ruffled his hair. "Don't beat yourself up; this is totally fair! She was left out to wander, she won't be found there. You know that her parents aren't going to care!"

Mendel stared up at Carl. "No, that's it. I'm done."

Then he turned on his heel and he started to run.

When had the snow picked up so severely? And how was he suddenly back at the berm? The boy had no time to mentally retrace his steps. He was already scrambling up onto the berm, branches scratching at his legs as he hoisted his body into the snow. Mendel's pajamas did nothing to shield him from the snow's horrid chill as he collapsed on his knees, heart beating hard as he grabbed his head.

He began hyperventilating. Mendel's breath came out in quick gasps of mist, barely taking in any oxygen. His legs burned with cuts and scrapes he only felt now. He felt tears once more threatening to roll down his face.

Mendel had shed so many tears over the past two days. But why was he crying *now?* He was safe, wasn't he? Carl had helped him and there was nothing to worry about. He shouldn't have anything to bother him anymore... right?

Mendel didn't truly know anymore. He remained on the berm, kneeling in the snow. Feeling the oxygen leave his lungs in bursts. He didn't care that he was freezing. In that moment, he wanted nothing more than to curl up and die.

And perhaps, Mendel truly *would* have died, had it not been for a pair of headlights suddenly shining through the darkness.

Mendel didn't look up as the spotless white minivan approached him. He didn't acknowledge the pretentious classical music blaring out of its open windows. But he did recognize *her* voice.

"Oh my *god!* Daddy, stop the car!"

With the clinking of snow chains, the minivan slowed to a stop just a ways in front of Mendel. The passenger door opened, letting out a burst of warm air, as none other than Cinder stepped out of the car, clad in fur-lined, woolen princess pajamass.

If Mendel had wanted to die before? Now, he wanted to *kill.*

"Mr. Miserable, is that you?" Cinder cooed, prancing up to the kneeling boy and looking him up and down. "Going on a lil' late night walk in your pjs, are you? You *know* the snow is supposed to pick up again, right? Huh?"

Mendel still didn't look at her. He couldn't find it in himself to muster a good response. Or, rather, one that wasn't simply him screaming wordlessly at the sky.

Luckily for Mendel, as per usual, Cinder's social agenda proceeded without any outside input. "God, *poor* thing... all lost and alone, out in the cold." Cinder leaned over and gave Mendel a condescending, almost painfully forceful pat on the head. "Do you need a ride back home, you poor thing? Does big sissy Cinder gotta help her little Mr. Miserable find his way back to his mommy?"

Still not looking up, Mendel bared his teeth like a rabid animal, his voice hissing like a snake, "Can you just—"

"*Okay, fine!* You've twisted my arm!" Cinder announced to the world, taking Mendel's actual arm in a vice grip and hoisting him to his feet. "Rev up the Thomas Mobile, Daddy! Ms. Cinder Claus has a gift to deliver to the Naftali house!"

"Right away, Princess," a somewhat hoarse, American-accented male voice confirmed from the driver's seat.

Despite his rising anger, Mendel felt a spark of curiosity as Cinder dragged him towards the door to the back seats. For all her incessant nagging and bragging, Mendel had never actually *seen* either of Cinder's parents. A supposed 'Mr. and Mrs. Thomas' had long been discussed between the school staff, as well as the few kids who were granted the *privilege* of visiting their esteemed abode. But as for putting a face to the names? This would be a first.

"Oh, uh, sweetheart?" the voice piped up again, as Cinder led Mendel into the car. "Can your little chew toy sit on the floor during the drive? Daddy *just* had those seats cleaned, and your sister will likely be filthy as it is."

"But Dad!" Cinder let out an agonized groan. "This might be Miserable's only chance to feel like one of us! Please? For him?" She widened her eyes in an attempt to make a pleading expression. Really, it just made her look even more unhinged than she really was.

Mendel still couldn't see Cinder's dad past the large, cushioned driver's seat but an unmistakable sigh could be heard from up front. "Sorry, little sugarplum, but the doggy sits on the floor where he belongs."

"Okay, fine...." Cinder bemoaned, plopping down on the left back seat and wasting no time in shoving Mendel down into an uncomfortable squat on the floor beneath the right seat. "So *anyway*, Daddy, you should *obviously* know where to go from here from what I've told you: Just take the first right, and you'll see his sad little neighborhood."

"Right, right, I remember that," Cinder's father replied; his tone was not very enthusiastic. "And, what house is his again? Don't want to drop the rat off at the wrong bum's—"

"First on the left," Mendel quickly piped up. As weird as it was that Cinder knew where he lived, he *also* shared her father's desire to not be dropped off on a stranger's doorstep in the middle of the night.

"Oh, so you *can* speak." Mendel swore he heard a 'huh,' added onto the end of that statement. "Alright, buckle up, boys and girls: Next stop, The Miserable homestead."

"Yay! Thank you, Daddy!" Cinder cheered, bouncing in her seat.

"Thank you, Mr. Thomas," Mendel muttered half-heartedly as the truck started to move.

Shifting so his body was parallel to the seat, Mendel pulled his legs close to himself. Even with the almost excessive warmth of the car (impressive, since they simultaneously kept the windows wide open), the boy still trembled slightly, rocking back and forth.

Cinder, meanwhile, having completely neglected to fasten

her seatbelt, stared down at Mendel with a curious expression. "So?" she drawled, stretching out on her stomach and kicking her feet expectantly.

"'So?'" Mendel repeated flatly.

Cinder just scoffed, rolling her eyes. "So, why were you out in the cold, Mr. Miserable? *God!*" Cinder threw up her hands in exasperation. "See what I have to deal with, Daddy? He's just so *dense* sometimes!"

"I could say the same thing about you," Mendel huffed quietly... except, he soon realized it wasn't quiet enough.

"*Excuse me?!*"

Mendel jumped as Mr. Thomas suddenly turned backwards in his chair. A small pair of rounded glasses doing nothing to distract from his wrinkles and prevalent crow's feet, Mr. Thomas leaned straight into the back seat with the most furious expression Mendel had ever seen.

"*The fuck did you say about my daughter, you Jewish shit-stain?!*" he screamed, mouth gaping so wide Mendel got a view straight down his throat.

"I-I..." Mendel stammered, scrambling back in the car; even Cinder looked distraught at her father's words. "I-I didn't—"

"*Well, boy?* Spit it out!" Mr. Thomas reached out and grabbed Mendel by the collar, hauling Mendel back towards him with an iron grip. "Give me *one* good reason why I shouldn't lob you back into the snow!"

"Daddy, the road! Watch the *road!*" Cinder pleaded, tugging desperately on her father's sleeve.

"*God fucking—*" Forcefully throwing Mendel back to the floor, Mr. Thomas spun around and grabbed the wheel with both hands, the car swerving across the lane as he did so.

And just like that, as quickly as Mr. Thomas had snapped,

the car went quiet. Mendel lay on the floor, heart beating hard in his chest, as he listened to the man seething through his teeth. Cinder stared at her father, her eyes visibly glimmering in the car's overhead light.

"Sorry, little princess," Mr. Thomas finally apologized, his breathing ragged. "I didn't mean to scare you like that."

"It's okay…" Cinder replied. Mendel had never heard her voice so quiet. "Just please be careful… and promise you won't hurt Mendel, alright?"

"I promise, sweetheart."

"Okay Daddy…" Cinder sunk back into her seat heavily, pulling her seatbelt slowly over her torso. It was hard to see but Mendel swore he saw a tear trickling down her face.

Watching her, Mendel felt that hollow feeling come over him again… but this time, there was something else beyond it. Somewhere, in that gaping hole in his chest, beneath the dread and the loathing, there was… pity?

"So…" Mendel began, somewhat awkwardly. "Why are you and your dad out driving tonight?"

Cinder looked over at him, pulling her arms close around herself. "As if you care," she pouted, almost to herself.

"Well… maybe I do." To his surprise, Mendel found he meant these words. "Is everything alright? What's going on?"

Cinder eyed him quietly, her hair shifting in the wind of her open window. She glanced back towards her father and for a moment, Mendel thought she would actually talk to him.

But then she simply scoffed, turning back a spiteful glare. "What's it matter to *you*, anyway?" she barked. "This is our own business and it doesn't concern you, Mr. Miserable."

Mendel felt genuinely taken aback at her words. "I'm sorry, I was just trying to—"

"Well *don't*, okay?!" Cinder snapped; her face was turning red and her eyes were watery. "I didn't *ask* for your feedback; if *I* want to talk to you, *I'll* talk!"

A stab shot through Mendel's body and his voice started to rise. "Okay, fine, then I—" Mendel stopped himself, looking towards Mr. Thomas nervously. The man remained focused on the road ahead. "Fine, I'll... stop."

"Good." Cinder crossed her arms and leaned back in her seat, glaring straight ahead.

Not sure what else to do, Mendel curled in on himself pitifully, resting his head on his legs. He was so, so tired. He couldn't think clearly anymore.

At this point, he just wanted to go to bed and get up the next morning to his dad pulling up in their rickety old Geo Metro. He didn't want to think about burying dead kids, or some weird talking snowman, or how he had felt himself pitying this girl who had tormented him for years.

Mendel was at the end of his rope. And his grip on it was slipping with every passing minute.

He felt his body shift as the car turned onto his street. There was a jolt as Mr. Thomas stepped on the breaks, bringing them to a stop.

"Alright, up and at 'em. Here's your stop," Mendel heard Mr. Thomas say from the front. "I assume your deadbeat father earns enough to afford a spare house key for you?"

If it were anyone else, Mendel would have retaliated at that. But he didn't want to provoke this man further. "Yes. Thank you again for the ride, Mr. Thomas."

"Don't drag this out, Miserable," the man growled in response. "Get inside and get yourself to bed before the snow gets any worse."

Mendel's eye twitched at the vitriol in those words, yet he forced himself to remain quiet for his own good. Obediently, he pushed open the door, inching across the floor before dropping down into the snow with a small *crunch.*

Before Mendel could walk back to the porch, however, the sound of shuffling came from inside the car behind him. "Hey, Mendel?"

Mendel hesitated. Cautiously, he turned back around... and was promptly slapped across his cheek by Cinder.

"You better have a happy fucking Hanukkah, Mr. Miserable!" Cinder sneered, shaking off her hand. "Because our Christmas week is turning up total *garbage!*"

That was the last straw. Mendel's actions flew out of his control. Lunging back up towards the car, he seized Cinder by the hair, pulling her straight off the backseat and out into the snow.

"*Aaah!*" Cinder exclaimed, coming down hard on the icy ground, only to be forcefully hefted to her feet by Mendel. "What the hell are—"

"*What is wrong with you?!*" Mendel's eyes were wide as he practically *spat* the words at Cinder's horrified face. "What did I ever do to you? I didn't do *anything!* I just wanted to live my own life, and for *that* you've harassed me every *goddamn day?! Why?!*"

"Let me go, you psycho! You're hurting me!" Cinder yelled, trying to yank her hair free of Mendel's grip to no avail.

"Then *answer* me, Cinder! Let me hear you say *why* you hate me so much!" Mendel demanded through his barred teeth, pulling her hair hard. "Is it because of your dad?! You need to make *me* feel worse, so *you* can feel better?! Is it some religious bigotry?! It is just because I *have darker skin?! What do you want from m*—"

The only forewarning Mendel got were two hands

forcefully clamping down on his shoulders. Moments later, he was lifted from the ground and sent hurling through the air, smashing forcefully into the wall of his house.

Everything hurt. Pain shot through Mendel's body as he tumbled down head over heels into the snow. His system was overwhelmed by an agonizing feeling in his legs, and all he could do was scream. A stream of tears poured down his face, soaking his shirt as he clutched at his leg, a red stain beginning to spread through the fabric of his pajamas.

Mendel thought he heard Cinder scream. He thought he saw a light turn on across the street. But he couldn't stop *screaming.* The pain was worse than anything he'd ever felt in his life. Worse than when he'd sprained his ankle during PE. Worse than when he'd been pushed off the slide as a toddler. Mendel screamed and screamed as Mr. Thomas lifted him out of the snow by the arm.

"Do you feel that, you fucking brat?" he seethed, staring at Mendel with indescribable fury. "Lay a hand on my daughter again and swear to the Lord above I will make the rest of your life a living hell!"

"Mendel?! *Mr. Thomas,* what are you doing to my son?!"

"Mom?" Mendel could barely make out her mother's voice over the sound of his own screams.

"I'll tell you *exactly* what I'm doing, Mrs. Naftali!" Mr. Thomas dropped Mendel unceremoniously into the snow, another burst of pain shooting through Mendel's body as he landed on his leg.

"*Bubeleh!*" Ines exclaimed, running down the steps to try and reach her child, only to have her arm grabbed by Mr. Thomas.

"*Don't* you fucking go anywhere, you Canadian *cunt!*" Mr. Thomas hissed, jabbing a finger in Ines' face. "*Your* son has been *harassing* my daughter this entire night! We found him freezing to death in the snow and now he has the *gall* to insult and *belittle* my baby girl! So what I'm *doing* is giving him his *goddamn* just desserts!"

In one swift motion, Ines yanked her arm from Mr. Thomas's grasp. "Disregarding that doling out punishment to *my* son is not your duty to undertake…" Ines' tone went cold as ice. "What righteous man of Adonai—of *any* faith!—sees it fit to *break the leg* of their neighbor's child?!"

Mr. Thomas reeled back his arm to slap Ines, but she grabbed him by the wrist before it could connect. Spinning him around, Ines twisted his arm behind his back. The man let out a roar of agony, her grip far stronger than he'd expected.

"Do *not* cite the Lord as your argument!" Mr. Thomas growled through the pain. "My actions are fully validated by the words of the Good Book: Spare the rod, spoil the child!"

"That phrase is not printed in *any* such book!" With considerable effort, Ines thrust Mr. Thomas forward, sending him tumbling face-first into the snow. Flakes of frost flew up into the air from the impact, mingling with the steadily increasing snowflakes flying past on the wind.

A few of the neighbors had stepped outside their houses from the commotion; a scarce few of them had cellphones, others simply watched from their porches. But Ines hardly paid them any mind. Immediately upon relinquishing Mr. Thomas, she ran to kneel at her crumpled son's side, running a hand over his bloodied leg.

"Oh, my baby…" Ines choked back a sob, carefully wrapping her arms around her son.

"Mama… I'm so cold…" Mendel stuttered, barely able to speak through the pain.

"Mama's here, Mendel... I'm here." Pulling Mendel close, Ines turned to glare back at Mr. Thomas, who was pushing away Cinder as she tried to help him to his feet. "Take your daughter and get off of my property, *Christopher*. Gabriel and I will see you in court."

"In *court?*" Mr. Thomas snarled, punching a fist into the snow and pushing himself up on one knee. "My lawyers will have you *and* your syrup-sucking husband in a fucking cell if you even set one *foot* inside a courthouse!" His eyes narrowing, a grin began stretching across his face. "Besides... I fully intend to resolve this *tonight.*"

"*Daddy, no!*" Cinder pleaded, running to grab at her father's shirt. "That's enough, that's *enough!* I'm okay, I forgive Mendel! But we need to keep looking for Aurora before she *freezes to death!*"

Mendel felt something click inside him.

"Aurora?" he questioned softly.

Immediately, Mr. Thomas's eyes were locked on him. "You know something, *boy?*" he demanded, taking a step closer.

"Christopher, I'm warning you!" Ines began, shifting her son further away from the approaching man.

"Who is Aurora?" Mendel asked hoarsely, though slightly louder this time.

Cinder was the one to respond, her voice shaky. "She's... my little sister."

A picture was becoming clear in Mendel's mind. "And she's lost?" he further inquired.

Mr. Thomas let out a heaving breath at this. "Good Lord, you really *don't* listen, do you?" he seethed, placing his hands on his hips.

"Christopher. *Answer my son,*" Ines demanded, meeting

his eyes with a steely gaze.

Mr. Thomas scowled but complied. "Aurora's our youngest. Pumped her out a few years back; she's not in school yet but she likes playing in the snow. Since it's Christmas, I let her go out the other day to build a snowman. I had *assumed* my wife would know I let Aurora out and would let her back in... but it's been a whole day now, and Aurora's *still* out there, screwing around in the woods somewhere."

"And I'm getting really worried about her!" Cinder interjected, looking at Mrs. Naftali desperately. "We're supposed to leave for my sweet thirteen celebration tomorrow but none of us have seen her..."

"Sweetie, like I *told* you back home, she's just rolling around on a road somewhere again," Mr. Thomas groaned, brushing snow out of his thinning, gray hair. "This is *exactly* why I shouldn't expect your mother to keep track of time anymore..."

Mendel began trembling.

"*Bubeleh?*" Ines whispered cautiously. Mendel moved Ines' arms aside, rising to his feet. He took a slow step towards Mr. Thomas.

"I know where she is." Mendel ignored the searing pain with every step. His face didn't visibly process the sensation. Mr. Thomas's eyes locked onto the approaching boy like a target reticle.

"The hell are you saying now, boy?" Mr. Thomas demanded, kneeling so he was level with Mendel.

Mendel stopped just before him, frozen in place. Snow began to gather in his dark hair. "I've seen Aurora. I saw what happened to her."

Cinder couldn't prevent herself from gasping. "M-Mendel, what...?" Cinder tried to speak but her words failed her.

"*Bubeleh*, what are you saying?" Ines questioned; she too was becoming concerned.

But Mr. Thomas did not share their hesitance. "You what?!" Once more, he took hold of Mendel by the collar. "Then where is she, boy?! Where's my baby girl?!"

Mendel began laughing. Mr. Thomas began shaking him. "*What's so god damn funny?!*"

Mendel kept laughing.

"*Fucking answer me when I speak to you, you little—*"

Mendel's hands clamped down on Mr. Thomas's arms. "You want to know what happened to her?" Mendel asked, as the older man's sentence died on his lips. "We'll show you."

A howl roared across the yard. The wind picked up, snow falling hard. It pelted Mr. Thomas so, of my presence he would not know. The ground began to tremble, quake; this man had made a bad mistake.

"This god damn snow! I cannot see!" Christopher ranted ceaselessly. Mendel just laughed and laughed some more; he knew quite well what was store.

His mind was blank; his thoughts, were me. His summons I answered so swiftly. Rising up from 'neath the snow, coal eyes sparked with a flaming glow. At last, frostbitten jaws spread wide, revealing icicles inside. I reached out and grasped the grown up's hair; I think he'd more than earned a scare.

"Hello, Christopher," I did state. "It would appear, you've sealed your fate."

He struggled, still blind as can be. "And who are you?!" he demanded of me. "I'll beat you down! You want a fight?!"

And that was when I took my bite.

His skin was frostbitten, chilled through and so fresh. Both the Naftalis screamed as my teeth pierced his flesh. His daughter cried out. My teeth punctured his bones; I'd finally tasted a wound of my own. And oh, what a taste! How I hungered for more! My claws tore off his leg, ripping fabric and gore.

"No! This must be a dream! This can't happen to me!" Cinder tried to charge forward, fists swung futilely.

But strong hands snatched her up, put her under an arm; Ines had swept the princess away from due harm. And Mendel was there, hanging so limply, too.

"What of Adonai's creations are you?!"

I looked up at Ines' words with a visceral grin; my teeth stained with penance for Christopher's sin. "Why my dear, I found form through your little tot's mind. He's seen quite a lot, I think you will find."

"A demon! You demon!" Cinder did decry, a stream of her tears pouring down from her eyes. "You took Daddy's leg! You should go burn in hell!"

I laughed. "Oh poor child... you don't know me so well."

I discarded her father, beseeching his God. Left him to bleed out, and approached at a plod. "This all was a process, I think you will see. We've been on a journey, Mendel and me."

His mother stepped back. Looked around at the snow. Hoping for aid... but yet she didn't know. "Your neighbors won't help you," I gently informed. "It's only us four, 'til your son's heart is warmed."

"I won't let you take him," Ines vowed with a quiver. The sight made me smile, if only a sliver.

"Who said I meant him?" I swiftly clarified. With a roar, then, I pounced—

—but she dodged to the side. Quickly turning tail, Ines ran straight towards the street, the frost harshly stinging her own bare *feet. Sinking into the snow, how I laughed at the sight.* "You cannot run from friends! And I will end her life."

Ines ran blindly through the wailing wind and snow, Cinder and Mendel held tightly underneath her arms. She had no idea what she would do or where she would go; all she knew was she had to get them away from that creature!

"*Peekaboo!*" Carl sprang up from the snow in front of them, claws raised and bloodied fangs bared in an unnaturally wide grin.

Cinder screeched. As Ines desperately altered her course, Cinder flung her fist straight into the snowman's eye. "*Get away from us! Go away, devil!*"

"Cinder—" Ines started to address the girl but was cut off as Carl's claw whizzed by her face. Truthfully, Ines didn't know what she had wanted to say; so instead, she simply bolted around Carl and fled further into the surrounding snowstorm.

On and on Ines ran, being forced to adjust her course by Carl suddenly lunging from the snow beneath them. Cinder was sobbing and kicking the entire time, begging Ines to go back for her father. At this point, Ines wasn't sure she *could* go back. She only prayed Naomi had somehow slept through the commotion.

Mendel, meanwhile, hung limp in his mother's grasp. Legs dangling behind her, arms swaying without any input. He was breathing, at least... but since Carl's appearance, Mendel had become dead silent.

"Mendel, *bubeleh,* can you hear me?" Ines asked, looking down at her son even as she continued to run. "If you can hear me, I need to know what this creature is! How do you know it? Is there any way to placate it?!"

Slowly, Mendel raised his head to look at Ines; his

expression was unreadable. Ines felt a twinge of fear at the sight... then, her son gradually turned his head forward, raising a hand meekly.

"We're in the forest."

Looking back ahead of them, Ines blinked in disbelief. Somehow, without her realizing it, they had entered a dense, snow-covered forest. They were coming up on a clearing, three trees arranged in a triangular formation.

"But... how...?" Ines tried to rationalize the situation in her head but all logic failed her almost instantly. "We were heading for the road. I kept us heading towards—"

"Present for you, Mrs. Naftali!"

Ines couldn't react in time. Lunging from beneath the roots of the closest tree, Carl sliced his fingers across Ines' face and she toppled to the ground. Cinder and Mendel rolled out of her grasp, tumbling helplessly through the snow. Mendel smacked painfully into the foot of a tree, letting out a yell on impact.

Mustering the last bit of strength he had, Mendel forced himself to sit upright against the tree, cringing in pain. Cinder lay on her side in the snow a few feet to his right; his mother was about a yard away from them, hand pressed to her face as blood seeped between her fingers. And thumping through the snow towards him was Chilly Carl, smiling like it was Christmas morning.

"Well, that was a fun little game, I suppose!" Carl mused, flicking drops of blood off his twiggy fingers. "But I've still got one last little holiday gift to deliver! And frankly, Mendel old friend, I see no reason to delay this any further."

Carl landed heavily in the snow next to Cinder. Realizing the snowman was looming over her, the girl let out a shriek, and attempted to crawl away from him but before she could make any sort of progress, Carl promptly hoisted her up by her hair.

"Now, now, young lady. This is long overdue." Carl tutted, drumming a finger on Cinder's forehead.

"Don't... hurt her!" Ines groaned out, the pain of her deeply scratched face straining her words. Desperately, she tried to climb to her feet.

"Uh-uh-uh! This isn't your call to make, Mommy Dearest," Carl chided. Raising his free hand, he snapped his fingers. On cue, two pale arms shot out of the snow and seized Ines by the ankles, pulling her back down to the ground; two more arms promptly grabbed her wrists.

"Mom!" Mendel exclaimed, looking at Carl with a horrified expression. "Carl, stop! She's not part of this!"

"And I am?!" Cinder screamed, tears flying off her face. "And my dad?!"

Before Mendel could reply, Carl jumped in for him. "Yes! Yes, you both very much are!" the snowman confirmed nonchalantly, before looking back to Mendel. "But you're right, buddy: Even at our worst, I've never taken issue with your mommy. So after this, I'll let her go, safe and sound. You just need to give me one, *final* push."

Pulling Cinder's hair further back, Carl raised his other hand into the air, brandishing his fingers in a claw. Mendel stared at it, eyes wide.

"Why are you doing this?" Mendel asked flatly.

The question had no purpose. He already knew the answer, and Carl knew he did, too. But the snowman nevertheless entertained him, smiling patiently. "Like I said before, Mendel: You made me. I'm your special guide that steps in when you're stuck. And the way I or rather, *we* see it?" Extending a finger, Carl traced it through the air over Cinder's neck. "This right here? Is the fastest way to wrap up your problems for good."

"Mendel, you..." Cinder sniffled, straining her eyes to be able to see. "You, don't *really* think that, do you...?"

Mendel stared back at Cinder without a word. He stared at her red, tear-streaked face, her lip quivering as she held back tears.

Then he looked at his mother. Lying on her stomach, held down by arms of ice, Ines was shaking her head, staring at her son with a mix of horror and disbelief. Finally, Mendel looked up at Carl. The snowman, now with a fully-emotive face, looked down at him expectantly... no, *eagerly*. And Mendel understood what that meant.

"Just say the word, Mendel," Carl reassured him. "I know you're hesitating. It must feel a little crazy, actually experiencing this moment for yourself. But you just need to put your trust in me, one more time. Even one quick little nod, and I'll gladly turn this snow into strawberry snow cones for you."

Mendel's breath came out in slow puffs of mist. He took in Carl's genuine face, the truth burning in his eyes. This was what they'd wanted for years. Mendel knew that all too well. This was his chance to be rid of his biggest source of grief. His chance to find closure for the *negligence* that led to Aurora's death. Revenge.

But as he looked towards Cinder one more time... Mendel paused. And when he spoke, his answer surprised not just Carl but himself. "No."

"Buddy?" Carl questioned. "Ha, you're not getting 'cold feet' on me, are you?"

Mendel didn't look at Carl. His eyes remained focused on Cinder as he replied, "This shouldn't have happened."

"What?" Carl suddenly sounded nervous.

"I *said...*" Propping himself against the tree, Mendel rose to his feet. "That this is *not* what I want!"

Carl reeled back as though he'd been punched in the gut, losing his grip on Cinder as he clasped a hand over his chest. "Of course it is! That's why I'm *here*, pal! When you saw her sister—"

"I should have told my *mom*," Mendel interrupted. "And I should have told the cops. And I *should* have told Cinder because it was the *right* thing to do!"

"You—" Carl buckled over, mouth gaping open as he clutched at his chest. "That's... I *told* you—"

"You were *wrong!*" Mendel snapped, jabbing a finger towards the hunched creature. "I made something out of *nothing!* I beat myself up over a death that *wasn't* my fault! And it was only by *listening* to you that I was *actually* becoming what you made me think I was!"

"Ugh—" With a fleshy squelch, a thick glob of snow slipped off of Carl's head and landed on the ground. "You're lying to yourself, Mendel! I know what you really—"

"What I wanted was *wrong!* It's bad enough I allowed you to hurt Mr. Thomas but if I let you follow through with *this?* I would have only continued the cycle of hate that tormented me for *years!*"

"You...! You...!" Carl began moving towards Mendel, his entire body sagging and sizzling like meat in a pan. "Do you really think anyone will be able to help you, Mendel?! That anyone could know you better than me?!"

One step. Two steps. Until Mendel was standing right in front of Carl's disintegrating form. He raised his hand, curling it into a fist. "*I* know me. And I know *us.*" Mendel fiercely punctuated his words: "And we! Are not! You!"

In one blow, Mendel smashed straight through Carl's

torso once more. The snowman let out an unholy screech, arms raised and fanged jaws hanging open as its body began melting into pungent, rotten slime. The hands holding Ines trembled and decomposed, dissolving into the same substance as Carl. It bubbled and boiled, revealing a distorted collage of the past day's events, its components wriggling against one another like panicking, swarming insects.

Ines scrambled to her feet at the sight while Cinder screamed and covered her eyes. Mendel didn't flinch, as snowflakes—*real* snowflakes—flew down on the breeze from above. They swooped downwards, attacking the clinging memories, bombarding them until they each were reduced to dust. Once the ground was clear, the snow began to spiral around Mendel, Ines, and Cinder, picking up speed until they were nothing but an icy blur, the surrounding forest lost in the expanse of white.

Finally withdrawing his arm from where Carl had once stood, Mendel smiled softly. Raising a hand, he placed it over his eyes. "Hear, O Israel: The Lord our God, the Lord is One. Praised is the Lord by day and praised by night, praised when we lie down and praised when we rise up. I place my spirit in His care, when I wake as when I sleep. God is with me, I shall not fear, body and spirit in His keep."

Mendel woke with a start. He was back in his bed. It was still late at night but he was home instead.

For a moment, he thought, had it all been a dream? But promptly he learned, things were not as they seemed. In rushed his mother, breathless and scared; for such strange events, she had not been prepared.

"Oh Mendel, oh bubeleh, I am so proud!" It went without

saying but she said it aloud. Ines took him in her arms, held him tight, held him near. There was no more danger; no need for fear.

Mendel looked at her cheek; Her wounds, they had closed. He shifted his legs; they could move unopposed.

"Your face... it's okay!"

"I... suppose that is true! Perhaps all was undone, when the nightmare was through?"

Ines had no time to think, someone knocked at the door. A guest at this hour? Could it be there was more?

But no, when they checked, it was only a man. When Ines opened the front door, he extended a hand.

"I think," he began, "that I had a bad dream. I thought you were threatened, but... that's not how it seems."

Ines simply smiled. "Thank you; we're okay."

The neighbor nodded back. "Well, I'll be on my way."

As they closed the door, mom and son shared a look. If doubts had remained, that was all that it took. It had happened, no question. Those events were real.

Mendel had fought back his darkness, and now, he could heal.

Sleep wasn't an option. They sat on the couch. When Naomi woke up, Ines carried her out. They sat, contemplating, while drinking some tea; Naomi sucked on her bottle happily. They stayed there that way and gave thanks for their lives. After some time had passed, a van pulled into the drive.

The mood had turned sour. Mendel knew it well. Would Mr. Thomas come through and make their lives hell?

But now, on the porch, Mr. Thomas did hold, the body of Aurora, still so deathly cold. Cinder stood next to him, tears in her eyes.

The hateful old man asked, "May we come inside?"

Ines chose to comply. She made them some tea. For now, she would show some hospitality. Mr. Thomas explained, while on their couch he sat, "She was out on the berm. Next to my father's hat." The man hesitated. For once in his life, his unshakable anger was broken by strife. "But, that couldn't be. That demon, it wore—" He sipped on his tea. "It had this hat, I swore."

Mendel and Ines felt perturbed. Oh, where to begin... that it was not a demon, but a symbol of sin. A concept that all of us have deep inside. That tempts us in waves, like the flow of a tide. To make such corporeal would be so surreal... the prospect of explaining, did not appeal.

"Christopher, please know that I feel for your loss. But for what you are saying, I am at a loss." Ines glanced at Mendel, they quickly agreed. "Please, take your girl home. Allow some time to grieve."

Mr. Thomas shot upright. "The hell do you mean?! I know you were there! I speak of that snowman with teeth like a bear! For the love of our Lord, he bit off my leg!'"

"Daddy, please... that's enough," Cinder somberly begged.

The father looked at his daughter then at his intact limb. His gums flapped in silence but words escaped him. "Perhaps, I am tired," he finally said. "I just can't believe that my daughter is dead...."

"Mr. Thomas?" Mendel spoke up, raising a hand. "I'm sorry this happened. I do understand."

"If you ever need us, we're here," his mom also added. "Our faiths are no reason we should be separated."

Mr. Thomas eyed her and then let out a huff. "Thank you, Mrs. Naftali. This week will be tough." He got to his feet. "I suppose we'll be off." A lump teased at his throat; he cleared it with a cough. "It's been a long day and far too long a night... and it seems that I'll now have to cancel our flight."

And away he strode, pushing open the door. Who knew if these households would meet anymore. But before she left, Cinder turned to look back. Her request was strained, her voice threatened to crack. "Have a good Hanukkah. If just in our stead."

Mendel didn't reply, but he nodded his head.

Cinder stood only briefly and then she departed. A shame that his promise was only half-hearted. But if nothing else came from this night that was not, Mendel had found truths he might not have got. And thus, he and Ines at last went to their beds. Gave thanks to Adonai, then rested their heads.

Such a heartwarming tale as we come to the end. It was such a pleasure telling it, my friend. But before you depart for your Wintertime fun, I hope you realize this story's just begun.

Mendel wasn't so special. His mind's not unique. We all possess darkness, longing to speak. So learn from your shadow, discern the real you; separate falsehoods from what's really true.

Or else, my good friend, you might happen to find...

... that I'll rise from the snow and take hold of your mind.

thirteen

An Isotopy of Shadows
David Mecklenburg

he orchids bloom in their kingdom: the deepest part of the forest. It is a kingdom defined by the expanding growth of the cerebral, patient fungus that slowly entangles every thought of the trees, the orchids, the vines, and creatures that eat its fragrant, vermillion mushrooms. Each life form consumes another beneath the sky.

Two orchids bloom together from the same ancient nurse-log of a tree. They drink the same water that falls to coalesce in the tender moss. They both yearn toward the flickering sunlight that carpets the leaves, humous, and rotting wood. Like a tapestry, the sunlight covers them in both shadows and glimmers, and they hold each other through the day and night. While the other orchids wait for a special wasp or fly—they use a manifold of color we cannot see and smells that range from our knowledge of rotting flesh or dragon fruit and out to unimagined aromas—the two orchids need only each other.

When the rare wind blows through the forest, it carries the deep boom of a waterfall reverberating against the trunks of countless trees. The orchids join and caress anthers and labellum, penetrating to the deep stigma and gynandrium—their most secret canal.

The orchids dream in their union, that they may never know a moment apart from one another, while the trees count time in their rings. The fungus? Its temporal considerations approach the geologic pace of the mountains and glaciers. Yet the Sun passes into the West and the night extinguishes all other shadows in its comprehensive embrace.

I don't know when the night swept over me on the little train, more of a tram car fading from opulence. The train moved through the darkness over rails and sleepers, six beats to the measure—the rhythm of my journey. The melody was far above me in the scattering clouds that swept before the moon. Shafts of that pale light broke through to illuminated grassland and copses of pine trees: spectral and primitive in their congregations. I imagined they made their own songs as the breeze blew through their boughs and needles; the light and sound of the train was only a fleeting theme, one that spoke of solitude and novelty.

Alone in the train-car, I had only the reflection of my face in the window. The conductor had long ago validated my ticket and had retired to the far end of the three cars. I listened to my breath and the rhythm of the train. I was a secret borne out here and yet in plain view of no one save the darkness and the abstract lies waiting for the Sun to return when it rose over the broken horizon to the East.

The tracks bent closer to the sea, and I could make out a shoreline. The Moon cast its light upon the waters it drew towards itself; they came forth and foamed briefly in the darkness and left a wide stretch of dully reflective sand: a river of gentle light that eventually disappeared into the darkness only to be renewed by the influx of another wave.

I am never sure where these events begin, but then who of us can ever say so with surety?

Before me, the waves performed their chorus as the tide ran out, and their once eager incoming iterations became improvisational phrases, arguments, and surrenders. I could smell the sea all around me, like a zinc-laden oyster opening her folds to the air to join the vegetal kelp and pervasive brine—a sharp drone that wavered on chaos. And yet... strangely, I only *knew* I was on a beach, perhaps *the* beach when you passed me.

You walked beautifully—a fluid reciprocation of muscle and bone beneath crisp white linen, and your dark skin touched here and there by the sharp contrasting points of moonlight on your salient contours. Your angular suit contrasted against the organic, complicated performance of your long, braided hair—a deeper black than the healing sleep which lies beyond dreams. I could smell the hundreds of intricate coils and pleats of your hair, all oiled with the verdant afternoon of olives that carried galvanized notes of eucalyptus.

I followed you. Always moving toward the Moon and like the water, we never reached it. I watched the regular flexing of your calves beneath the linen and could see the tendons of your ankles—you were barefoot. I had not noticed, but we had climbed away from the surf and walked upon dry and finely textured sand. You turned then. Then, as now, your face matched the rest of you: strongly arched eyes, prominent cheekbones, and the sensual lips of a Pharaoh. Your wide nose widened further as you smiled.

"It will be here," you said. "This is where they will fly away."

"Where is here?" I asked.

"Here is where you bought a ticket for, ma'am." And suddenly, I was asleep again, by which I mean that I was awakening and aware of the threadbare velour vest and rosacea on the nose of the old conductor who smelled of tobacco and camphor. "Karmiguel Station. The resort is not too far off."

"What time is it?"

"Just past two o'clock in the morning. Always seems strange at first if you're not here to take the cure, but most of the people who come like arriving at this time."

"Yes," I said, getting up and wobbling. We were not yet at the station itself, so the train still moved in six beats to the bar. "The cure would be most effective, now I suppose."

"Seems odd to me as well, but I can't really sleep very well early on in the evening as I've gotten older, so they moved me to this line."

"How much further before you sleep?" I asked, yawning.

"Do you mean that literally or metaphorically?" he asked, winking and getting my suitcase out from its strapped down location during the ride.

"Let's just stay at literal for now," I said. "Metaphor is too vast a territory for me."

"There are no other trains coming down this line until this one tomorrow. I wouldn't concern yourself with us. The train will glide into its platform, and we'll sleep there awhile until we return down this line."

I thought of the conductor and engineer sleeping peacefully—like children in some illustrated holiday book—upon the bench or in a hammock slung up in the foremost car as the train pulled into the brick platform of Karmiguel.

The Sanatorium and Hotel had gone back to horses and wagons, partly per regulatory compliance but also due to the picturesque charm of it, and so had sent a driver. Her conveyance was like a large, fanciful wagon and I was the only passenger to the wide bed, which was spread with cushions, blankets, and duvets like an enormous bed. Its canopy had been flung back; the weather, although brisk at night, was dry.

"You're more than welcome to sleep, ma'am" the young woman said. She climbed up to the driver's seat, arranged herself and cracked a signal bolt for the horses to move forward. "Most do. It's not entirely comfortable for sight-seeing and most come here prone anyways."

"And what about leaving?"

"Same thing, ma'am."

It was not long before we came to the Sanatorium and Hotel. I could hear and smell the ocean not too far off, but the clouds had grown thick again, with fog rising from the land to meet them in an all-blurring mist. Two vast, darker blots became apparent, and I recognized them for the two famous, massive rocks that differentiated this place from the rest of the coast, which otherwise smoothly reclined to meet the ocean. Deep in the crevasse between the rocks, the hotel rested between them, and there it lay in its safe shadows. We arrived at a set of stairs, and lower, wide carriage doors built into the rocks and walls of the building.

I was the only passenger there although there was another on the edge of the driveway waiting to meet the carriage. I thought of the train, still coursing through the night to distant Manduken and the sleep-break of the conductor and engineer. Yet I was not concerned for the passenger who possessed all the time in the world by waiting in an elegantly constructed coffin.

"We'll load him up tomorrow when the train returns," the young woman said. "The main door is this way. It's very dark, but you'll get used to that."

Her description was apt, for I found myself in some sort of

miner's hunch, trying to look at my feet to see if I were really walking on the gravel or some kind of illusion. The darkness swallowed us as we walked beneath the eaves of the hotel and the high outcroppings of rock above us. "Steps here, ma'am." She then opened a louver on an old-fashioned lantern, the kind in which its light could burn brightly and yet save that light for the chance opening to show me the way into the massive entrance. Inside, it was somewhat brighter, for faint diodes glowed like phosphorescent worms in an Art Nouveau tracery around the wide front desk, made more desolate by having one pale-faced man behind it.

His head was shaved so that he also seemed to glow, but his lids were heavy and cast his eyes downard toward the ledgers and registers on the desk.

"Your key, Madam Ludenow. Dora, will you show her to her room?"

The hallways loomed vast and empty, although there were shadows of people moving around, more than I expected at that time. Although every shade of skin, every physique, every gender, and age moved up and down the halls, they were all uniformed, for everyone wore some shade of black. Well, it's true, some of them had dresses or trousers of charcoal grey but in the gloom of the Karmiguel, only a black-and-white photographer could perhaps make out the different shades. Some nearly walked into me. One short woman, elegantly dressed in black silk and with some kind of hat made of raven feathers (perhaps, I could never be sure), bumped into me and lifted her head with an apology at her lips. She wore sunglasses so I could only make out the faint, distorted reflection of my own dark eyes.

"I'm sorry. You must be new," she said and moved off.

"That's Mrs. Dalrimple. She's been here for decades. I

don't mean to be rude, but is this your first time here, ma'am?" Dora asked. I liked her, if for nothing else, she had taken off her wide black hat at the desk to reveal a tight French braid of blonde hair, which made it easy to follow her through the hallways and up the stairs of the Karmiguel.

"Yes, I'm not a patient."

"I know that. I was told not to talk to you because you're an Inspector from the Syndic, but being a rude mute seems to be kind of stupid to me."

"You're very right, Dora."

We turned off a flight of stairs at a long corridor that stretched off into a darkness that hid its central perspective point. There were rows of doors, barely discernable, and the same soft glow of the wormy lights stretching partway down the hall. Aside from the darkness, it looked like any other hotel hallway save for a most marvelous carpet runner in the middle of the floor. I tried to set some reminder to study it more in the light, if light ever came there, because unlike the dark ebony-finished paneling of the walls and doors, it was a mixture of light and dark.

Understand that it did not strike me as some kind of glowing chiaroscuro of geometric pattern, but it did remind me of the paintings of Caravaggio in that all manners of figures writhed in a contrast of limbs, legs, tables, rooms, furniture, and drama down the hall. And the pattern did not, ever repeat itself. Entranced, I had taken many steps down it toward the darker gloom to see if the pattern would repeat, when Dora called out softly.

"Your room is here, ma'am. Oh, hello Mr. Conrado." Just then an older man came out of the dark shadows down the hall. I saw his hair first, for it was beautifully silver although disheveled in the way short hair can be when the owner never combs it. He had a long nose that hung over his lips. His suit was somewhat baggy; it had once fit him better in life. His hands, though aged, were beautifully shaped and no knob of arthritis marred them. I noticed this because he held one out and smiled.

"Pleased to meet you. My name is Jawethil Conrado. You must be new here. You seem so healthy. Ahh! *Bletilla,*" he said.

At first, I thought it was some kind of greeting then I noticed his fingertip tracing the silver embroidery on my black dress. I had some notion of the place beforehand and thought it would make sense to dress accordingly. He continued in gentle tones:

"*Bletilla:* Chinese orchids. That is a very beautiful dress. You must be visiting someone here?"

"In a way, yes I am."

He peered closer. "You are healthy, Ms.?"

"Ludenow. I should hope so."

"That is good. Then you won't be staying long. I never meant to, but the place sort of grows in you." He turned then to his door, opened it, and removed into the utter blackness inside.

"Don't mind him, ma'am. He's very sweet."

I tipped Dora well, and once the door to my room was secured, I searched for some way to increase the light. It was not difficult. The place had regular light switches, but no one used them. Once encased behind my own dark door and papered walls, I turned on as many lights as I could and felt better. There was a shuttered window and although I could draw back the curtain, the finely joined shutters seemed impossible to open at first. I did not care. I was tired and wished to sleep. I have slept in many strange places and this temple to shadows did not bother me. Indeed, the room was so soft and silent, with only a whisper of the sea making its way through the shutters that I fell soundly asleep. I suppose that is why I never heard the note as it was shoved under the door.

The Karmiguel has some of the best coffee I have ever had. Appropriately, I took it black there, although in the massive dining hall, you could barely tell, save for an occasional brief reflection of some rebellious light.

"You can see the guests and patients are quite comfortable. We ensure them a good diet. In addition to this food, they have regular high doses of cholecalciferol," said the Director.

Director Carnell was a vivacious man of medium height. In the low light I could not tell if his skin was a natural dark brown or tanned, but he seemed to smell different, as though he went outside in the sunlight as much as possible. Next to him sat the Assistant Director, Dr. Brucilla, a middle-aged woman, with a statuesque bearing, a narrow face, gold-rimmed glasses, full lips and a thick natural afro that dissipated out into the welcoming shadows like a black moon. She seemed exhausted, for she yawned mostly behind her hand. The Director noticed my attention.

"Dr. Brucilla normally works the day shift here, which means the night shift to you and me, Ms. Ludenow."

"I thought this smelled like dinner," I said. I meant it. There were roiling smells of roast beef, fiery clay pots filled with noodles, a very full dim sum cart, Caesar salads assembled tableside and countless other dishes.

"Yes, well we find that feeding our guests well can be a challenge so far out here away from normal supplies, but it is worth it for their therapy." Dr. Brucilla added.

"Are they all here for the same reason?" I asked.

"Yes and no. Yes, in the sense that the patients here are undergoing Dark Therapy as a way of contending with trauma and neuroses, but no, in that our clientele range from the curious, the afflicted, and the bored and each of them has their own pathway into the despair of living," Dr. Carnell said.

"As with every other being on this planet," I said. "Still, it seems a bit odd. One would think so much gloom would affect them negatively, like Seasonal Affective Disorder."

"As I said, we keep their psychochemical balances in order through nutrition, and we do not skimp on talking therapy. You see, Ms. Ludenow, that in the darkness, their own shadows seem paltry and insignificant. They can forget them here, or they can slowly negotiate with them."

"But not get rid of them."

"Are you sure any of us does?" Carnell said. "What sort of secrets do you cleave to without even knowing it? In the Darkness, one can apprehend such…"

He was cut off by some kind of aid, or orderly—a nondescript woman in a black tunic—who whispered in the director's ear. "…I am afraid I am called away. Please enjoy your breakfast. And perhaps enjoy the scenery. The clouds, which we normally welcome here, are particularly uniform outside."

I raised an eyebrow but said nothing else. The doctors arose and went out.

It was then I could pay full attention to the card I had read that morning.

"Ms. Ludenow. Welcome to Karmiguel. I don't think you are in any danger, being an Inspector and all, but do not let them drug you or you will never leave. Be careful of the carpet. Your shadow is somewhere inside of it. Perhaps not on this floor but somewhere. Do not stay long or it will find you."

The stationery had a distinctive imprint of two intertwined orchids at the top.

"He seems a bit strange, don't you think?" said a woman who was sitting next to me. Like everyone she was dressed in black, but she wore a finely tailored black suit crowned off with what I took to be a cravat made of heretical green silk. At least it appeared green, for the terrible light in the dining hall desaturated nearly every hue.

"He somehow fits this place. Ms. Ludenow," I said holding out my hand. She did not take it.

"Ms. Myrtle. It's important for you to know that not all of us here are so bad off. I like to get out a bit during the day, but I was a night owl before I came here, so it fits in an upside-down way."

"And what was your occupation?"

"Oh, I was an assistant secretary to a business concern. It must be exciting to be an Inspector. Always going somewhere new! You must get a chance to listen to many kinds of music."

"Are you a musician?"

"Oh, no. Not really. I played piano when I was younger, but not anymore."

"I'm somewhat surprised they don't play any music here in the dining hall. Even something recorded."

"Oh, no. The Dr. feels that any kind of music may be triggering to some people. It's a powerful evocation of emotion you know—the closest thing to the true expression of universal Will."

"You read Schopenhauer?" I asked.

"Oh, no. I mean I know of him through other sources."

I gathered 'Oh, no' was Ms. Myrtle's way of starting nearly every sentence, as though life was an unending cavalcade of surprises, which I suppose it is from the right perspective.

"Well, I am no longer hungry, Ms. Myrtle. You should read Dear Old Arthur if you can. His misogyny is a bit tedious but easily dismissed when you know a bit about him and his mother. The rest of him is... interesting."

"Oh, interesting?"

"We don't have time now, but perhaps before I leave, I can explain further. I will simply say it is a pessimistic philosophy that has the allure of reinforcing the negative cognitive bias many sensitive souls seemed cursed with."

I rose and left and was going to inquire about a way outside, when I remembered I wasn't wearing my boots, and the soft flats I had on were entirely inappropriate. I went back upstairs, along with several other patients who were wearing sunglasses and navigating the darkness with aplomb, but I was alone when I reached the landing. However, something was happening just outside my door. There was a gurney parked outside Mr. Conrado's open door and the people inside spoke in hushed tones, albeit not quite whispers.

I walked silently to the door and peered in. It is my job after all.

The lights were on and four people were in the room. Five if you count the body on the floor. Jawethil Conrado lay contorted, as though he had fallen from a height and landed there, but it seemed he had had some sort of seizure or fit. His neck was unnaturally twisted, and the left side of his face rested on the floor. His mouth was open, and Dr. Carnell was scooping some kind of black sludge, or oil—something viscous and absorbent of all light—onto the carpet. The procedure left his gloved fingers blacked and yet the sludge disappeared into the carpet and faded from his hands. Dr. Brucilla was writing notes.

Two orderlies stood nearby, looking down. I looked again at the face of Conrado and then it struck me. As if the disappearing substance weren't enough, his expression did not match the seeming agony of his death. His eyes were blissfully closed, and his old mouth with ragged lips lay open, not in the stretch of pain or surprise, but rather in the sensual projection of an open kiss.

I was not supposed to see any of this. That much became clear and I glided back away from the jamb. I kept my cautious steps as light as possible and the strange carpet, of which Conrado had warned me, accommodated almost too well. I experienced a feeling of compressed warmth rise through my feet, ankles, and calves.

"Time of death, perhaps two hours ago." Click. I loudly put the key into my door. "Hello? Ms. Ludenow?!, are you here?" came Carnell's voice.

"Um yes. I forgot to put on my boots. Is anything wrong?" I paused, wondering if I should act blissfully ignorant or pretend to go about finding my boots. *No, it would be better to go over there and be blocked entrance.*

Which is exactly what happened when I walked over to the open door. An orderly stood in the way. I could not tell what his expression was for he was wearing sunglasses, obviously an old-timer here.

"There is nothing to worry about. Clyde, please." The orderly stepped aside, and Carnell oozed out of the door taking off his surgical gloves. "I'm afraid the guest here has passed on. Heart failure. Happens to all of us eventually."

"How unfortunate."

"I apologize, of course."

"For what?" I asked. He smiled at this.

"You would do well here with that sort of *sang froid*, Ms.

Ludenow. Anyway, we will wait until later when the guests are asleep at noon and will extricate him and notify his family. Did you know him?"

"No. He only introduced himself last night. He was a retired horticulturalist. That is all I know of him."

"Yes. I see. He does not have a wife or any children, only an older sister."

"Perhaps that is for the best," I said.

"How so?" Dr. Brucilla approached and asked.

"Not as much grief to go around?"

"There is enough for his sister," Brucilla said.

"Dr. Brucilla, let us return to our duties here and let Ms. Ludenow go on her expedition outside."

My journey that day was the beginning of many "expeditions outside." That first day it was a relief to simply get away from the oppressive darkness and consider how I was to carry out this particular assignment. Since my instructions are always vague and the Code of Syndic Regulations points in as many directions as Kali at a SoHo nightclub, I found no guidance in that regard. I walked down the steps toward the sea and began to walk on the beach. The grey sky ponderously diffused all the light upon the sand, the water, and me and the thick salt air seemed to mute the rhythm of the waves. But as I looked at the beach, its contours and direction, I remembered that I had walked there with you.

The woman runs across the sand. There are a few others, who, being bundled against the cold, simply stand there, and observe. Like old pilings from a pier that has long ago disappeared, they seem randomly placed, faceless and indistinct. The running woman wears tight athletic clothing, and were it not for the gray sky, her tanned skin would sharply contrast against the white waves and seafoam she moves over. Her feet arch beautifully in their strides, poised with each step to grab the wet sand and propel her forward.

Beyond, and far behind her there are others running, but they are so far away we can barely make them out. We stand there, together. We are wrapped in coats and shift our feet from side to side in the cold. We are not running like her. We are perhaps another marker. Yes. We are markers. I see that now. I count. The runner's strides are so perfect in execution that you can count them easily. The waves, undulations of contrast: the dark sea water and white foam, splash and engulf her feet then recede.

I do not know what time it is. It seems irrelevant at first until I notice it's absence. No. Time is never absent, only its passage and here beneath the grey sky, there are no shadows at all save those faint spots that appear just before the runner puts her feet down. Why is she running?

"To win," you say.

"Win what?"

"The race. The course. The beyond."

"The beyond?"

"That is where she would like to go. Winning one race always leads to others and when you are built to win—look at her: body, technique, pace, all perfect—it means there will always be another race until…"

"…Until the body cannot."

"Or else she leaves the course. There is always that option although many cannot see it. We are here in our intervals. The sea would wash away the more pedestrian constructs of physicality. We would only pay attention to them, to her progress. But stop.

Just listen to her."

The woman breathes hard, but not in any painfully stressed way. Her face seems strained in that particular expression of pain that all runners share, which strangely conceals an ecstasy of performance. I sometimes run so I know it. But I do not run like this. There is a power in her lungs that speaks of depths beyond mundane shouting or sexual pleasure. I am jealous and so I admire her. I listen and am transported beyond the gray beach and this race. It is why I did not see the other runner catching up to her.

A cipher is doubly secret. It conforms to the basic description of a secret since it is known to a few, sometimes only one—if you consider the complex parliament of your being in the monadic convenience of that term. Yet a cipher also *does* something: it conceals and therefore what it conceals is also a secret by this very act. I have thought of this before, but in the Karmiguel, the richness of the cipher, its use, its theory became manifest in the black lines of phonetic symbols known to only me, and probably you.

After what I had seen in Mr. Conrad's room, which was obviously a secret, my cipher seemed the best tool at hand for recording the scene as I have described.

My room was full of shadows, even though the lights were on. I noticed them. Finally. The darkness beneath the bed: familiar to all of us since childhood; the shadow of the lamp's base; the black line beneath the door of my closet; and even the form of my hand cast in the beige darkness on the paper.

In the list of names I had learned, the menu, and the liquid anthracite that flowed from Mr. Conrado's mouth, I moved unthinkingly into other shadows and memories: the elegant darkness which lay between our hands when my lover and I walked together; the empty chair she once sat in; the figure of my mother behind the shower-curtain.

I sensed the presence of my black hair as it fell to either side of my face, as if it were straining for the ink. The action seemed to reveal an answer, or at least a clue. I have always been secretly proud of it. Since adolescence I have thought it one of my best features although I told no one of this secret. There was always too much holding it back, like a hair band. Was it modesty or self-loathing? The paradox of a matter of pride occluded beneath something like self-loathing seemed ridiculous, yet at the writing desk, I felt disconnected from the old emotions that had guided my steps, my hands, my body for so long, so I could study these feelings with a cool equanimity. I remembered a few of my lovers saying "I love your hair, it's so beautiful. So black" and I felt as though they had learned my secret in the best way possible: through love and so I did not have to break the silence myself.

It is this place. This library of shadows. I wrote that and then stood up. I heard movements outside my door, and murmurings although they did not sound like conversations, but rather the muffled echoes of statements made to no one in particular. And yet in the acoustics of darkness—that is the only synesthetic assemblage I can manage—the sounds recomposed themselves into the mode of conversation. I was not dreaming. Time did not slowly flow in lengthy epochs of seconds as it does in nightmares or even tedious work-dreams. It flowed quickly around me and my writing like a black river. And then, I opened the door and stepped out into it.

Into the crowd. They move, not silently. From slippers to high heels, they make the sounds of muted footsteps, but most definitely the footsteps of the living world. Or, this particular living world. Most of them are old and move in the deliberation of age. They are the guests, but like everyone they are shrouded in tailored black clothing. Some of it is very fine—couture cut for their bodies alone—and I can imagine blind tailors measuring with only their hands and cutting and sewing through muscle-memory so acute it no longer needed sight. Some of it is simple. Off the rack as it were and uniform.

They walk past me for the day has past and the last invasive hints of sunlight no longer infiltrate the windows. There is only the dim light of the hallway's curious lighting. They are awake now and going to breakfast. Some, friends perhaps from here or whatever the memory of their younger life was, lock arms. Some lean on canes.

And yet from all of them, faint shadows rise. It is difficult to see because of their clothes, but I can see the shadows extend and undulate like pythons or wings and detach. All manner of shapes: bottles of shampoo and Scotch, furry black spheres, pendulous members, and boxes, boxes everywhere exude from the people walking by me and slowly drift to the floor. And there, the carpet lovingly absorbs them, becomes them. I close my door and step backwards into my room. I leave every light on. I ring for coffee even (left outside in a porcelain pot that proudly displays the obscenity of its whiteness). None of these methods work. Sleep comes, and yet in that shadow I am unmolested. There is only the erasure of consciousness that lies beyond the metaphors of my senses.

I performed my duties over the next few days. I inspected this and recorded that. Kitchens, laundry, heating, ventilation and air-cooling systems, steps, baths, plumbing, paintings, and the leather couches where people would speak with the Doctors. And at least once a day, perhaps more often, I would witness convolutions of shadows in the carpets. Sometimes it was simply a shudder that ran out like a rogue wave. Sometimes it was a circus of acrobats, runners, riders, freaks, clowns, and mentalists. The patients radiated these forms, walked through them, carried them in some cases that were at once pathetic and sexual.

Is it any wonder I went outside as much as I could?

My stay was supposed to be short. I looked for and considered the clues, the facts about Karmiguel. Insofar as doing anything, *nothing* suggested itself and that phantasmagoric ontology—that only language can describe—neatly underscored everything I could say.

I walked from out of the shadows of the great rocks and saw, near the entrance, a woman standing by the carriage, or wagon that had brought me here. Dora was nowhere to be seen and I knew the woman did not belong here. Beneath her purple surcoat, she wore a dress that had the appearance of crème de menthe. No, it wasn't just the color. It was the texture, like a liquid hung about her in defiance of physics. I felt drawn to her, to see how the illusion revealed itself upon closer examination.

She was not wearing sunglasses. She was older, but beautiful in the way some women can simply *be* beautiful whether they are eighteen or eighty-one. An expert had cut her gray hair into a sharp bob. I looked at her perfect bangs and thought of my own rough-cut handiwork and grew embarrassed. Her clothing was all silk. I could see it better once I was near her. In the finest threads of silver, I saw the same orchids that adorned my dress although they were done with much better skill. The sunlight then touched her—it came unlooked for from between parted clouds—and I marveled at the sight of it reflecting from the green silk and silver. It seemed such a novelty that it took me a moment to look beyond her at the black wooden coffin waiting to be loaded onto the hearse, for that is what the vehicle now was.

"Hello," she said. "You don't look like a patient." Fresh tears moved down her face.

"I am not." I stammered this out and regained myself. "I'm sorry, you are obviously not a patient here either. That is a beautiful dress and surcoat."

"My name is Lisa. Lisa Conrado-Viktumbu," she said and held out her hand. Her hair, her bones, the way her nose hung, the cast of her lips. Though I had only seen her brother once, I knew Lisa to be his sister.

"You are here…"

"…to collect my brother. Yes. He did not have any spouse." She sniffed as she said this and dabbed at her eyes and nose with a handkerchief made from the same green silk. "I told him he never needed to come here. That this place would be the early death of him. But he believed what they said. Needed to, I suppose."

"I am sorry. I am not fond of this place either, if I may trust your confidence."

"That is not good news for them, for I can see you are an Inspector. You can trust my confidence…?"

"…Ada, I am most sorry. Ada Ludenow."

"Trust is an important thing. But sometimes it can be a prison. And yet only the fewest words can open it. I learned that a long time ago. My brother. Never could. Or would."

"Would?"

"Yes, you know by now this place is where people try to forget their deepest secrets." She leaned close to me and whispered, "It's why they are so profitable. But the greatest secret is if their patients ever really told someone their secrets, they would go bankrupt. So, they keep that from them. This place keeps their secrets close by."

"The carpets."

"Yes, I saw them just now. There is a large pair of orchids outside my brother's former room."

"Really?" I searched over my memory for these, but I could not picture them. "I did not notice. His room was next to mine."

"How did he die?" she asked.

And I told her. Maybe it was her smile and tears? I do not know. I simply felt unburdened in a way my ciphered journal could never accomplish.

"I see. I thought so. Do you see these flowers?" She pointed to the embroidery on her dress.

"Yes."

"They are a kind of orchid. One that, like most orchids, seems to flourish somewhere that's far away. There is a species that grow like these: two blossoms from the same stem. It's not that unusual, but these orchids have a way of growing together, fertilizing each other during certain conditions. My brother was a horticulturalist."

"Yes, he told me."

"He loved these flowers. They reminded him of me. And him." She looked at me then with an expression that seemed blank, but under her gaze I felt an enormous world of time and thought. "Yes. Some could say that I killed him. But that is not true. When we were young, we had what most people would call an inappropriate relationship. I was older. But had we different parents you would have known us as a beautiful couple. Doomed, like most of them are, our lives went separate ways. I lived, and grew, and married. My brother... did not."

"But you loved one another." I stood there and thought about this. In the presence of the secret, the memory of the oily slick in his mouth, I could see. And how, *or why* was I to judge?

"You do not need to judge," she said, her words hitting so closely that I could feel my eyes widen and my skin blanch.

"I realize that. And... I assure you that is the reason for the strange look on my face."

She laughed.

"I believe you, Ada, because strangers really are the best confessors of secrets. We do not have all of that baggage of knowing each other's lies."

At that point, Dora and two of the bigger orderlies came around a corner and proceeded to load Jawethil Conrado into the hearse.

"I'm sorry, but Ms. Dora. When are you leaving?" I asked.

"Soon ma'am. Your bags are not here. I hadn't heard you were leaving."

"I can be very quick. Would ten minutes suffice?" I thought it a long shot, but one worth taking.

"Ten minutes, and then I leave, ma'am.

I ran back into the Karmiguel, but upon reaching the main staircase, I ran into Ms. Myrtle, the woman I had met at that breakfast on my first day. She descended the staircase in a careful, frail way and I had to stop myself from running her down.

"Oh, Ms. Ludenow," she said. "Such a hurry."

"Hello Ms. Yes, I'm afraid I am. I apologize. I must catch the carriage back to the train."

"Oh, no. You are leaving? A pity. We never got to talk about Schopenhauer."

"No. I never got to hear you play the piano," I said as I politely moved around her and then I stopped. "Tell me, why did you say you quit playing?"

"Oh, it was a long time ago," she said, faltering. "I don't even remember the reason now."

"That is not entirely true. I believe you wish to forget, and this place—your being here—is part of that, is it not?"

"You will miss your ride Ms. Ludenow. And I must get to the dining hall."

"Ms. Myrtle, are you running from something?"

She turned away from me and hurried down the steps. I was not surprised to see a faint shadow rise from her back. It was large, almost shaped like a manta ray but with four spindly misplaced legs. The broad leading edge of it had teeth. Of course they were teeth. They had been teeth, of a sort. Eighty-eight of them.

I turned and ran back up the stairs and collected my things but even as I clumsily closed my suitcase and turned, I felt somehow the task was hopeless. I still went back downstairs as fast as I could to the front desk to check out.

"Ms. Ludenow, I did not know you were leaving. I am sure Director Carnell would wish to say goodbye."

"Yes, I'm afraid something urgent has come up. I am in a hurry to catch the ride to the train."

"Oh, but Ms. Ludenow, I heard Dora's signal bolt crack a minute or so ago."

"Are you sure?"

"You may go check. I can check you out while you see."

I left my things near the desk and walked as quickly as I could across that wide black lobby. I went through the double doors and the carriage was gone. *Never mind, you can take it tomorrow.*

But when I turned around, I saw Director Carnell and the Assistant Director coming toward me.

"Ms. Ludenow, is something wrong? We hoped you would stay longer, even though I will admit this place takes some getting used to." He said this with a genuine smile and held out his hand.

"Yes, I have an urgent message from my agent. I need to return to the City as soon as possible."

"That will have to be tomorrow."

"Yes. I understand."

"Well, you can spend one more evening then," Dr. Brucilla said. "Or day, as our guests call it." We walked back toward the desk. Dr. Carnell walked a few paces behind us.

"I hope the Karmiguel has met your standards," he said. "Tell me, did you have an enlightening chat with Ms. Conrado-Viktumbu?"

At this I turned and felt the needle slide into my arm.

"Alfred, Ms. Ludenow will be staying with us but I'm afraid she is unwell. Please have her bags taken care of…"

"You bastards."

That was the last thing I remember. The unnerving thing about modern anesthesia is how quickly and completely it works. It is a marvel to our consciousness—still huddling in caves or trees—that a small amount of chemicals can so completely eradicate the universe for us, underscoring the frightening conceit that we are merely a bag of accidental elements and nothing more. Fortunately, we are all a little different. Red heads are famous for needing more anesthesia. I myself am tall, much taller than most women. I can only guess that is the reason I came out of it before Dr. Carnell had planned; perhaps my shot was a dose for a shorter, and therefore lighter weight woman.

Not that coming out of it did me any good really, but I could hear them chatting. The room was full of light so being cast out of the memory of the lobby into the examination room equally shook me.

"She fought so. I had my fears. She is much stronger than she looks," he said.

"I had warned you about that. I had warned you about everything. This will not look good." Dr. Brucilla's voice.

"I will take that chance, Doctor. Your concerns are noted."

"But she is an Inspector. What do you think the Syndic will do? They will send more and then? We cannot keep doing this."

"Oh yes we can, Amanda. You object and you differ, yet you are still complicit. Oh, she seems to be waking. You had better give her the injection," he said. They both walked toward me. "Ms. Ludenow. I am sorry, but you seem to have swooned. Don't try to talk. You really can't you know. I will be looking forward to hearing *your* story. What secrets you must have. The carpet will be most thirsty for them. Dr. Brucilla, if you please."

He was right, I could not speak. While I was not bound or gagged, none of my muscles would obey any sort of command. I felt weak, as though my involuntary nerves were on the threshold of death. This powerlessness, and knowing what was going to happen, flooded my body with adrenaline that had nothing to work against. All I felt was the sweat coming to my forehead, my armpits, the curves behind my knees.

But I could see. As I said, *this* room was flooded with light, so the droplets sparkled on the end of the stainless-steel point.

"Just a pinch, you know," he said. "And then sleep. We will slowly draw you back from it, but I am afraid you will be here for a long time."

My mind was filled with profanity even as Dr. Brucilla lifted the syringe and moved toward me. I was not ready for her to turn slightly and stick it in Dr. Carnell's arm.

I heard him collapse and hit the floor like a heavy bag of grain or potatoes being thrown down. Dr. Brucilla leaned over me.

"I'm afraid you will return to sleep, but you will not awaken harmed. I must talk to you clearly when you are ready, you understand. There will be much to do." She said this without smiling. She was clearly worried, but her dark eyes were kind and stolid. Even in my state, I could tell as much, but she was also right. I felt exhausted and some sort of last kick of the anesthesia was coming back. She rolled my gurney out and the darkness of the Karmiguel engulfed us. All I could see was her white coat. That, naturally stuck with me as I began to slide backward.

There is only the wide dark hall, so tall I cannot see the ceiling. The floor is not carpeted, but bare and dark, and the cool wood feels good against my naked soles. Before me there is light, diffused but strong behind a vast curtain of linen. It comes to me just as I walk toward it and I am enveloped in it, not a shroud but a swaddle. I feel your arms come around me, not in a lover's embrace, but to lift me with so little effort that I must be a child. Yet I can feel my long legs, my breasts, the length of my arms. I am not a child, but I am carried.

"The night is black; the day is gray. The wind is blowing in from across the ocean. Sleep for a while."

"You have slept a long time," she says. I hear her next to me. I sit up. I *can* sit up. My hair is a mess. And there she is. Her. I know it is her although she wears a linen surgical mask as white as the terry cloth robe wrapped around her. I wear the same thing. My eyes are clouded, half asleep but I would know her anywhere.

Her hair is silver now, almost white, and longer than I remembered, but her eyes still flash in an impossible violet. I lean toward her to see the gold and amber inclusions in her irises are still there. She remains impossibly beautiful, but I remember. I remember her form leaving the door. I remember the angry phone calls and I remember her absence in our bed. I remember the cold, static form of her. The gaze that was always considering somewhere else toward the end.

We sit in some sort of capsule. There are windows all around us. She sips black coffee from a bone-white cup. She taught me how to enjoy black coffee. She turns gently then back to me with a cup.

"Here. This is what will bring you back into the world."

"Are we in some kind of spa?" I pinch and fluff the robe. It is thick and delicious.

"Of a sort. And not at all. We are here for a moment."

"You are not a secret. I have never kept you a secret."

"But I am a secret. You know that. And you are a secret for me."

"How can that be? We loved one another."

"Consider that word 'love.' It makes secrets."

"Even if many of them are phantoms. Phantoms behind a mask."

"Come now. You know we have to wear these masks. It's the only polite thing to do. The smart thing to do. Many have no choice in what mask they wear, while more privileged people, like you and me do."

"Your words are a mask," I say.

"No, words cannot be a mask. Ada, I still do love you. We will always have some connection. You yourself told me in Berlin: 'words cannot be a mask save in metaphor. I believe the word you are seeking is *lie*. But words cannot be lies, they only bear them.'"

I did say that to her. In Berlin.

"They are getting on with it. It's time for you to go."

"But I have so many questions."

"So do I, but we'll have time for that later. Go." She leans forward in the capsule and opens one of the windows which swings upward like a hatch. Outside, the world is gray sand and gray skies, yet still the nuanced shadows in the clouds gives them form and shape and reveals their swift movement.

I step out of the capsule still wearing my robe. "He will guide you," she says and closes the hatch which disappears into the wind.

And you are here. You take my arm and walk with me across that beach we know so well. We walk toward the pyramid and the smoke billowing from it.

"There, you see," you say and point toward the pyramid. Around it stand the shapes of men and women. The pyramid blazes with orange and apricot light and all of the orchids, the pianos, the chain link fences, the broken dolls, the rings—thousands of rings—the running shapes, the snakes, the clocks become clear in their darkness to evanesce in the wind and updraft from the fire.

Dr. Brucilla stands there near us. "We are burning the carpets. You should not be up yet, but I am glad for you to see this. I did not want to. But it was a slow descent into that lie. There will be no more Dark Therapy. Slowly I will bring them into the light. I promise. But I must do it. I know them. You won't..."

"No, I won't."

"I am glad you are returning with me," I say. The train is clacking in the familiar rhythm, although it is day now. "Your linen suit is crisp and perfect. I don't know how you do it."

"Yes," you laugh. "An absurd privilege of the state of affairs. Tell me, you are troubled. I understand the cipher and know the story. The events must be troubling, but perhaps I can help?"

"I worry for her. That place is so full of shadows. I wonder if her secret will be her undoing there, even though she makes amends for all of the others."

"Do not worry for Dr. Brucilla. Think about it, Ada. It is not her secret alone, but yours as well. And now it is mine."

"There are so many shadows in the world. I feel as though this was a small victory in a very uncertain war."

"That may be true. There are many shadows in the world, and they will continue until there is no more light. Yet it remains a victory worth fighting for."

The train moves—six beats to the measure—across the wide salt marshes, beneath the gray sky. I am grateful that the day is long.

author biographies

JANUARY

Bree Indigo is a poet and songwriter. She enjoys tarot, exploring Washington State's Olympic Peninsula, and tending to her menagerie of pets. She has been published in all four volumes of *Unnerving* and both volumes of the women's poetry and essay collection, *Rise*. Indigo lives with her wife and their family in the Puget Sound. Her first memoir, *Unreliable Narrator*, is forthcoming from Blue Forge Press. Find her on Instagram @bree_indigo

FEBRUARY

Gregor Fjellrev is an author, musician, actor, martial artist, woodworker, strategy game enthusiast and black hole of carbonated, fermented, and distilled beverages alike from Auburn, Washington. Among his proudest achievements is being called "unreasonably reasonable" by one of his non-online friends, of which roughly three exist.

Fjellrev's other published writing includes the *Universal Defender* series of both novella and novel-length works as well as other books available at www.BlueForgePress.com. Find his albums at www.BlueForgeRecords.com

MARCH

James Lowell Snyder was raised in Arizona. He worked as a civilian logistics specialist with the US Air Force for over twenty-five years, which included writing and teaching instructional courses. After retiring, boredom set in so he decided to write fiction. He contributing several short stories to J.W. Capek's *Ever Aequum*, part of the *Deerwhere Codex* series. Emboldened by success, he decided to create his own fictional sphere.

APRIL

Hailing from Tacoma, WA, Lauren Patzer has been an information technology guru, actor, writer and film producer among other pursuits. His love of horror began with a non-stop reading of *The Amityville Horror*. With two novels and over fifty short stories published now, his most recent work is the horror novel *Granny Bael*.

MAY

Angela Faro is an artisan of many skills who resides in Washington State. She is an author, an award-winning filmmaker and actress, a musician, singer, and journalist. Her previous writing includes a novelization of the *Ghost Sniffers, Inc.* episode *Wild Things Waking*, various short stories, poetry, and articles for *Arts Ex Machina Magazine* and a reoccurring column in the *Northwest Karaoke & Entertainment Guide* called *The NW Film Focus*.

JUNE

Pauline Ugalde is a visually-impaired writer, gamer, amateur musician, and voice-actor. Her favorite genres are sci-fi, fantasy, and horror, and her creative influences are Stephen King, Mark Z. Danielewski, Toby Fox, and Daniel Mullins. Her favorite scary movie is *Get Out*.

JULY

A PNWC and Bumbershoot award-winning poet and Seattle Times bestselling novelist, Jennifer DiMarco first toured nationally as an author when she was nineteen years old, having written novels since the age of ten. The first sixteen years of her career included the publication of contemporary drama, high fantasy, science fiction, poetry, and mystery novels as well as the production of two short films and three stage plays. During a twenty-year hiatus from prose, DiMarco married, raised two children, and worked as a filmmaker writing and directing more than a dozen feature films, half a dozen mini series, and more than a hundred short films. She returned to prose with *Hannah at Night and Twelve Other Stories* in 2020 and will celebrate forty years as a storyteller with the re-release of her bestselling poetry collection, *Season of Fire*, and an all-new creative memoir, *Sabbath Rising,* in the winter of 2022. DiMarco lives in the Pacific Northwest with her wife, composer and actor Brianne, and their adult children, author and illustrator Maxwell, and actor and illustrator Faith.

AUGUST

From reading children's books to grade school students, to creating the Senior to Senior Intergenerational Communications project, J.W. Capek has always appreciated the art of storytelling! Growing up in Arizona, teaching high school and raising a family in California, J.W. moved to the Northwest to be an author. Her *Deerwhere Codex* trilogy creates a world with quantum computers, epigenetics, and three unique genders. J.W.'s short stories span the human experience from tragedy to ridiculous. Check out www.jwcapek.com for current information.

SEPTEMBER

Born and raised in the Pacific Northwest, CM Kane was fed a steady diet of sports, particularly baseball. Having this love of the game instilled in her at an early age, she found that nothing was better than getting lost in the game. Storytelling was another gift that was encouraged in her youth, and she's taking to the written word to explore a new aspect to the game she loves.

OCTOBER

Marshall Miller retired from Homeland Security and police enforcement to more deeply explore the human condition and what drives us a species. Framed with the arrival of alien Apex predators who see us as little more than a food source, Miller is best known for crafting his series, *The Tschaaa Infestation* that dares to ask: Are we truly superior and do we deserve to survive? Find out more about his work at www.tiny.cc/marshallmiller

NOVEMBER

Michelle Lee is a Pacific Northwest native with an imagination open to possibilities. Growing up, people often saw her with her face buried in a book, and not much has changed in that regard. She's living her life's dream of writing books and exploring the possibilities she sees in the mysteries of the land around her.

Michelle's eight book series *The Raven's Journey* and her novella-length series *I.S.P.I.* can be found online at Amazon. Keep up with Michelle on Facebook at www.tiny.cc/MichelleLeeWrites

DECEMBER

Author, illustrator, and award-winning actor and filmmaker, Maxwell DiMarco has been writing professionally since he was a pre-teen, with stories and novels published in *Tales of the Slug, Super,* and *Ghost Sniffers, Inc.* In addition to these family-friendly adventures, DiMarco has written stories for all four volumes of *Unnerving,* where he explores the darker aspects of society through both physical and psychological horror. He lives in the Pacific Northwest, where he works as a special effects editor and the host of the weekly children's series, *Seriously Cereal.* He is a huge believer in community, acceptance, and seeing the world from all perspectives, striving to always provide his readers with an intriguing, thought-provoking narrative, no matter the genre.

THIRTEEN

David Mecklenburg was born in Sacramento, CA. but at the age of 22 he moved home to the Pacific Northwest, where he received his MFA in Creative Writing from the University of Washington. In short fiction, novellas, poetic essays and novels, he unveils worlds upon worlds in the fabulist tradition that reveal the multivalent condition we call being human. His short fiction has appeared in Silver Blade Magazine, Adelaide Literary Review, The Dark Fiction Spotlight among anthologies, such as Blue Forge Press's *Emerge* series. His longer work includes *The Nightingale's Stone,* a fictional memoir, along with Graphic Illustrated Essay collections such as *Hyperborea* and *Deukollectrum* also available from Blue Forge Press.

www.ingramcontent.com/pod-product-compliance
Lightning Source LLC
Chambersburg PA
CBHW060236100726
47907CB00003B/657